BRODIE SELZER

Sentinel 1

Cover design and illustration by Rafael Andres.

Second edition

ISBN: 9780645065800

This book was professionally typeset on Reedsy. Find out more at reedsy.com

To my family and to my younger self, who thought it'd be fun to write a story...

Contents

1

Chapter 1 A Sighting

"She'd better come out quietly." Three police cars surrounded the small corner apartment and all its exits, leaving no opening for the tried criminal to escape from them again.

"Chief, something is barricading the door, and there hasn't been any response from inside." Said Detective Billings, second in charge of his precinct, Hawthorn, Melbourne. He spoke to the chief, Captain Deer, over a vehicle's in-built radio. Billings and his team had already been there half an hour and midnight was closing in.

"Okay Billings, take your team and knock it in, the wife's already waiting, and we don't need to drag this out any longer. The felons in there, why else would she call? That's the weird thing about criminals, sometimes they do a crime, and, for some reason, feel sorry for it, so why do they do it at all?" Billings nodded, forgetting that the chief couldn't see him.

"That's not always the case, sir, but I'll have the team ready in five minutes to breach. Don't you think, it's a little strange, that she called, I mean, she's evaded us for weeks, why now?" Billings asked, walking from his vehicle's radio to the central team, positioned in and around the armed truck that had cut off traffic to the street. He switched to his private radio.

"Don't try to fathom the minds of the criminally insane Billings. It will make you insane. Leave that for the professionals. I'm coming onto the main road now, so I'll be there just after you breach." Billings reached the group and took his hand down from his face.

"Alright, prepare to breach in four minutes," Billings said. He turned around and, facing the door to the apartment building, spoke to the chief again. "Are you sure you don't want us to wait, sir?" Billings's group started moving into action, mounting the handheld battering ram and giving their weapons a twice over, before the siege.

Billings heard the Chief sigh through the radio, followed by a progression of honking.

"I'm in a jam, some old man's car just broke down in the middle of the road, looks like he fell asleep. You know the drill, besides, it's about time you lead your first siege, we want to make you captain by September still, don't we?" Billings smiled and realigned the badge on his chest.

"Yes sir, okay then sir, be careful with your old man, I'll radio when we have her."

"Over and out." The radio made a short crackling sound for a moment before the transmission died and Billings reclasped the radio to his hip, looking once more to all the windows of the apartment. Turning back to his men, he prepared himself for his first breach.

"Okay, are we ready?" He said, entering the truck and passing the other seven officers to get his helmet from the rack. He stood with them. "Jennings, Ford and Burrer head the first team, you'll carry the ram and Burrer will cover the windows, while Boris, Damon and West will breach the other side. When it breaks, leave the ram and enter, with caution. We don't know what to expect. Still, one of the neighbours said she was the only one renting an apartment. Time yourselves, from," He paused, "we breach, in one minute, starting now." Billings gave the order, and he and his team went for the front door, boots landing heavy on the wet ground as the rain started again. The other team went down the alley down the side of the building, passing another four officers that pulled out to let them through.

"Thirty seconds." He reminded the ram holders, looking back to Burrer and confirming there had been no disturbance on the upper floors.

Billings wondered again, why the criminal had called the police herself, there seemed to be no sense behind it, she knew she'd be captured, that they'd find her. Why?

"Ten seconds." He muttered, unable to stop himself. He straightened his helmet, clipped it in place and felt the first bead of sweat drip down his cropped hairline.

"One." He breathed deeply, nodding to the other two.

"Breach." He yelled, and the ram fell against the door with great force, ripping the softwood from its hinges and breaking the makeshift barricade all over the floor of the hallway as they burst in.

As they did, another shout came from behind and their radios blurred alive.

"Wait!" yelled Burrer, going for his gun and turning to the side alley. A window had smashed.

Over the radio, a surprised voice shouted to the officers.

"We have movement on the left side! I repeat, window smashed on the fifth floor, assailant was seen on another

3

building rooftop, all officers' available head to location." Billings continued running up the stairs, gun out and ready to fire the second an unknown person reached his sights.

The other team searched the first three floors, while Billings went straight for the fifth floor, where Annabelle had been said to be staying. *There's no way she jumped, and made it across a two-lane road, it's a trap.* Billings thought.

The rooms got increasingly messy as he climbed to the fifth floor. The wood creaked under each step and dust-covered everything that he passed.

"Breaching apartment room," He yelled breathlessly into the radio without unclasping it as he came to the fifth landing. Seeing the door of room five-zero-three, he moved directly for it and kicked against it will all his might, surprised to feel it give way easily, it wasn't locked or even closed properly.

"What the Hell!?" He yelled, moving into the room and seeing Annabelle, in the middle of her lounge and facing him.

"We're on our way up, Billings what do you see? Is she there?" Billings nodded, bewildered by what he saw.

"Sorry to report, the escaped person is nowhere to be found, no details other than that they wore black, nothing to report otherwise, how did the arrest go Billings?" Another officer reported over the radio.

"Annabelle Ruffton, you are under arrest, you are free to talk, but know that everything you say and do will be used against you."

"Good lord!" The other officers had reached the landing, seeing what had surprised Billings so absolutely. Annabelle was on her knees, tied down in the centre of the room. Her mouth was covered with cloth, her hair as black as night and frazzled like a birds nest. She looked tired and terrified by the officers that had barged into her room. She was battered and bruised.

"The window behind her is smashed. That's where the attacker must have escaped from, it's them they saw escaping," Billings grabbed his radio and went to the window as he motioned for the others to begin cutting her loose. "Get around to the surrounding buildings, look for anyone suspicious and get them in, if they were dressed up, their probably changed by now, so go about to dumpsters and pick up anyone with a bag."

With her arms free, and her mouth still clothed, they cuffed her, making sure there was no escape if this was all some kind of plan. Then, as her legs were freed and she stood, Billings confronted her.

"I'm going to ask you this once, and I don't feel like being spat on at this late of an hour, or someone might add some more bruises to you. Tell, me, who did this, what was their name?" Annabelle gulped several times before answering, a few tears streaking her face.

"I, I, don't know his name. Please, just get me away from here. I'll tell you everything I know." She went quietly, looking at the window that was shattered. Then she stood, as straight as she could, left leg dragging slightly as she limped down the stairs of the building, two officers supporting her.

Billings talked to Burrer, who had just come up while they were leaving.

"Burrer, get forensics up here and keep radio checks for any mention of this attacker. Whoever he is, he was looking for information, and Annabelle will tell us everything, to keep her at the station or, probably in prison." Burrer's eyes squinted slightly as he stepped into the room and looked

Billings straight in the eyes.

"Jee, Richard, I get the whole, we just got a criminal mentality, but, did you see her? She was battered, broken for this information she may or may not have." Burrer winced as he saw the window and the weapons across the floor.

"It's Billings, Burrer, and it doesn't matter, a criminal was beaten by another criminal, it's just another case." Billings slapped him roughly on the left shoulder as he went for the door, and Burrer chuckled for a second.

"And that is why you are aspiring to be Chief, and I'm still fine being a detective." The two of them left the room as other officers, including forensics, entered the scene and begun to tape off and study the crime scene.

"All officers, remain radio dark, no word of the attacker gets out until we can explain it or have a link between the two criminals." The radio went silent again after a confirmation from each officer on the scene, and the holder of the radio turned it off, and clipped it back onto his belt.

"So, they're going to take her to the station, and she's afraid. Good." The figure waited, as the sounds of a police car drew near and passed, throwing a small fountains worth of water into the alley. The rain had let up slightly, but he exited the path with his hood drawn tight and no umbrella to hinder the bullets of water from quickly saturating the hoodie. Running across the street, he went down another alley and, expertly flicking the keys from another holder in the belt, he unlocked a small two-door car and entered it. The vehicle started and the driver took off the helmet he'd worn in the interrogation he'd just had with the known criminal.

"Annabelle Ruffton," he said calmly into a small recording device on his chest, another function of the radio. "Small-time thief and narcotics runner." He turned the vehicle around the corner and into another alley, with no lights on, he avoided the police in the next two streets and made it past the patrol.

A quite shrill sound came from the bag in the passenger seat, and he stopped the car almost immediately in the centre of the road to take the call from the block style phone inside. Pushing aside a tie, suit shirt, and two wallets, he stopped before grabbing the phone and picked up an id card.

Smiling, he read Melbourne University and saw his picture on the card, it was two years old. The face he saw looked almost nothing like himself now, the small rounds of subtle blood stubble gone and short hair had grown, longer and brown instead of its old blond. He threw it back into the deep-set bag and picked up the phone, eyes widening at the caller number, one he remembered well.

He flipped it open and moved the car to the side of the road. Pressing a button, he made a black covering go over all the windows of the car, he turned off the engine, and it began to pour outside again.

"Hello Samantha, it's been some time." He said, voice smooth and well modulated. On the other side of the phone came a scream that caused him to move the phone away from his head for nearly a minute as the caller calmed themselves enough to not blow out his eardrums.

"Athien! It's been forever, where have you been, I've been trying to catch up with you for ages?" He smiled, slightly distracted by sirens coming from in front of the car.

"Well. I've been busy, went around the world and I'm in Melbourne. Did my father give you my number?" Athien sat calmly back into his chair as the sirens past without stopping or slowing. *Good the covering works.*

"Of course he did Athien, yeah I already know about the world venturing. Well, I'm going for my first role casting tomorrow, so that's my schooling finished if I get it." Samantha talked with a high pitched voice that caused interference when she spoke. Her acting skills must have improved since last they had met, as Athien had heard her say she would never make it in the acting world.

"Well, thank him for me, it's been busy for me, and I didn't want to bother you, well you had a lot of study to do, so did I." He heard a scoff from the phone, as Samantha laughed, the sounds deepened slightly, and it sounded like the funniest joke had just been said.

"That's never meant anything to you though, Mr Dickens, you're just like the man himself was, you've never tried on those silly exams." Athien nodded and laughed in turn. He spoke again, ear going to the radio on his chest.

"Officers there's no sign of the attacker, hold off at three blocks and bring the search inwards, we won't find him by spreading ourselves thin." Came the officer called Darius's voice over the radio.

"I'm better than that Dickens was, smarter and stronger, and I don't get lost on trips that I plan." Athien spoke sarcastically and begun shuffling through his bag again with his free hand.

"Yeah, I know that!" She said, as Athien found a bottle of water and took a long drink from it.

"Ah, not that I don't enjoy the call Sam, but do you think we can continue it tomorrow sometime, you realise what time it is here?" Athien asked, turning the engine of the car on again and unlocking the windows.

I should leave before they widen the search again.

"Oh my! What are you still doing awake! Get some sleep

for your exam tomorrow, good night."

"Good night Sam, talk to you later." Athien ended the call and stared at the small phone for a moment, watching the light fade to black, before he turned the key and brought the engine back to life. The street was tranquil, no lights on any houses and only one street lamp that worked, shone from the far corner of the end.

Before he turned into the main road, Athien touched the monitor on his dashboard, and a list of settings came up. He found the setting labelled security and begun switching things from off to on and vis versa. Cameras in the neighbourhood, houses and businesses alike, would all meet a slight malfunction in due time as the vehicle approached.

The rain continued to pelt down on the car as Athien drove through the suburb, avoiding cars and people the moon, obscured by most clouds, still managed to give a little light off for the driver.

As the buildings became more updated, the city-style spacious streets became present. Athien turned off to Richmond and followed the train tracks to the southern side, past the station and close to the outskirts. In the night, all of the houses in the area looked the same, small, or medium-sized, but similar builds and materials used to build them.

As he approached Scholar Street, Athien tapped at the dormant digital screen on the dash of his car, glaring slightly as the bright light came on. He navigated to the security tab he'd created on it and turned on the signal scrambler and slowed the car to a halt as he came up the drive to his home. The garage door opened thanks to a hidden proximity key under the hood of the vehicle.

"Well, that was an eventful night." Athien stepped up from

the small car's seat and into the dark garage, he clapped once, and the lights came on with a snap.

The room was sparse in design and contained only metal cupboards, two tables at the back of the room and a punching bag. On the far wall, beside the tables, Athien went and stood next to a padlocked tool cabinet combo with a blue chrome rim.

"Hmm." He breathed deeply, changing into a casual button shirt and pants. Unlocking the lock with a key in his belt, he placed the combat suit he'd worn and the mask inside the draw, ensuring he didn't get either snagged on the draw when it closed. A slight reverberation sounded as he left it and walked into the house from the door inside the garage, the lights turned off behind him.

2

Chapter 2 Exam

Beep, BEEP!

An alarm sounded at eight o'clock, and Athien rose with a slight growl to his voice, thumping the clock with a closed fist. He'd accidentally broken the two small bells on the top the first time he'd used it.

His bed sat beneath the window of the room, a queen-size with natural grey cladding and white sheets. The space was empty besides two cupboards and a desk, which was covered with school papers and old photos from years ago. One, an image with himself and a grown man outside of a massive skyscraper in a busy city street, caught his attention.

"It's been a while since I've been home." He turned to the other photos and smiled before changing.

Can't go back.

"Word arrived today that the new Aus Brand satellite will be going live in just a couple of days, making downloads and uploads exponentially faster." He began to drink his water as he walked to the lounge.

"There was a raid at the late hours of last night, a known drug smugglers home. Annabelle Ruffton was found in Hawthorn, where the siege took place. It's been reported police were called to the scene by the criminal. She was found tied down and unable to resist the police." Athien tuned into the Television as he continued to drank water from a glass, sitting in the lounge of the house as it covered the attack he'd been at last night.

"Police also state that there was someone else at the scene, but failed to elaborate further." He watched as the news anchor relayed several photos of the broken apartment building.

Another alarm, this one from his watch, signalled that it was time to leave. Athien grabbed his suit jacket and satchel before leaving the house, careful to lock the garage with a portable button key he took from his pocket and quickly pressed. The street he lived on was complete with a boring sidewalk, plain houses and a tram stop at both ends.

With his satchel in hand, Athien boarded the tram and tapped on his boarding card, almost slipping on the last step into the over-crowded vehicle. He managed to catch the landing pole by wrapping the satchel around it and flung himself in as the door abruptly shut behind him.

Athien readjusted the jacket he wore, black and form-fitting, before he began to feel a tingling feeling in the back of his neck. *There's, something wrong.*

The tram was packed to the walls with passengers, and all of them looked either comfortable or very uncomfortable. There was a group, at the back of the tram though, that Athien thought seemed very hostile.

Why is it always on an important day, that there's trouble? He walked calmly to the end of the tram, seeing three men crowded around a teen that sat beside the door, head and shoulders down with a mop of black hair that hid his facial features. The rest of the occupants in the tram seemed oblivious to the hostility. All too busy on their phones or talking to someone about their night.

Athien was within a meter of the men, when the one closest to the boy, a big burly man who wore a bright green vest too large for him, with a tangled brown beard, struck the boy in the chest where he sat.

"Hey!" Athien reached the men and grabbed the first, swinging them into the wall of the tram. The other two, one with two different coloured eyes and the other with a large scar on his chin, stood defiantly as their friend slammed against the doors on the left side of the tram.

"What's the deal man, we're just getting our due from this snitch here, nothin' for a pompous fool like you to get yourself hurt over. Just back off and we'll be done here shortly." The multi-colour eyed man stepped in front as his comrade went for the boy again. Athien looked around, his coat swishing slightly as he did so. He took in the passengers, no one was paying attention to them, and those that were eagerly awaited the next tram stop.

"Why have I not seen you men around here before? And what does he," Athien motioned towards the boy with a nod and a shake of his hand and the boy looked up slightly, teeth clenched as he doubled over from the punch. "Owe you?" He finished and took note of the situation.

The one ruffing the boy up is the leader and has a dagger he might pull out of his left leg pocket, but judging by the way he grabbed the pole to the right himself, I'd say he's left-handed. The one at the back, has a lot more bulk then the others and seems to be the muscle.

13

"What does it matter to you what he owes us? We're here to collect as we do when we need to." The tram began to slowly move as the men talked, Athien was happy to see many of the occupants close to them were leaving the tram to catch another. There were no security cameras on the tram. Still, Athien could see multiple other teens at the other side of the tram that had phones out would be ready to record if anything happened here.

I'll need to get them off the tram if anything happens.

"Look, there's a lot of things he could owe you, and I'm not sure what it is he did or, for that matter, what you all do, considering you're trying to ruff up this guy, on a public tram, at day time." He emphasised the last words he said, making it sound very patronising as he put a scowl on his face and leaned towards the men.

The tram stopped, and even before the doors opened, Athien saw the leader of the three come towards him, hand going for the dagger he had.

"We don't take kindly to low life remarks or people butting in on our business, now buzz off, before I make a mess of you." He spat into Athien's face as he spoke, teeth showing in a slightly enraged looking, savage smile.

Athien nodded, watching more people leave the tram.

"Okay, please, just leave the tram and this boy alone, there's no point in starting a…" Athien started to say, as the main man came at him with the dagger in hand, thrusting forward with speed and force enough to plunge the blade straight through Athien. Athien dropped his satchel in the chair closest to him and stepped away from the attack.

"No," Athien said triumphantly as the blade snaked danger-ously close. He was easily able to grab the man's wrist with both hands, applying a thumb to the vain cluster under the palm of his hand and causing the man to drop the blade. Then, in one fluid motion, Athien pushed against the point and used it to throw the man back. He fell into his comrades and against the closing doors. One of them got stuck, the multi-coloured eyed man and was thrown out onto the damp bitumen ground, leaving him behind.

The muscle man came at Athien, his feet sideways to each other and arms up like a boxer fresh inside the ring. Athien stood straight with his arms by his side and a slight sneer formed on his face. The brute stepped forward, throwing a low arching punch towards Athien's temple.

Athien ducked slightly, right arm going up to knock the punch sideways as his left fist collided with the man's stomach. The attacker collapsed as Athien went around him and used his shoulder to push the man into some seats. He landed on his side and crashed to the floor with a groan.

The teen stood as the brute went down, dodging Athien as the tram slowed. Athien and the last guy rounded off, both watchful as the doors opened and people filed out.

"You runt, come here so I can crush you." The remaining figure dropped his guard and suddenly rushed Athien, who was almost struck by the leg of the downed man that lashed out at him. Athien grabbed the man running him down and took hold of them from under their arms while he jumped away from the kick of the other holding tight to the bigger man's body as the two fell over the third. Athien rolled out from between them as they angrily fought against each other to stand and come after him. It was at this point that Athien looked behind himself and saw that one of the other passengers had risen and even come close to video the fight.

She was older than Athien, an adult, around twenty. Brown hair went down to the small of her back. She also had a smooth, oval face.

Also goes to Melbourne University. Athien read the name off of her hoodie, a grey one with the cities university symbol on the front in blue and black.

"Back up now," Athien warned, as he took several steps back from the two men, both of whom were scattered brained and angry at how badly their attacks had gone. Athien felt a hand on his shoulder as the woman held him back from the fight. She stepped forward.

"I'll have you both know that I videoed this from the start and have clear evidence I'll give to the police, of the two of you attacking first that boy and now this one." She smiled at Athien, stepping in front of him fully and addressing the men with all of her attention.

"Boss, let's go." The brute said, looking back to his boss and motioning beside them to the doors, newly opened by the driver, who had called the police and stopped the tram.

"Run!" The boss yelled, and the two of them took one last look at the pair that had disrupted them, before running out the door at a sprint. A police car rolled past seconds after, in hot pursuit of the two attackers, Athien saw that the other attacker was already in the back of the vehicle.

Athien shook off his jacket and evened his short hair, before making sure that nothing had happened to his satchel, which had fallen to the floor from the chair he'd put it on.

"Most people would say you know, thanks for helping me not to have to fight someone. But it looked like you could handle yourself well enough, so I'll let it slide this time." The woman turned to face Athien, eyes briefly taking him in, seemingly searching him while her phone went into her right pocket. She smiled to herself.

"Yeah, well I have an exam, so I couldn't really afford to have a police report to write up." Athien grabbed the satchel from the band and hooked his fingers around the handle on the bag itself, for added support.

"Oh, that's fun, same here, doing a degree in Biology. I have two today," she hesitated for a moment, before putting her hand forward for Athien to shake. "Oh, it's Nicola, by the way, pleasure, to meet you."

She thinks quickly. Athien churned over her ability to change topics and tactics so fast, her eyes kept darting around the place as the tram moved and looked at everything they could.

"I'm doing a degree in Computer Science, looking to getting a job in that area while I finish the degree." Nicola looked surprised, blinking three times while her smile continued to shine on her face.

"I didn't expect that, you look so young." Athien nodded, preparing his response as the tram moved on from yet another stop.

"Yes, everyone does, no matter the facial hair, it seems I am forever cursed with a young face. I'm almost seventeen," Athien paused for a moment, letting that sink in and watching the other passengers. "This is my second year in the course, and I'm looking forward to having it finished."

Nicola didn't respond to either facts. Instead, she opened her phone and started to scan through what Athien reasoned was photos, as the light that passed her face was too bright and colourful to be writing.

She looked up again, staring straight into his face for a split second, before nodding and exclaiming;

"Oh, that makes sense!" She dropped her voice as Athien brought his hand up and dropped it down quickly, motioning for her to keep her voice low. You're the Dickens boy, Athena, Athien." Athien chuckled, using this brief moment to the assertion that in two stops, they would reach their destination.

"That's me, generally smart boy, shot in the head and disappeared for two years while he did an online university course and travelled the world." Athien watched the tram stop for the second last stop, multiple fire trucks and an ambulance raced by on the tram line next to theirs, another problem.

He grimaced slightly before looking back to Nicola.

"Well, it's a pleasure to meet you, Athien, your father's business is one that I hope to apply for after I've finished my course."

"No need to wait, apply now, I'll put in a good word for you, after all, you stopped me from having to fight off some tough opponents."

"Ha, like you needed help, where did you learn to fight? Surely there are bodyguards for that type of thing." They both saw the tram stopping and moved towards the end of the tram to exit onto the university grounds.

"Well, that, would be what the travelling was for. Of course, that's what any rich boy does with his time." Athien mocked, stepping from the tram onto a drenched street, right outside of the university.

"And why have I never seen this rich boy around before, if we both go to the same uni and catch the same tram?" She asked, walking beside him as they moved into the covers of the roofs of the buildings, inside the campus grounds.

Athien dodged a group that came from a side corridor to the outside path and offered his explanation.

"Well, in truth, this is the first exam I've actually sat in on, and I've only recently returned to civilisation of this magnitude. Travelling has allowed me a certain clarity, to these busy and crowded spaces." Nicola stopped walking and drew Athien to a building that was four stories tall with one level being a full glass front.

"That, does not surprise me at all, but this is me," She said, pointing at the building. "So I guess I'll see you around Athien, good luck with the exam, something tells me you'll have no problem with it." They both stood there, watching each other for a moment, before Athien replied.

"I won't, and I hope yours goes as easily, or if not, at least time passes by quickly." Nicola scoffed at this, moving through the doors of the building, she walked backward.

"It's actually the opposite, things always seem to go really slow for me. Sometimes it feels like I'm a step out of time." Nicola laughed softly, her eyes glossed over as the door shut between them, leaving Athien with a slightly questioning face, his eyebrows and lips curled.

Walking through the college Athien made it to the classroom, a lengthy lecture room with seats enough to fit two hundred people. Every position was covered with the same black and blue cushioning, same as the carpet floor. Only two other students were already there, their names being ticked off and waiting the half an hour that was left before the exam opened.

Athien made his way to the front of the room, the lecture room's main door came from the side, so that classroom students wouldn't disrupt the lecture as they came and went. On the table were a set of cards, all white with the Melbourne University signature and each card had on it a name, a student identification number, and a small picture. Seeing his face on a card, Athien found it and went to the examiner.

He was a wiry man, with a face full of brown hair that slightly greyed at the tips of the hair and beard. With a black suit jacket, dark blue tie and lighter shaded shirt, he looked like another piece of the university. He wore his name tag with a shallow amount of pride as he watched Athien approach, eyes looking above the rim of his glasses in a particular fashion.

"Mr Morrison," Athien said, reading the name tag he wore. "I hope you have enjoyed your day thus far, Dickens sir." Athien showed him his card and smiled to resemble the photo finish he'd been forced to assume when it was taken. Mr Morrison looked at the photo a good while longer than he should, clearly confused as his eyes darted from the card to the boy standing in front of him.

"It's good to finally see you here in person, Mr Dickens, though I was expecting to have to call your tutor, Mr Mark, was it?" Morrison gave the card back and stiffened his slightly stooped stance, his mind racing as to the reasons why Athien would show up to this exam out of all of them.

"Aha. Unfortunately I have dismissed Mr Mark, I'm back in the country for a long stay and might as well make my time spent here worthwhile." Athien said politely, moving from directly in front of Morrison and climbing the first of the steps to the second row.

He wasn't the examiner from last year, so the only way he knows Mark is if someone, the last one told him, or Mark did. Keeping his face devoid of any outward expressions, Athien sat at the seat second from the column, bringing his satchel down to the floor to rest. At the same time, he opened its zipper to expel his writing utensils, two pens and pencils, plus an eraser and a drinking bottle.

20

Mr Morrison looked downward, seemingly upset for a moment, but then smiled again, cheery faced.

"I like your optimistic thought process, Dickens, and it's good to see you here with us today." He said again, motioning to the rest of the room and two women who walked in at that moment, carrying multiple bags of shopping and sporting colourful hairstyles.

3

Chapter 3 Miss Kali

His exam finished, Athien caught the next tram back home. There were two officers there from the start of the line to the finish, added security from the day's events. Nicola wasn't on the tram, neither was the boy from earlier, and Athien didn't see any sign of ruffians.

As he walked down the road towards his house, he passed multiple families out on a short walk to the shops or who played in their back yards. It was a family orientated neighbourhood, and he still felt slightly out of place living here, in case anything happened.

If I'm careful enough, though, nothing will ever happen here. Athien was two houses down from Kali's, when a car came by from behind him and swiftly turned into the driveway of his house. This caused him to smile, it had been some time since he'd seen his boarding partner, he speed up and jumped the front fence as the door to the garage closed behind the car.

As he opened the door, he heard the garage door open as well. He waited patiently in the hall as the person walked into the main entrance and missed him, walking straight to the other side of the aisle and entered the kitchen.

Athien scoffed silently, and looked at the old ladies tea knitted wares and crochet that were spread across the long side-board that ran down the hallway and on all of the dark wood cupboards.

"Aunt Kali, it's so great to see you again, it's been a week and a half you know. Did you forget where the house was?" Athien entered the kitchen and found an elderly woman in front of the coffee machine, her attention drawn from his entrance as she busted a sachet of powder into the machine.

"How many times do I have to tell you, it's Kali, to you, and to everyone except my dead husband? And I happen to have just as much memory as you do, and a great deal more to remember, Mr. Dickens, so why don't we skip these questions and you make me some nice tea?" Athien laughed outright as he went to the small cupboard and examined the mugs that hung on their individual hooks. He picked the one that she liked the best, one he'd made for her seven years ago, while in grade four, it was white clay that he'd hardened in a smithing test with his father. During which he'd emblemised it with a white daffodil, her favourite flower. He stood and watched Miss Kali as he waited for the coffee to boil.

She was eighty years old, an excellent marketing assistant and eventual tycoon in her lifetime, as well as an outstanding developer in online code and professional mechanical technician. Her hair was short, kept to her exacting standards by a weekly Barbour shop cut, her eyes, despite her age, and had not gathered the slightest amount of mist to them. Athien knew that behind her sharp cheekbones and well-kept sweater and pants that her bones were cold. She found it hard to move sometimes in the winter months, but she was always creating ways to get past the typical elderly problems. Her mind was one of the most brilliant that Athien had witnessed in terms of what it could remember and strategize. Though, Kali was retired now and just did a few days at a nursing home as a nurse, she was an influential doctor as well, and Athien had the up-most respect for her.

"The tea's ready," Athien said, pouring the now smooth liquid into the mug. He took it to her where she sat at the dining table, her hand going for the kitchen T.V. remote as he placed the cup by her side and sat down with her.

"So how did your exam go today? Was there any challenge to it?" Kali asked as she scanned the channels, finally settling on a news channel.

"There wasn't anything I didn't know already, a bit hard to not know what you know with our memory." Athien mussed over how easy each exam had been over the years. He'd been gifted with two intellectual parents. Though his mother had mysteriously disappeared, Athien had had a brilliant learning life for those first eleven years. He had close to a photographic memory with both words and numbers. His father's endless pushing at learning everything had also pushed Athien to read anything he could get his hands on.

The news started to play, and the news anchors talked about the steady increase in crime in the city.

"Yes, though I still find it surprising, if your father hadn't been there the night you were shot, you mightn't be able to remember anything. Athien winced slightly, though it had been years, he couldn't forget that night.

He was with his father, Prometheus, at his workplace in Alazarath City, U.S.A. Three hundred kilometres up the coast from New York, it housed some of the finest technical minds in the world, Prometheus being one of them. When they exited the building, a lone gunmen supposedly aiming for a shot at Prometheus, the C.E.O. had missed and hit Athien instead. He would have died from blood loss had Prometheus not taken him back inside to stitch him up.

Athien felt the back of his head, though six years had passed since then, he could still feel the icy cold that had seeped into his body after the shot.

"It was just a flesh wound, the scar isn't even there anymore." Athien stopped thinking about the attack, as an exciting scene was displayed by the news channel reporters.

"Today there was a murder at an infamous bar in downtown Melbourne. Police say that the man killed, a Mr. Boss, was being searched for after a mugging earlier in the week, and have not yet released an official report on the matter. Meanwhile," The screen changed from showing the bar to the front of a hospital. "There has been an admission inside this hospital for another wanted man, Mr. Barns, who police say was also a part of the mugging on a tram earlier this morning. Mr. Barns has sustained multiple heavy injuries to his head, arms and legs, and it is reported that he and Mr. Boss were both shot, by someone inside the bar at the same or near the same time. It should prove very informative if police can gain access to the video surveillance of the shop. if Mr. Barns can answer any questions they have for him too, thank you, Dale, this is Mara Star, out." Athien stood and apologised to Kali, who wasn't surprised by his interest in the criminals. She smiled as he left the room.

"Don't go driving my car again Athien, you're going to need a bike or something soon, and you're underage." Athien nodded absently to himself as he left the room and turned into the garage, the lights still on from when Kali entered earlier.

"Computer!" Athien yelled across the room as he passed the punching bag and sat on the spinning seat he left here. It was blue, with a black rim and tall arched back, like a gaming chair.

The computer screen lit up with a volcano background, shot in Italy, which he spent a short time of his holiday in, before moving to Tibet.

He put in the password and immediately opened the file folders of the pc. There, he scrolled through a multitude of files in his structure, he passed, Suit upgrades, Side projects and landed on Case Files. After putting in the encryption code, fourteen files appeared, all of which had names of people he'd been after, such as Annabelle Ruffton. Above these were files of different branch members for criminal organizations, ones he knew in the city.

That's even more definitive after today's events.

"Okay," He said, testing the audio device he'd input into the computer for ease of information transfer. "Today's the twenty-third of March, and we have two new suspects of organised crime, the name is still unknown. Mr Boss and Barns…" He talked to the air, the computer taking down his words and writing them onto a new document.

He'd just finished, twenty minutes later, when the phone in his pocket began to ring, it emitted a small bell sound that sounded like a cat's neck bell. Samantha.

"Hello Sam, my exam went well, how was your audition? Sorry, role casting." Athien asked, as he stood, closed the window of the garage and sat down again. Samantha was on a busy street, Athien heard multiple horns and shouting on her end of the line.

"Well, I did the parts I was told to, and added a little MORE to the role, so I hope they enjoy. I should get a notification on it in a couple of weeks, and that's great! And that's your last one?" She huffed and took a long breath from her lack of pause.

"Yes, just the one for this term, the other two were assignments. That is good to hear, though I'd think it would be dangerous to play it up on your first try at an actual role, you are you, after all." Athien leaned back and watched the sunlight as it left the sky, it got darker with every minute.

"I know, but, hey, I can't help it, I'm too creative to just DO a roll, I have to BE the character. Anyway, I'll tell you now that I'm coming down to Melbourne with Prometheus. He's keen to see you again." Athien smirked, logged quickly onto the internet and loaded up a news article he'd thought he'd seen on the paper he'd passed this morning. There was a talk happening between lead technologies firms in Melbourne on the weekend, two days from today.

"Yeah, there's a conference here in two and a half days, your time, but okay, I'll make sure to meet you both at the airport. Hopefully, there aren't as many reporters as last time." Samantha chuckled on the other side as the sounds got quieter.

"I've just stepped inside, yeah, we don't need you to break the media away from the company's view again, do we." Athien's return from his trip had created an enormous media storm weeks ago with his father searching frantically for him due to a killer on the loose in Alazarath.

"No, we don't need that again." Athien closed the internet tab and turned the computer off fully.

"Well, I suppose I should leave you now, seeing as we'll have plenty of time to catch up over the weekend, and yeah." Athien got up and walked over to the tool case he'd locked last night.

"Okay Sam, I'll see you then, I've got somewhere I need to be anyway, so I'll talk soon, call me when you leave Alazarath." Athien put the phone down as he sought the key, hidden inside a false lid to the top of the giant wheelbase box. Though he had locked the wheels and indented them in concrete, so it couldn't be moved easily.

"Okay, see you soon, Athien. Bye." The call ended as Athien unlocked the box. The last of sunlight passed over the back of the house as he pulled out his uniform.

4

Chapter 4 Introductions

His suit was a thick mesh similar to the seat at his desk's covering, only thicker and more rigid. He wore a belt around his hip with a grapple gun and his helmet, a titanium black chrome front with a d3 centre, kept his head safe from any attacks as he searched the night for information on the organised crime units. In other compartments, he passed guns and other, harsher methods of attack, settling with his average fists and thickened gloves. His quiver sat behind the box, in another compartment, along with real bullets.

Kali is right, I need a motorbike or something fast at least, and more manoeuvrable.

Athien put a coat over himself and placed his helmet and gadgets in a duffle bag. He could hardly be caught with the gear and being an underage driver. Still, most police wouldn't question his age, the licence card he had told of a different era and name anyway and it was simple enough to hide the bag in a false compartment in the car. He'd gotten the I.D while travelling the world, something he didn't want to do again, not like he had.

He went to the car Kali had driven in and put on forged plates. The ignition shaky, he revved the vehicle five times before he opened the garage door and drove onto the street.

The sky had cleared dramatically since the morning. Only the last dregs of the storm were left in the sky, wispy clouds with no volume and a bright, yet faded orange light from the set sun basked the top of the clouds in its glare.

The streets were quiet as Athien drove, his mindset in the zone as he thought over how he'd complete this next mission.

Barn's is in the hospital, it's in Hawthorn, so I know which one it is. The problem will be getting in there without being seen, but I think there are taller buildings then it, so maybe a grapple shot could do.

As he drove, Athien thought of how the last few weeks had been, of his escape from travelling and how he ended up in Melbourne. He was unable to go back to the city he was born in and unable to keep out of the fight, for the other side. Now he fought against the people that had bought and trained him to make their killings.

It had been a long two years, after the shot that had nearly killed him, Athien went travelling and finished high school abroad, seeing the world one stage at a time. It was on the trip that he forged the frame of mind he was in now, concentrating on the need to have this one thing done, and knowing it would most likely lead to something else. The Order of Mark, was their name, the people who had bought and used Athien, and though they were a small, enclosed group, their power was intense and demanding. Athien learned a lot of what he knew of vigilante skills from them, but running away from that was the best choice he'd had.

He turned onto a busy main road towards Hawthorn, the

evening traffic surged past him at high speeds, filtered and smooth. He had a good view of his surroundings, multiple heavy trucks on his left one of which was branded with M.A.K.E. Industries on the back, a challenger in his father's business and a giant bus on his right.

The sudden sound of sirens caught Athien's attention. He saw in the rear-view mirror multiple emergency service cars as they moved up behind him from further down the street. They moved towards the tram line that crossed the next side road so they could avoid traffic. Athien turned into the left lane, behind the trucks and waited for them to pass. He tuned into the radio frequency with the cars specialised radio, like the car he drove the night before. They turned off the street and Athien was able to merge back into the centre of the road. His radio blared, and he quickly turned it down. Kali liked loud music and was slightly short of hearing.

"There's been an attack on The Vampire's Drool nightclub, officers are scrambling at the scene, but it seems the attack was from one of the patrons and a customer. Don't know how The Vampire will get himself out of this one." The nightclub was notorious for expensive food and drink, but acclaimed for its dance floor and musical performances.

Athien tuned out the radio noise as he entered Hawthorn, a small and old suburb but complex in its heritage and architecture. Some of the buildings were used in everyday use, and had been for over one hundred years, Athien liked it there, there was a casual atmosphere, and though it was close to the CBD, it was still its own place.

The hospital resided just off of the main street, and Athien drove up to it slowly. He saw a wild commotion of miss-parked vehicles and wildly clicking camera flashes at the front of the building.

Well, at least I know the places I can't go through. All the entries will be covered by reporters wanting a scoop. There was also multiple police officers at the hospital, three Athien could see inside the doors, monitoring the entrances into the building in case someone came for Barns that shouldn't.

Athien drove past innocently, not wanting any attention and parked the car in a side street half a block around the side of the building.

He grabbed the duffle bag and moved from the vehicle, the key he took and, after he unzipped the bag, Athien placed it inside a small notch on the belt of the uniform. He zipped it back up and left the car.

Time to go to work.

The spared light of twilight made it difficult to see what lay before him. Still, Athien was practised in building environments, and he climbed the fire escape nimbly, using his feet and arms to ricochet off of the ladders and the walkways.

The building he climbed was an old brick design and was positioned two buildings away from the four-story hospital, a huge concrete building.

Athien put the duffle bag behind a stairwell outcropping on the second building, unzipping the bag, he prepared to change from his jacket to the helmet.

He stood seconds later, making the bag as inconspicuous as possible, and monitored the building. His radio was tuned on his chest to listen to the officer's positions.

"Nothing's happening on the third or second floors, how is the ground and first?" An officer reported in from the elevator as Athien saw him walk past a window, radio to his lips.

"Brook, you're just reporting here, I'm captain on this one.

And the ground is secure, first as well, crew one just responded. Crew four respond." The captain, probably on the ground floor, was very attitude orientated at Brooks.

A former captain perhaps, or a trainer.

"Four is secure, we've got two up here." Athien cocked his head at these words, most likely to be the words of the men who guarded Mr Barns. Athien continued to monitor the radio channel, every three minutes there was a report back to the officer and no one missed the beat by more than a few seconds. There was a differentiation between command priorities between one officer and the captain, one wanted to leave the hospital, with the prisoner, but the captain believed it was safer there than in a cell.

Athien watched as the third and fourth-floor monitoring team and the first and second, passed each other on different floors, thirty minutes after he appeared on the scene. Beneath him there were still quite a few journalists, occasionally being shepherded from the scene when they got too close. Some had accepted into the foyer for a professional doctor's report on the patient, Athien read over the news as he watched their patterns.

He grabbed the grapple gun from his side, finally satisfied he'd gained as much knowledge of paths and people as he could.

He stepped onto the side of the building, aimed for the roof above him, and fired. With a repressed release, the grapple launched into the air. It carried itself straight into the wall of the adjacent building's top stairwell. Once it latched into the wall and stood fast, Athien pulled back and stepped off the building. The winch that was housed in the gun sprang into action, pulling him across the gap and onto the roof.

He landed at a run and smoothly stopped a meter from the wall, where the grapple disengaged with another tug. Athien opened the door to the hospital and donned the helmet he carried, eyes covered by the one-way glasses.

He entered the stairwell, consciously aware that the next watch would reach the fourth floor in two and a half minutes. The stairwell was white painted, old and scratched from age, and the stairs themselves were unclean and had chunks missing. Athien made his way to the third-floor door, two minutes before they went to leave.

His radio came to life as he reached the third floor and Athien quickly sidestepped halfway down the platform to the second floor, afraid he'd missed something.

"There's commotion on the ground floor, all supporting officers reconvene downstairs and cover all entry points. Suspect shooter appeared with several others, drove past seconds ago. Danny, get up with the prisoner and the rest of you, get down here and stop these other criminals if they cause any trouble."

Athien worked on his grapple hook and quickly shot up into the top of the stairwell again. He propelled up even as the door to the third floor opened, and he just stopped as they entered the stairwell.

Holding steadily to the roof, he waited with bated breath as five policemen rounded the stairwell, the last two hit the ground floor without so much as a check of the upper floors.

He breathed as soon as the door closed, dropping down to the floor. There was an evident problem with something downstairs.

I've got to move a little quicker now.

Athien wondered if the building was being watched, and

if he'd triggered an attack, to stop some kind of important information from being released by Barns. He moved quickly to the third floor, eager to look for the room of the criminal that had more valuable information than Athien or the police thought he did.

He checked every room that was open, sure to be quiet and avoid his shadow being seen in the room of the patent. Then, he went into the corner room of the west side.

Mind at racing speed, Athien went for the door. He put his ear to the surface. Officers with too great a curiosity as they talked about the goings-on outside.

"Ya think it's someone for this loser? Jeez, we might get promoted for this." To which the other officer remarked in a harsh and bored tone.

"No, this is just an act by whatever gang he's cooked up with that he owes money to. They won't do anything, cept make him scared to say anything, which is why I agree with Deer on this, should have taken him straight to a cell." Athien pressed with a false resolve to go straight in and tell the two rookie sounding cops to do thief job with more of a serious matter.

Athien pressed a button on his chest, under the radio band turning the volume up to its highest.

This way, I teach them a lesson and I get into the room, with minimal fuss.

Just then the radio blared from inside and outside the room.

"Group four respond, still tense down here but nothing of note yet." Athien heard one of the officers curse as the other answered the radio.

"Yes sir, everything is fine here, the prisoner's still in his bed and unhappy." The radio went quiet just as Athien moved out of the room and back into the hall.

"Did you hear that report come from the other room too? Is that where Danny went?" Athien wondered what had happened to the sixth cop, as he saw the handle of the door rustle and heard the fall of the officer's foot behind the door.

"I don't know, but I'll just take a loo…" Athien sprang into action and used the open door and the officers off guard nature to slam the door into him with a kick, which sent him back into the hall with a hard hit to the side of his head. Following the door, Athien rolled into the area just behind the fallen officer and came up before the other, knocking the gun from his hand before the officer knew he was under attack. Then his hand came up and made contact with the bottom of the officer's chin.

Athien lent back as the other officer came up again and attempted to get a look at his attacker. At the same time, his hands both went for his radio, he then landed a kick against the officer's back that sent him into the floor in a crumpled heap.

Athien stood and looked at the criminal he'd come to question for the first time, and saw a mixture of calm and defiance in tear-stained eyes. He nodded.

"I want you to tell me everything you know about the people you work for, before, whoever it is that's here to kill you does so." He made his voice shallow and silently thanked the room for being so tight and small, it made the voice he put on menacing and deadly.

The prisoner, Barns surprised Athien by nodding over and over. Apparently he agreed wholeheartedly with Athien. He shook so violently that he began to gag on a cloth in his mouth. It'd been put there by officers.

Athien, sceptical of the man's motives, took a corner of the rag and pulled it out, careful to check that the rest of Barns was strapped down, so he wasn't attacked by a frenzied man on deaths' row.

Barns gargled several times, before he spat on the floor on the opposite side of the bed that Athien stood on. Athien, reproached, stepped two steps back to avoid any future phlegm.

"I can't tell you much, but if I do, can you help me get these ugly brutes off my back, I know they work for someone big, and I was hired through a contractor of sorts." Athien smiled beneath his mask and nodded for Barns to continue.

"I'll keep you alive if you tell me what you know now." Barns, seemed relieved by this sentence, and breathed a deep sigh, before he shook himself out of a groggy stupor and talked to the person who'd just downed his only protectors.

"His name is Caretaker, I learned today when his men ruffed me up and shot my friend at that bar you saw on the news. We were working for a tuff, strong player in the city, but never once did we hear his name, not once. Too low on the food chain. But the Caretaker, he hired us out, Boss and I, to this mystery man, who apparently has a small army under his sleeve. They're probably here to stop me telling the cops anything, oh please," Barns started to break down as his mind raced to an untimely death in a hospital robe. "Please help me stay alive."

Athien moved forward, his hands grabbed Barn's shoulders as he hoisted the bigger man up a few inches and looked right into his eyes.

"I need you to tell me anything else, where is The Caretaker, any other workers he has, the places he visits. Anything." Barns shuddered, but nodded again.

"The man that shot me, or his pal, one of them had the name Mordacai. Big guy, Caretakers best. That's all I know, I was just a shake downer, and there are a lot of tiers to this business." Athien nodded.

"I know."

"So can you help me?" Barns looked desperately at Athien as he stood there, suddenly in another world.

"Shut up, there are people in the hallway." Athien motioned with his hands for silence and crossed the room, he shut the door with next to no noise and waited for the bodies to pass.

"Group four, reports, there's…" There was a loud boom sound over the radio as Athien tried to turn it down.

"We are taking fire, I repeat we are taking fire." The radio fuzzed out as Athien quieted it, but the bodies were still in the hall. They both heard the door to their right slam open, a foot kicked it in.

"You have to stay quiet." Athien grabbed the cloth he'd taken from the man and shoved it back into his mouth, much to Barns detest. Then Athien crossed the room and stood behind the door as multiple pairs of feet stomped outside their room.

Now the fun begins.

The door shuddered as a hand pressed against it, the handle wriggled as they attempted to open, just as Athien turned the lock to lock it. He looked to Barns as the attackers prepared to barge through and attack anything in their way, and motioned with one hand, palm down, for him to get as low as he could.

Barns began to wriggle down the bed as far as he could, as the boot slammed the door. The hinges shook, and the lock broke through the thin board that stopped it. Athien stamped his foot against the bottom of the door, hitting it straight back into the attacker. They stumbled, flailing backwards.

The attackers wore standard combat gear, a makeshift version of Kevlar armour, majority of which was just hardened materials and thrown together with scraps, but the helmets were police raid grade. Athien dropped the first one, the helmet of the second stopping him from instantly halting the next, who ducked slightly.

He grabbed Athien and his head slammed into Athien's open gait, and pushed the two of them deeper into the room while four others climbed over their still knocked down comrade.

Guys have some form, I'll give them that. Athien acknowledged his weakness in numbers, and immediately went into the steps he needed to do to even the odds.

As they moved into the room, Athien sidestepped the brawl as they collided with another bed and sent the man straight over and into the wall on the other side. His next move, after he surveyed the area, was to engage in close-quarter combat so their guns would be used with the least effect.

"Hey!" Athien yelled as two attackers went for Barns, and threw himself at them. He kicked the first, a shorter man with a semi-auto rifle. Then swung their falling body into the path of the second, bigger man, which sent the two falling into the ground.

Athien grabbed his grapple gun and shot straight at the leg of the man closest to Barns, he'd just made it to the end of the bed. The body fell haphazardly onto Barns, who kneed the head as the body fell, sending the shout that sounded into a faded gust of air.

He dropped the grapple and turned his feet in an L shaped stance, before he shifted the weight to his front leg and kicked with the back, two quick and concise hits. One into the downed man's head and the other into the other's torso, giving the man a cracked rip.

Athien saw the man at the door stand, another rifle pointed in his direction, but then a shout broke differed his concentration.

"Stop! Hands in the air, don't you move." Athien turned a half step towards Barns and saw the attacker he'd thrown over the bed and into the one who hadn't been hit by the grapple. They stood over Barns, two guns pointed at him. A rifle to his chest and a low hip-pinned handgun to his face.

"Aren't you going to do that anyway? That is why you're here." Athien faced them head-on and raised his arms into the air, eyeing the other near the door as he came slightly closer, gun pointed straight at Athien's centre.

"Knowing why there's two dead cops in here is more of an issue, and you've just downed three gunmen in a minute. Who are you, and what did he tell you?" Athien scowled himself for letting them get to Barns, but he still had the upper hand here.

The man's arms shaking, he wasn't expecting a fight, they got in without the police knowing like me and whatever is happening outside is just a massive diversion. I can move before the doorman pulls the trigger, but how to stop two guns and dodge a third at the same time?

"Hey, stop avoiding the question or we'll kill you both right here and now." Athien grimaced under the mask.

"You kill him, and you get no answers from me," He barked. "Then I'll beat you all until there's not a bone unbroken and the police can have what's left. Who I am doesn't matter to you, all that matters is that I'm here, and he's told me nothing, yet. But now I know he's important. Thanks for that." Athien cooled, after he realised the doorman fingered the trigger like it was his best friend.

The handgun user looked Barns square in the face and pulled his head up.

"I don't think you told this nutter nothing, hell I would have, you did, didn't you," The man's voice grew with malice. "Didn't you!" He yelled, the gun he held bumped against Barn's head hard as his whole body shook.

Barns screamed, but with the cloth in his mouth, it came out as a strangled gargle as he furiously shook and nodded his head. He was desperate to be out of the room and the world at the time.

"He's under stress and gagged, witnessing two cops go down and a fight between gang soldiers and a random, you would be shaken too, or worse." Athien yelled and hoped it would defuse both the man's outrage and Barn's weakness to interrogation.

The handgun turned on Athien, whose arms instinctively drove down with his head to protect it, so fast he didn't even see the gun stop in its movement towards him. *That was quick.* He thought. He peeked from behind them and saw the man, who stood, sweat profusely dripping from his scalp, with his mouth slightly gapped.

"There's something really off with you, man. I should put a bullet between your eyes and see if you rise from the dead." Athien moved his feet slightly, pretending to look casual, but, in reality, he lined up his foot with the cord of the grapple gun, the end pointed at their body.

"Look, there are two things you need to know here. One, I'm about to drop all three of you guys, and there is nothing you can do to stop me, and second," He readied himself to move quickly and watched the man closest to Barn's the most. "The name I carry, the one you'll carry to whatever big boss it is you work for. The boss I'll end by the way. My name." He stepped onto the cord and pulled it back towards himself as he turned around and leaned forward, avoiding the trigger-happy doorman's rapid-fire. He fell, his finger letting one shot off before the gun left his hands.

Athien whirled towards the doorman, who desperately back-peddled to keep the distance between them, but failed to realise the ajar door, and tripped on his way away, the gun dropped. Bullets sprayed the ground at his feet as Athien reached him. He forced the gun up and into the man's chest as his fist collided with the other man's face. As he fell, Athien grabbed the door with his left hand and slammed it into the falling head, the man knocked out with heavy bruising before he hit the floor. As the other two recovered, Athien wasted no time in eliminating the man close to Barns, who was confused from hitting the wall earlier. He took two steps and, having grabbed the gun from his last foe, threw the weapon across the room and rolled forward. He avoided the handgun bullets that whizzed by his head and behind his accelerated body.

The man attempted to dodge both, pushing the gun onto the bed, as Athien's legs crossed in between his and brought the man down. Athien then grabbed at their head and head-butted it, before punching them three times, aiming for the clavicle and the bottom rib. It was enough to make them growl in pain as Athien rolled back over himself and stood in front of the other fallen man, who'd rounded the bed.

"The name's," Athien grabbed the man's gun with both hands and clasped his wrists as well, looming into his face and deepened his voice.

"Sentinel. Deliver it. And if you haven't been caught or handed yourself in by two days, if I find you again, I will make you wish you just had broken ribs." He twisted the gun from

42

the man's hands and held tight to his wrists.

Tears crawled from the gunmen's eyes as he looked in disarray at the scene around him. He then stood straight, sniffed snot back up his nose and spoke with a hate spitting tongue.

"Yeah, he'll hear, got it. Sentinel hey, I like it, got a nice ring to it and all that. But, you got to know, he means business, and if you go after him," He looked briefly around, as if expecting to see whoever he worked for to be standing right behind him. "He'll take whatever good there is in your life." Athien let his hands go and stepped back, giving him space.

"You have two days, and there are police on their way up here right now. I have no fear of whoever he is. Oh, and, those cops," Athien motioned to the cop behind him and the one next to the bed. "They aren't dead. It's simple to tell." He pointed towards the door with one hand, the other going for the gun of his grapple.

"Now get out. I don't want to see you again, unless it's on the news or, in the likelihood of your boss lashing out, dead in a river." The man took off at a run, turned right, and headed directly for the stairs to the left, Athien followed shortly after.

"Don't speak of me, or you'll meet what they met." He left the gag in Barn's mouth and got to the stairwell just as the officers moved in from the elevator. He turned the radio into the officer's frequency as he climbed the stairs, eager to be out of the building and the suburb before more officers arrived to clean up the mess.

"They're mostly gone now, we got two of them and…." The lead officer on the third floor entered the room and gagged.

"What the hell happened here? Where is Danny?" They checked the officers and the criminals alike, as Athien escaped from the rooftop without incident, seeing that the door to the stairwell his bag hid behind was open. In contrast, before it was closed, he could hear the faded echoes of the gunmen he'd let go.

Well, what an eventful night. He grabbed his bag and jumped down the fire escape side in a controlled fall for two stories, before he caught the last ladder and dropped safely to the ground.

He took off the helmet, after he made sure the coast was clear. Then he changed into the coat, shirt and pants he'd carried with him. Athien put the rest into the duffle bag and zipped it up, taking the key out before he did so and entered the car, the bag flew to the back as he threw it.

The main street was full of people and cars as he passed back after doing a half block, closed off to traffic as more police and hospital crew engaged with the injured. Athien saw Barns being escorted to the ambulance as he turned off to another side street adjacent to the hospital, and rounded his way back to the house.

There were a lot fewer cars on the road, and the travel was fast as a result, but as the car drove closer to home, Athien noticed a small, yet piercing, burning he felt in between his shoulder blades.

He pulled over, dulled the windows and turned on the lights. Remembering what it felt like to be bitten by a snake.

Athien pulled his jacket down his arms and unbuttoned his shirt, then turned and whistled as he felt pain slice up to his neck and brain as he saw his back muscles twist around so he could see in the rear-view mirror.

A thin crevice ran over his muscles and blood spread down his back from the wound. It would be difficult to stitch or clean by himself.

He replaced his shirt and jacket and returned to the road, mind going over all the things he'd learned throughout the night and ignored the growing pain he felt.

Going to need some help with this wound. Must have been that handgun shot he fired as I moved against the guy at the door.

He arrived at the house just before ten, the T.V. off, and no other lights present in the place that he could see from the drive passed.

Athien stepped out of the car and closed the door, when the lights came on not of his doing, and he spun around, already back into a fighter's stance, though his back slowed him.

Kali stood in the doorway, hands on her hips in a matter-of-fact way. Athien noticed the computer was on and the files tab showed that she'd opened all of them.

She smirked.

"So, what's wrong tonight, Mr Dickens?" She motioned for Athien to sit on the desk corner near the door. He walked over slowly and peeled off his jacket, blood droplets falling to the ground from his shirt.

He grimaced as she grabbed an alcoholic swab and pressed it onto the wound.

"Thank you, Kali." He said through slightly clenched teeth.

Mordacai, you'll lead me to this Caretaker. Then I'll find Barn's handler and the other major players, the war against Melbourne's crime, starts now.

5

Chapter 5 A night of thought

"There's a lot of crime in this city," A News reporter said through a radio. "An increase of over two hundred per cent in the last few years has seen the outskirts and even the CBD hit with varying degrees of success. But it's not all bad, the rise of crime has fleshed out the single time crooks. It's made policing the city more of an ease for the authorities and a good thing, because now their job, while not being any easier, has been a whole lot, simpler."

Kali, ever listening, spoke up as the broadcast ended.

"Is that why you're doing it here? Because there's so much crime?"

"I'm not fighting for the law, that's not the goal or the means. What was done to me as a kid, an accident meant for someone else, it doesn't make what I do about justice or revenge." Athien stood in his combat suit as he surveyed a small warehouse in the business district of Richmond, close to the train station. He talked into his mask's newly developed mic piece.

"That's good, I suppose, no need to go beating on people for just having a little bad luck." Kali talked on the other end of the call, her voice sounded like it was frailer to Athien than it did in person.

"I'm giving the injustice criminals give back to them, and stopping crimes before they're committed by ending the circulation of the system. Though no one will sign up for a trip to Painesville." Unknown to Athien, Kali laughed at that, not the idea, but the fact he could say it at all and then make a joke about going after people to hurt them.

"You're one to watch, I know I wouldn't want to be in that town." Athien moved from where he'd been standing, seeing three trucks turn on almost simultaneously as workers gathered up boxes to put inside them. It was a quiet place, at four in the morning, and Athien wondered what he'd do for sleep before the airport in a few hours. Samantha had called last night to say they were leaving Alazarath, one day after Athien had learned about The Caretaker.

"I'm also going to end the Order, but to do that I've got to weaken them, Melbourne is one of their biggest assets, just one of their stock rooms I'd learned of while working for them gave me all the gear I have now." He walked to the back of the warehouse and grappled to the roof, sure to be as quiet as possible. He rolled as he landed to avoid any unnecessary damage or noise.

"Well, whatever you commit too, I'd bet on you completing it. Most people don't go after people doing the wrong thing, especially with a graze down one of the most moved parts of their body a day after nearly being shot at point blank range." Athien looked down and counted the men he could see, while waiting for the truck drivers to leave with the cargo that they so desperately wanted to creep with.

Twelve workers, three drivers and three guards for each, all with guns and moving the largest assortment of oddities I've ever seen. He summarised, it seemed one of the last packages being loaded onto the truck on the far left, a chair of sorts.

The trucks were all black canvas, white metal lined, single container vehicles with the same bland front design. The warehouse was vacant, besides the gear, causing Athien to believe they were just objects to sell, a flush of cash offered to the business. It'd be useful for a criminal organisation trying to hide its real wares inside everyday objects or hidden within the bundles.

"Okay, I've got to go now, got some skulls to crack." Athien stopped the call and readied himself to pounce, as he moved to the next outcrop of the building's roof and prepared to jump the trucks as they neared to leave.

He'd received a tip from the Barns, who'd signalled him on live television using the address covertly as the police escorted him away from the camera.

SMASH!

Athien slammed onto the truck's roof, his foot almost slipping from the edge as he used a knee to hold his body in place.

The drivers already in the vehicles were taken aback as the two on the outside saw the sudden attacker. Another panicked and started the truck, which roared to life and chucked a mammoth of smoke into Athien lungs as the brief wind blew it straight back towards the warehouse.

Oops.

He rolled from the roof of the truck and kicked the driver's door shut next to his own, the one on the left and ran at the back of the trucks where four men were prepared to fight him, guns dropped in the interest if their cargo was safe.

48

Expensive furniture.

Athien ran into the group, his head snapped back as the first punch went straight for it. He caught the attack and sent a knee right into their stomach, then dropped as another came for his hip and another around his side to flank him.

Athien jumped up, took the punch to his right shoulder and turned, following the energy, the man's hand acting like a magnet as Athien took it to the ground. The one who flanked him dug two punches deep into Athien's side as he pushed the other to the ground. Then they found their leg being taken from underneath as Athien sideswiped it with an arched leg attack.

Hurt by the punches, Athien breathed profoundly and shook off the pain as he rounded on the last man, the drivers got out of their vehicles by his sides and got the rest of the men to attack him. The last one tried to get a truck away.

Athien punched the man in the face then quickly kicked both his knees from the inside, leaving the body to fall in agony as the other five workers came up the side of the truck.

They yelled as the other two trucks turned on and more smoke bellowed into the morning sky.

Athien tapped the two trucks before he confronted them, his arms and shoulders squared up to cover the whole space between the trucks.

"I am Sentinel!" He yelled back and immediately blocked a kick aimed for his stomach with two hands pushing it from the side, which caused the man to kick the truck instead.

The trucks began to move away as Athien combated the rest, and he disengaged as the third truck came into view, running at it like a beast as the group followed. He reached the back as the truck left the yard, and tapped the end, before turning back and against the of the warehouse grounds, so the others lost sight of him for a moment.

He clotheslined three of them as they came around the corner and kicked the other two's knees out from behind as they passed, beating each one a few times as they attempted to rise again.

"Kali," Athien called her back as he pulled them back into the yard, the others there too injured to fight back or just scared he'd beat them again. "The trucks are tapped, follow their movements and tell me where they end up, I'll call the police and have this lot arrested before I head back for the night.

"I think you mean day, sir, and yes, I can see the three dots leaving the suburb as we speak. Good luck with your interrogation." She ended the call, and Athien knelt slightly before his victims, all of whom stared at him with a mixture of feelings.

"Where can I find The Caretaker, and which of you knows his man, Mordacai." He said with a deepened voice, his mask faced each face in turn as he asked.

They stayed silent for several seconds, and Athien shook his head and flexed his knuckles menacingly.

"Well then, I guess the bones start breaking." He grabbed the one closest to him, a man with long arms and a drug smelling breath, with pure white skin and oversized clothes. He drew the man close to his face, holding him with both hands.

"Wait." Said a man behind him, in the middle of the group. They were wet and muddy from the fall outside the grounds. Athien kicked him over.

"Start talking." He said roughly as he stood over the criminal.

Athien arrived back at the garage, his body bruised and slightly tired, but alive and with enough information for the night not to have been a total waste.

Kali sat in the big chair, asleep, with the screen of the computer on and a video of his night's events taking up one half, paused before the interrogation. The other half showed an enlarged map of the city and five red bleeping lights.

Athien took off his gloves and coat, and moved to the computer and Kali's side, having not realised she was asleep, he exclaimed.

"They've stopped at the convention centre." Kali awoke with a slow moan and yawned, before giving the screen a second of her attention.

"Think you could change the brightness setting on this?" She croaked, blinking rapidly to adjust to the light, as Athien watched the interrogation.

"Sure." He reached over and pressed a button on the side of the screen, which dimmed the light.

"He, he doesn't go by any name, not to us, we never saw him." The man in the video shouted.

Athien paused it again, pulled up an internet tab and used it to search the building's trucks he'd stopped.

"It is. This is the building that Prometheus will be giving his talk in this weekend. In a matter of days, now. Why would they take all that old equipment to that, building in particular?" The site he went on showed the buildings standard information, it was a convention centre, made with spacious seminar rooms for private viewings and an ample open space for everything else, complete with office spaces in the higher up floors and a large kitchen for meals.

"Seems like it would be a lovely place to steal from valuable people, or maybe cause some chaos." Kali offered, her hand scratched an itchy spot on her neck as she answered.

51

Athien's eyes skewed up as he thought of what could be the reasoning behind the location of the truck, and what whoever they were from wanted with the presentation.

"What if it's an auction? Or they're letting some of the stuff be taken by someone at the convention? Someone who works with the person responsible for the trucks, or even larger?" Athien wondered, before he glanced at the clock on the computer and noted the time it would take for him to get to the airport.

I'll need a few hours' sleep if I'm going to be staking out the entire convention centre tomorrow. And an extra pair of eyes at least. He looked down at Kali and put his hands against the table, he leaned slightly and breathed.

"You're going to need me to be watching cameras, aren't you?" Even though she was tired, Athien saw a little light spark in her eyes as she anticipated the challenge. Kali had grown up with computers and technology, and loved the chance to prove her prowess.

"Yes, please. Could you drive me? I need to go meet Samantha and Prometheus at the airport, but after that, could you drive me to the convention centre?" Athien asked without pleading, but with a slight bit of hope to his voice. He knew she liked to help with his adventures as Sentinel, even though it meant she had to patch up his worse injuries herself.

She nodded and pushed the chair aside as she stood.

"I've watched you, your father and your father's and mine grow to be some of the strongest people I've ever met. Whether it was physical, mental or, in your case, both. Your mother was one of my best friends as well and she was just like you. Except," Kali looked him up and down and grabbed the helmet on the table. "She had a better taste in attire, so

52

does your father." Athien smiled at that, took the helmet and begun to put his things back inside the box.

"I'm working on that, there are a few things I want to try, when this weekend is over, something I found on my travels that should make my attire a little more presentable and stronger." Athien opened another draw in the compartment and showed Kali a shiny and smooth piece of black metal.

She bristled and shook her head, while her hands reached form the pc' screen power button and the mouse to turn the tower off.

"I'll always help this family, it's what I do. You should have seen what your great aunt and I used to get up to in our younger years, back when the World Wide Web wasn't anywhere near as secure as it is now. Along with common security." The power to the device cut as it turned off, and Athien thanked Kali for her commitment and friendship.

"Thanks, Miss Kali." She headed for the door so he could change.

"Oh Athien, I'll see you at the airport. Good night." She opened the door and almost closed it, but Athien spoke again.

"Oh, what do you think about code names, while we're over the wire?" Kali stopped at the door while Athien took off his vest and replaced it with a shirt.

Kali poked her head around the door.

"Sentinel, was it? I'm fine with that, but I'm also fine with Kali, that makes enough sense as it is, being an offensive technical system." He laughed again, and she closed the door behind herself.

6

Chapter 6 Pickup

Athien awoke to a quiet house the next day. He could feel a developed bruise from the night before. He put on a suit with dark blue jacket and pants, and a red shirt. He finished the look with a black long tie.

"Well, it's time to get to the airport soon." He said to himself, seeing the twelfth-hour chime on his alarm clock.

He made breakfast, Weet-bix and yoghurt, with a warm tea afterwards from Kali's yellow knit covered teapot. He then sat at the wooden kitchen table, casually flipping through the channels until he saw something that caught his interest.

There was a reporter, at the warehouse he'd gone to earlier that morning. She talked about the attack on the men working there, and reported that they were all questioned thoroughly on why they were tied up. Athien turned the T.V. volume up.

"The workers report saying that they were attacked, they don't know what by and they are all scared. Police believe this might be the work of the same person who left Annabelle Ruffton's apartment shortly before police came. I'm here with Captain Deer, Mr Deer, what do you have to say on these last two attacks we've seen?" The camera turned and moved backwards so the viewer could see the Captain, his uniform perfectly pristine and eyes alert.

"We are yet to find proof on the matter as of yet, but it seems like there is a strange connection between the victims. Both sets were beaten, the attacker has the skill and knows what they are doing. But without any of the workers we met last night testifying to getting attacked by a vigilante, there is no action to be taken, besides everyone to be wary of this attacker." Deer looked directly into the camera as he finished, warning the audience, as well as the reporter, of the danger that the vigilante posed.

Athien rose from his seat, cleaned his bowl and turned off the T.V. The kitchen was faced towards the sun, so he had to squint slightly as he passed by, light reflecting off the white counters and the stove.

He went back to his room and grabbed his phone and laptop in the briefcase he always kept beside the door. In it was his gear that Kali would use to monitor the building. There was also a reinforced seal and it could act as a good weapon, the insides padded from most kinds of damage. It was also just a common-looking laptop, grey with white keys.

The street was busy, being a Saturday, there were families out with their kids on the lawns and the occasional lawn-mower sounds over the laughter. Athien walked quickly, tempted to talk to the neighbours as he passed, but knowing he was going to be slightly late, he decided not to.

They'll be there when I get back. They were friendly people, a young couple with two kids, boys, Jake and Tyler Bate. He liked them, both smart and imaginative, as they played in the lawn with their cars, they both talked about how they could build a ramp to propel the vehicles higher into the air.

The tram was still the same on weekends, over packed, no matter what time it was taken. Athien got on and managed to get a seat after three stops towards the city. His case sat on the floor under his seat, and he looked around the entire time he was one, ensuring he didn't see anyone doing the same thing as the men he'd seen before.

The tram stopped in front of a train station, Flinders Street, after an hour of travelling, Athien made on stop at the station before travelling on to it to Avalon airport.

Athien walked to the corner of the famous station, intent on walking straight in, when a shop at the corner of the station caught his eye. It was a hat store, tucked away as a set of two-story windows below the sidewalk and rows of hats on the walls in the shop as back. He stepped into the shop and immediately found a hat he liked the look of.

It was a dark red fedora with a blue inner lined thread, matched the colours of his suit entirely. The man at the counter, a stout man with wrinkles over his eyes and weedy arms and a relatively thick gait stepped around the counter and motioned to him with great happiness.

"It's a fine hat, and suits you perfectly." He said cheerily, his wrinkles lifted and Athien saw a young pair of eyes stared intently at him as a picked the hat from the stand and studied it. He'd meant to buy a hat for a time, but always had a problem finding one he liked.

Right on then, James. He thought as he turned to the seller, hat in hand, thinking about his only favourite T.V. character. Though, theirs usually was in black or cream.

He walked out with the new hat on his head, his blond mid-length hair hidden and briefcase in hand. Athien tapped onto the station with his transport card and boarded the train, three minutes before it departed. The conductor seemed to try to deafen him as she yelled into the microphone next to him.

"Train is boarding now, platform five boarding now."

Athien called a taxi from the station he stopped at next and made it to Avalon without incident. The rain held out still, even though the sky had gotten considerably darker, near black swirls contorted the sky, much different to the sun of the morning.

"Hello, I was wondering if the Dickens aeroplane has landed yet?" He asked the help desk, displaying his I.D. so they would verify he could ask the question. They replied saying it was in it was about to land, and that he should be pleased to wait at the bay, or go straight to the hanger, where a service bus would drive him.

The weight of my family's name holds strong with most walks of life. He noticed the airports pleasure to help out such a rich and influential person, but, it was customary, they did it with others, he was just used to it.

Minutes later, he waited in the hanger, driven by a luggage cart driver to the hanger. A slick black chrome plane stopped just as he sat there, with silver trim lines and two compartments. Athien waved to the aviator as he walked around to meet them at the stairs. They extended from the bottom of the plane to the ground near where he stood.

He saw two figures in the plane through one of the windows, waiting patiently as the aviator came into the back and talked to them.

"Athien! How are you?" Samantha stood at the door to the plane, then sped down the ramp and hugged Athien, her arms caused Athien's bruised side to react harshly, but he grabbed her back and hugged deeply for a moment.

"It's good to see you, Sam, I'm good, a little bruised, took a few punches the other day and I'm healing, but that's talk for later. You look well, and you got the place in the audition. Well done." Athien watched as his cousin glowed in his phrases. She did look well, hair brown, with the hint of urban, straight to below her back, a smile the size of her face and clean, intelligent eyes watched him with concern and playfulness. She wore a jacket, long-sleeved with a yellow chest.. Her jeans were black, and had plenty of pockets for her gear.

"Well, that's fine, and yes! I'm going to start in two months, I hope you're okay," She dropped her voice and looked around discreetly. "It must get tiring, killing people and beating up bad guys." She said quietly, hastily. Athien winced slightly, before checking himself how clear the coast was.

"I don't do that anymore. It was complicated. But yeah, the city has a lot of work to do, before I leave for Alazarath." Samantha hugged him again, as Athien watched a man approach the door and shake hands with the aviator.

"Just glad you're not with them anymore," She noticed his contraction of muscle as his lips tightened, looking past her. "It's not good for character!" She said aloud, loud enough to be heard by the man who stepped onto the ramp.

"Athien, it is great to see you again. How was the world? I see you and Sam are catching up again." Prometheus walked down the plane ramp and put out his arm, which Athien grabbed and hugged half his body.

"Prometheus, it's been a long time," Athien took in his father's kept, short blond hair, his three-piece black suit and white tie, and his tired expression was hiding well behind his brows. "The world was, educational, but I'm glad to be back in society, two years of solidarity is fine, but, I missed the city." He motioned for them to follow him out of the hanger, as the aviator and two workers took the cargo from the plane in a cargo carrier.

"So, do you have transport for us, Athien?" Samantha walked with him as Prometheus took a case that was run to him from the plane.

"Thank you, Clarence, insure the rest is taken to our hotel, will you?" Prometheus said, caught up to the others as they entered customs, Athien walked through the scanner as well, his and Prometheus's cases cleared through the scanner separately.

"Yes, I have Kali coming to pick us up, to take us straight to the conference building." They both waited for Samantha to be scanned, as she took her phone, purse, a brush, a notebook and a pair of clips from her different pockets.

"Oh, so that's who you're staying with, not where I pictured you, but, I guess I am picturing you from two years ago, perhaps you should write a memoir of your events." Prometheus grabbed Athien by the shoulders, unconcerned by his son's uneasy expression. He looked at the back of Athien's head and brushed the hair slightly with his thumb.

"It's fine, there hasn't been any change. If anything, my memory and thought processing has improved greatly, since last we met." Athien moved away from his father's hand, smiling back and directed them to the park off to the side, where a black, old-style limousine sat in the taxi section. Prometheus gave him a look as he walked behind the two young adults.

"Wow, I didn't know auntie owned any cars like that!" Samantha laughed, seeing the car and her aunt stand out as they exited the airport. It was American, so she stood on the sidewalk, not the road.

"It was our parent's. They bought it years ago." Prometheus smiled at the old, slick vehicle, and watched with Athien as Samantha ran to her aunt. She was Sam's favourite aunt, and they hugged deeply.

Athien sat in the back, with Samantha, as Prometheus shut the front of the car off from them, he sat with Kali in the front of the vehicle. The small wall that separated them was for privacy. Still, Athien knew Kali had put in security measures for the car, and that she could see him if he just looked at her from the window.

"Wow, it's been ages since I've been in this city, sure, it's smaller than Alazarath, at its centre, but, there is something, extravagant, about it." Samantha leaned out the window slightly as they passed over the Western Gate Bridge, hair wiped back against the side of the car as she took in the cities sights, cars raced past as they cruised the middle lane.

"It's busy, and the people here all have their things to do. But there's a lot that goes on here that nobody ever sees." Athien looked out his window briefly and wondered what was being said in the front, he'd never seen his aunt and father talk before. It was rare to see them talk about anything other than business. He looked at her from the review mirror, as she spoke to the bonnet, his father not seen.

"So that's what you've been up to, I caught some news as we flew over here. That there's been some, disturbances in the neighbourhood." She smiled while her eyes fluttered with concern.

"It's fine," Athien opened his jacket and pulled his shirt up slightly, revealing a blue and purple bruise that spread a few centimetres in an oval shape, on his side. Below his ribs. "This was a kick, I rolled before it got bad, but, it's been a while since I've been hit." He pulled his shirt down and sat back into the seat of the car, eyes closed as he remembered the incident.

"Well, you're going to need a better suit then, something that can actually protect you when you go up against whoever it is you're hunting." Athien's eyes opened quickly, Sam's voice had dulled as she spoke, and when he looked at her, for a second, she seemed hurt.

"Wait, who approached you?" Was it The Order?" Athien leaned forward again, ignoring his pains. Samantha nodded solemnly and grimaced as she shrugged.

"They didn't say much, man's name was Hazard," Athien's face skrewed up as she said the man's name. "Came to me, a month and a half ago, said he'd seen you meet me last time you were in Alazarath and that I should be careful with you around, that they'd always be watching you, even if you left." His jaw locked, Athien breathed three deep breaths, then released.

"Hazard, of course, he's, he has been a huge part of my life for far too long. But, he's retired now, so that angles covered," Athien swallowed and swiped a hand through his hair, a slight bout of nerves conflicting his ordered mind.

"Wow, retired? That's a thing that killers can do?" She said half-heartedly. The car bumped up slightly as they drove into the main CBD area and exited the freeway.

"Yeah, he's the one who shot me. Also, the person who I worked under while I was in the Order. He's good at what he does, I'll give him that, but I don't care if they're watching me. The fact that he came to you, that was his assurance against me, but I left before he could use it." Athien shuddered and looked outside again, throwing his thoughts out the window as he saw they were almost at their location.

Kali had stopped speaking to Prometheus, Athien saw her, eyes draw to the front of the car as she stared, unblinkingly at the way ahead. Every now and then, her eyes would dart to the mirror, whether to look at Athien or to see traffic behind, he didn't really know. Still, he smiled every time he saw her, a code to them both if she smiled back, everything was okay.

The car drove up a ramp, and Athien saw the front door to the convention centre was crowded with people, all streaming into the event with bags and cameras. Doubtlessly there would be technology exhibits and rival standoffs at the meet, even from here, he could see flags of other industry leaders on the walls of the inner room.

"Oh. Are we here already?" Samantha undid her seatbelt as Kali parked the car on the roof, their spot in a V.I.P. section.

"Yes, this is the place." Athien knocked the back seat of the car and pulled out his briefcase. Samantha was surprised, having not seen him put it in there when they had entered the car. Athien took out a pen, his phone, and a few other gadgets he put inside the jacket he wore. Samantha nodded, understanding there were things her secretive cousin would keep to himself. She exited the vehicle at speed, the clouds darkened further, and they all witnessed the first of the droplets fall onto the bonnet of the car as they walked to the elevator.

7

Chapter 7 The Convention

"Welcome, everyone, to this year's Tech-athon convention, where we bring you the tomorrow, of today." A presenter spoke into a microphone as they entered the main ground floor area. Kali, was already tapped into the building's infrastructure, she'd visited it before going to get Athien and the others from the airport.

The group were scanned as they entered the huge space, and Athien's father cleared the scan.

There came a light beep, as Athien stepped through the scanner. The guards did not look pleased as Athien looked confusedly at his attire and patted down his pockets.

"Ah!" He exclaimed, as he pulled a pen from his pocket and showed it to the guards, one of them approached and took the pen, not bothering to scan it. He nodded to Athien and smirked softly, pocketing the pen as he showed them through to the convention area.

"Excuse me, but that pen..." Prometheus took the man's shoulder as he meant to leave them, just a few metres from thousands of people gathering into the area. The guard turned, just as Athien broke the contact, he pushed his father's arm away. Athien shook his head, then jerked towards the people they were about to move into a room with, cameras guarded each person from all sides and the journalists and hobbyists themselves all had a device.

Something they could easily make a big deal over, of course, that much attention also puts me in a spotlight. So if anything goes down, it might be challenging.

"It's just a pen." He added for good measure, as Prometheus lowered his hand and nodded the guard away. His neck and chin uncurling from their locked positions, standard practise for a highly remarked C.E.O.

"Hey, Prom, where do you have to be? I think I'll go have a look at the displays, before all the talking starts." Samantha piped up as they entered the central area, the stage seemed miles away from behind the sea of people. Prometheus nodded as he proceeded to walk around the outskirts of the centre, eyes flying to each face, as he tried to find someone.

"Indo is here," Athien pointed discreetly to a man with a white moustache and brown hair. They wore an expensive white suit and talked with a shorter, fat man, in a very similar suit with full-length brown hair and no facial hair, who Athien pointed to. "And there's the snake, Euro." He was world-famous for having made the super-fast superhero of Alazarath, Bolt, in danger. Though no one could put him away for it.

"Who else is here, son? I can't make out a lot when there are so many normal people among us. Can you see the Bots, or that Sound Wavz hero girl, she's the C.E.O. now and a superhero, you know, after her father died." Prometheus remarked, looking about the room.

"They're both here, Nathaniel Bot and Sound Wavz, their

parents, must be up here too," Athien nodded to the stage as he passed it and entered the door to the stairs at the end of the room.

Sound Wavz, or Erica, was a lead scientist of her father's old company, carrying on his name as a hero after his death three years ago.

Athien put an earpiece, one of the pieces of equipment he'd grabbed from the case, into his ear and turned it on. He monitored the rest of the room as he and Samantha stepped onto the stage.

It was huge, covering a large portion of the entire floor, with blue L.E.D. lights that went widthways across the whole space, which made it look like a giant, side-on wave from the audience's perspective. Outside of that, the room curved around the stage, grey marble with floor L.E.D.s of blistering sunlight. From the roof, came the real spectacle, a completely blue-stained glass set of panels that were boarded with black chrome metal. The glass seemed to absorb all the sky within its folds. The forked lightning that begun to cross the sky, mixed with the black, swirling clouds, made the room feel like it was in the eye of a hurricane.

Athien wondered at it for a moment, before he relayed his findings to Prometheus. They had nearly made it to the other side of the stage, where a bunch of people were positioned and talking rapidly.

"Well, that Christopher Dale, the one who wouldn't sell his ore to you, he's here. And I see both Derrick Day and Nick West, the reporters for the A.N.A. Oh, and, of course, some of The Forge's greatest workers." Athien motioned to the lab coat wearing supporters of Prometheus's company, the building of which, he called the Forge. Finished with his list of anyone he

65

thought Prometheus would find interesting.

"We're up and running, sir." Kali suddenly said in his ear.

Athien merged with the fifty other people on the end of the stage, all of whom were talking excitedly about the presentations and their new projects. Luke Euro and Alexander Indo both reached the group first.

"Okay, let's get this operation underway," Athien whispered to Kali, through the earpiece. He heard furious tapping on her end of the line and frowned slightly.

"Operation Sparrow's Keep is underway," She replied. Athien was relieved that they hadn't somehow been caught already, he needed to find out what was going down with the equipment he'd seen before. "I can see you on, fifteen cameras, and there is a lot of movement all over this building. Though I can confirm that the trucks are still here, your tracking devices are offline. I'll monitor the other floors and rooms, you keep your eyes peeled on the ground, there's bound to be something happening, somewhere today." She continued to tap away at the laptop as Athien watched Prometheus clap shoulders with Euro, both men competed for the most smiling face. At the same time, their eyes stared daggers through to each other's souls.

"Samantha? Did you want to inspect the expo, before that presenter starts to yell at everyone again?" Athien tapped her shoulder as she stood, waiting for Prometheus to introduce her to someone on the stage. She looked at Athien with pleasure, having felt strange to have been in the same space as so many intellectually known people for so long.

"Thanks, yeah," She did a half curtsy and took his arm, then the two of them escorted each other down the stairs on that side of the stage and joined the throng of watchers.

The floor was a mess of people, and as the two of them moved within it, the objects they found ranged in sizes from a giant satellite replica in the centre of the space. It was tall and surrounded by rope and guards. Then there was the smallest on show, a new portable device that resembled a mix between a phone and a laptop.

"Wow, some of these look amazing," Samantha commented as they viewed the twentieth exhibit, plans for an orbiting satellite that would transmit internet downloads through the use of light.

"Yeah, because it's in space, the light will have little to obstruct it, giving communication another big lift." Athien laughed at his own joke and watched the presenter move towards the centre of the stage.

"That seems smart." Samantha followed his line of sight and saw the presenter tap his mic on his head experimentally. The sound of his finger tap echoed from all sides of the room.

"It's about to start, this should be fun." She said quietly.

"Athien?" He suddenly heard Kali's voice in his ear.

"Again, I'd like to welcome everyone here, to the sixteenth annual Tech-athon, hosted this year in this wonderful building and in the great, city of Melbourne." The presenter began to talk as Athien turned away from the stage, pretending to look at one of the exhibits.

"Kali, what's the matter? What's going on?" He asked, his face remained clear as he talked, though there was a crease to his eyebrows, it looked like he was thinking about the piece, not the situation in his ear.

"Something's happening, on the third floor, two guards just stepped off, and their security is off. I've got no sights there, but the trucks, there are a lot of guards there. You might want

67

to head to the third floor, before they do whatever they want to do, up there." Athien turned around again, his mind raced as he figured out the most direct route to the third floor.

"Athien, what are you doing?" He started slightly as Samantha touched his shoulder, bringing him back to the moment that was now. He looked at her, and wondered whether this was something he should include her in.

"Listen, I'm working right now too, I have to get up to the third floor." He whispered as he drew her close, people around them looked slightly concerned with their actions, moved around them to watch as the speakers of the day walked into the middle of the stage.

Among them, Prometheus was the tallest, had the most wide-mouthed smile and walked with the least amount of purpose, strolling into the middle, ahead of his fellow speakers. He waved with one hand, he's right, the other fixed the mic he had been given to sit just below his lips.

Samantha looked at Athien credulously, resolved that his actions were right, she nodded and begun to lead him through the crowd.

"Samantha, wait." He snipped though he let her lead him, so that they didn't draw attention. They walked quickly, but with the room, so that their movement wouldn't be noticed in the horde of people.

"Athien, there's nothing to be said, I'm an actor, you need a distraction when we get to the floor." Samantha talked with sharp sense that Athien felt was commendable, if she knew what she was up against, he believed she'd be less ready to act the part he required.

Meanwhile, the first speaker begun to present his piece, Nathaniel Bot, eighteen-year-old prodigy in electro-engineering and head of research at M.A.K.E. Industries, stood with his father for his first expo.

"Hi, you might not know me, but I know my father's company better than most people know their own faces, I'm Nathaniel Bot, and this, is our tech," He pressed a button in his hand. The wall at the back of the stage became a large projected image of a small mechanical suit. In it, a man ran on a treadmill, a pace keeper on the wall stated he was running at forty kilometres per hour. "The future of transportation on a human scale." His speech continued with an uproar from the audience that he joined in on. Athien and Samantha were already in the stairwell, unable to hear what he said next.

"Samantha," Athien stooped her once they were in the staircase and unseen by the audience. "Listen to me, these people might be armed, they might try to hurt you." She looked unfazed by this and attempted to listen to Nathaniel's speech as Athien trapped her in the staircase.

"Athien, I know how to defend myself. You've been away a while, and I've been training since we last saw each other as well. I want to be able to act as much as I can, so I need to be fit and capable," She said all at once, stopping to catch her breath before she finished. "So let's go do this, before Prometheus notices we're not in the audience and we both get into trouble."

"Alright, let's do this then." Athien turned away from her, thankful for her compassion to acting. He didn't show any indication that he was talking to anyone, but spoke to Kali as he walked on ahead.

"Catch-all that?" He asked the elevator insight as they rushed to the end of the building, few people on the floor at the back of the building, not even the receptionist office was open.

"Every word, always surprised me, that girl did. You'll have to watch her, she's good." Athien looked back at her as he pressed the elevator button and she crossed within two meters of him.

"Can you play Prometheus through the piece when he speaks?" He asked, not only for Samantha's benefit if they missed it, but because he also wanted to know what his father would be unveiling. Athien didn't know what he'd be showing off.

"Of course I can, good luck up there, I might lose you. I'll give you updates when you're in the elevator." she waited as Athien and Samantha entered the elevator.

As the door closed, Kali continued. "There are seven guards, two tall males with a handgun each and the others all look like regular guards, three females and two other males, ones on the short side and might prove a handle, he seems strong of mind. Like I said, they've just unloaded the truck and are about to start to make their way upstarts to you, it seems, and I have..." Athien waited for her to respond, and realised that there was definitely something going down on the floor they'd reached, if his radio had gone out. The elevator opened and revealed a cream coloured hall with white faded glass doors and windows the whole way down to a black wood end, the door had a gold knob and had writing on it.

"Okay, in a few minutes, we're going to have several people get up to this level and their bringing that equipment I talked about. We've got to find out what's going on here, without anyone knowing that we were here." Athien stepped into the hallway and looked at the first window to his left, the door read;

"Storage Wagon #1" And was dark as night inside the room, even with the light of the hallway.

"Okay, let's go see what that room is, after all, these rooms are too dark to see into." Samantha stalked out of the elevator, and straight down the hall. She tried each handle to the doors on the right side as she went. Athien was irritated by her straight forward approach.

Athien followed, using a similar approach at each wall he passed for any sounds of people or mechanics. He couldn't detect any noise in the rooms, and all of the doors on the left were locked. A large black door was standing before them.

"It says, Archie Buth's Pandemonium. Wonder what that means." Samantha tried the doorknob as Athien reached her and immediately stepped to the side as she began to push the door open.

"It's a shop, of sorts," Athien said as the lights came on beyond the door and they were struck with bright lights. Inside, the dark wood continued to shine throughout the office space they'd stepped into.

The main desk said the same thing as the door, and everything on it had some amount of gold on it, the pen, books and even loose-leaf paper. On the walls, stood all many of objects, small bottles and other antique objects. Athien saw swords that hung on the walls by their sheaths, and books that carried strange letters.

"This place is a hodgepodge with things, what is it?" Samantha asked, she picked up a small dagger that rested on the right side wall shelf, next to an old cash register of marked silver.

Athien looked for cameras, and when he found none, he went to the desk and checked the draws. He found, in the right top one, three ledgers, written in an old variant of Romanian

71

Latin, with scrumptious handwriting and an ornate ink quill and bottle.

"Whoever this belongs to, they are a collector. The gear they're bringing up here must be worth a lot more than it looks to be," Athien heard a clap in his ear, and realised that, somehow the earpiece was working again. "Take some pictures, please. If anything, we can show this to the owner of this building and get whoever owns it evicted."

"Athien, can you hear me? Prometheus is starting." Kali spoke to him near the earpiece, just as Athien heard the ringing sound of an elevator being called down to the ground floor.

"Kali, I can hear you, patch him through, those gunmen are coming up as we speak, whatever I expected to find up here, this wasn't it." Athien received a weird look from Samantha, her face showed concussion as she heard her aunt's name and watched Athien race to the door.

He closed it with a slam and thought to lock the door. Instead looked around the room to find if there was anywhere for them to hide inside.

"Done. They've arrived on the floor, you better hide." Kali watched the bottom floor elevator icon and saw it flash, signalling its arrival at their floor.

"Samantha, follow me." Athien moved from the door and quickly ran around the table, seeing their place to hide. She followed, looking to the door and back to Athien as he started to remove an old drapery from the wall. It depicted the Great Battle of Troy, with the giant wooden horse in flames and the wall in ruins as the Romans destroyed the city. At the top, there was a bladed soldier, Agamemnon, who stood with Odysseus, as they defeated the giant army the city held.

"Are you talking to aunt Kali? What, is she in on this? How

many others do you have pulling ropes for you?" She asked as he pulled the door handle of the secret door, he'd found it by looking at the top of the drapery, which was indented at the top, where it was hanged, thus meaning it was in front of a gaping hole. The door was locked, and Athien could hear the loud thumps of steps coming from behind the door they'd entered from.

"Only her, now stand back." Athien held up a hand to show her to stop where she was, as she too noticed the sounds that had begun to sound from the hall.

"They're coming!" She whispered furiously.

Athien heard his father's voice through the earpiece as he stepped away from the door, gagging how much time he would have after the door was opened to be completely silent.

"Get in there as fast as you can." Athien brought one leg up and kicked the door, just above the handle. There was a small splintering sound as the lock bit through the wooden brace it sat in. The door opened the full amount, hit the wall behind and bounced halfway back, Athien held it, and Samantha went through immediately.

"Ladies and gentlemen, there is a profound amount of work that goes into funding and forming events as grand as these, so let's start with a clap to all those who did so, for you all to enjoy the howling wind and brilliant display of lightning above us, here today." Athien looked around the room, he wanted it to look as perfect as he could, to hide their traces.

He saw the ledgers and put them back together, thankful for the thick gloves he wore as his finger-marks wouldn't be found. He placed them back as he'd found them and, seeing the rest of the room in shape, ran to the back room and covered the door again, the door falling back into place, even without the lock working.

"Athien, we're in a storage cupboard." Athien felt Samantha standing right behind him and breathed in the smell of dust and musty air. He could feel a breeze coming from somewhere near the floor as it brushed past his legs, it was clear that whoever owned the office hadn't been in the room for quite some time. The storage room was small and packed with boxes on top of boxes, but as he turned, Athien could make out some source of light, hidden behind the boxes and near the back of the room.

Probably a service door or something, a stairwell exit straying to the street below us.

"My project has actually been under development for some time over a year. It's been in its prototype stages since early twenty-twelve in fact, and features some of the most ground-breaking science of the century." Athien piqued his interest at his father's speech, he could name the number of prototypes his father had been developing at that time.

And none of them were significantly world newsworthy. Athien wondered what it was Prometheus was referring to.

The door into the other room opened with a silent wheeze, as many boots stepped past its frame. Athien heard grunts and groans, equipment they'd just lugged three floors, from the loading dock found even further behind the stage, came to rest in the office.

"Athien, there's another car that just drove in next to the trucks. It's a bulky Rover style self-branded car. There are gunmen. We're talking assault rifles." Athien grimaced, he had to think of what this event he was a part of was about.

"Kali, what does the main man look like, has he got black hair, past shoulders and a reasonably sized gut. He is probably also wearing a very thick and tinted pair of sunglasses." Athien remembered the man that Barn's had given up at the hospital, and the recount of his features by the first speaker of the trucker gang he met earlier that morning.

"That fits the description, he's walking them all into the building now. They seem to mean business," Kali babbled, as her sight of the newcomers decreased with every step they took. "Athien, this is becoming a job for the police." Athien shook his head, even though he was outnumbered, he wanted to keep the police as far from these men as possible.

"My son, you see, was shot, you might remember it, went all over the news for too long," Athien reeled as he heard himself being brought up in his father's speech. He regrettably tuned out so he could focus on getting out of this situation.

"Kali, I'm going to hand you to Samantha, you need to get her back to the stage and lead her from the back of this room, there's a special exit out of the wall," Athien spoke with urgency as he handed the earpiece to Samantha. She looked incredulously back at him and looked for the exit.

"Ah, okay I can do that, Sam, are you there sweets?" Kali spoke as Samantha adjusted the piece inside her ear. She nodded at Athien as he pointed for her to get going to the far wall as fast as she could.

This is a nasty plan. Athien thought to himself as he quickly moved some boxes from around the door up, on top of the others.

"Yes, I'm here, what do I have to do." Samantha climbed boxes as she talked and haphazardly fell over the last few in her gracious attempt to be silent. Several boxes of stuff fell onto the floor around the big gap between the door and the room.

"Kali, Athien, there are pills and weird plants inside all of these boxes!" Athien snapped to attention before he was able to chastise her for whispering so loudly.

"Of course!" He said with emphasis, his mind opened to the area he was standing in. Meanwhile, Prometheus continued to speak;

"I'm quite sure that the world will benefit from them, as I've seen firsthand, the amazing small things that they can do for the brain and the human body as a whole. Better memory, thinking, and reaction times are all just small benefits." Samantha was shocked to hear the sound of her uncle talking in her ear.

This is an unusual room, he only comes in from the back entry, which he can just cut the cameras to like he has on the third floor. The reason it feels so dusty is the degraded leaves that have obviously been broken in here for some time. A lost buy of drugs, or stolen from a competitor, Mordacai is planning something big.

Athien looked over to Samantha and asked what was going on, she looked shocked.

"Athien, you're dad, he's..." She started to respond, as Athien heard a commotion in the room next door and as Samantha was yelled to by Kali with instructions of where to go. She watched as Athien cleared more space around the door, and figured she knew what he was planning to do.

"Athien," He looked at her again with wide eyes. "Beat them up fast, then get down here so we can call the police." He nodded, and she opened the thick metal door. It was heavier than she imagined and, as it opened, they were both taken aback by a giant screeching sound that came from the bottom of the door.

"Hey, you guys hear that, sounds like it's coming from

behind the wall over there!" Samantha ran down the stairs of the escape way and saw that she was headed straight for the kitchen space of the centre, even there, there were fantastic glass roofs.

The rain and wind beat on her hard as she ran the two flights of stairs, tearing at her comparatively thin leather jacket and hair as it wiped into her face, stinging her.

"This chip, the Compact Set Memory and Neuron Stabiliser, or C.M.N.S., as we call it, could and will, revolutionise all manner of things, and, had my son's condition been any worse, I wouldn't have been able to use it to attempt to save his life from that crazed gunmen. So I know, personally, that it'd be a great help to the world. Thank you." Samantha caught the end of his speech as she entered the kitchen area, much to the confused chefs that ushered her from it seconds later.

Athien, meanwhile, made ready as the men searched for the source of the noise, one of them just near enough to the door that Athien could smell his breath through the cracked door. He opened the door with a quick hull, and kicked the person through the art piece, the full force of his front kick hit the tall man right in the chest and swept his body onto and through the desk. the desk cracked under the pressure and his weight. Athien ducked as he shut the door,and the other gunmen shot directly into the painting and at whatever had attacked his comrade.

Athien smiled to himself over the predictable actions of the criminals. Now their shots would alert patrons and others in the building, and the police would be called. He needed to secure a way out for himself first, and get the information they wouldn't tell the police.

The shooting stopped, and Athien could see into the room

through the many holes in the door.

"Get in there and check out what hit him, now!" The other gunmen stood in the left side of the room from Athien's perspective, trigger finger still on the gun as his allies stood in front of his line of sight. The one Athien had kicked into the table had yet to rise again, and Athien took comfort in knowing the pain. He felt now, and more he'd feel later, had been put to fair use.

Three others came before the door, and Athien turned against the right side of the wall, he planned to catch at least two of them and pull them into the room with him.

One ripped the canvas down, hearing the door handle wriggle as the door opened slowly.

"There's a door here, maybe we shouldn't go in, the boss was…" Athien heard a shout from the other side of the room as the gunmen approached, himself.

"Whoever is in there attacked us first, kill em!" He yelled at their faces and Athien shuddered.

The door opened fully, and Athien watched as two of them walked into the room first, the others waited for something to happen.

Athien grabbed the first, a women, by the shoulders with his hands and thrust a knee into her stomach. She dropped as the second heard the movement and saw the body dropping, he was unsure as to what had attacked, but he could see a white face in the darkness. Athien kicked at the man, the leg hit him straight in the face and caused him to fall among the boxes Athien had set up behind him.

His leg had appeared in the door's light, so the others were surprised when both of their other comrades were taken down equally quickly. Athien heard the click of a gun as he faced the door. He'd been spotted by another of the henchmen.

"I'm gonna kill you!" Bullets fired into the wall as Athien stepped over the women and barged into the man who had fallen into the boxes. Athien's intent to use that body and the disarrayed boxes as cover for himself.

The shooter grabbed the other two people and threw them both into the room as he reloaded the gun. Athien was relieved the henchman hadn't packed anymore as the other two came at him from over the boxes. Athien stood tall, ready.

"What the hell do you think you are doing!" An angry voice screamed from down the hallway. Everyone, including Athien, stopped to hear it, and the two that would have been pummelling him stepped away and into the doorway. The shades wearing man entered the room, flagged by his three armed guards.

"There's." The gunmen who had shot at Athien attempted to explain.

A gunshot sounded, this one more powerful than the last, and Athien saw a henchman fall into the doorway, the other two yelled and screamed as they crawled into the office and begged. More guns pointed at them too. Athien, driven by a sudden and quick shot of fear at the dead body and his lack of weapons, almost wanted to join them on the floor, but he knew they'd be gone soon too.

So far, Mordacai doesn't know that I'm here. He crept around the edge of the room, several boxes knocked over in his way to get to the door Samantha had left open. As he aligned himself with the doorway, the others grovelled in, Athien ducked and listened while Mordacai talked to them.

"You were meant to just deliver the goods, not die, not shoot up MY office and attempt to steal MY goods, for your boss.

There's an unspoken code between professionals, don't ever make it personal, you and him just made war against The Caretaker, against me and the rest of this cities underworld." He pointed at one gunman and then to them, while the other two men he motioned to check the room.

Athien rolled to the door and hit the metal staircase, making a lot of noise as he jumped from the first staircase to the second, landing heavily but he grabbed the rail to save him from damaging his legs.

There was more commotion upstairs, he heard Mordacai and the others move to the stairs as he raced to reach the bottom, his suit jacket torn on the last ring of the stairs as he jumped onto the glass roof. He slid to the ground, seeing Mordacai and his men on the stairs. He was unsure of how much of him they'd seen in the dark.

Athien walked into the kitchen with sweat on his face and messed up hair, he threw his jacket in the bin and undid his tie slightly. He was glad he'd left his hat in the car by accident as he stepped into the expo from the service entrance. The kitchen staff yelled at him and threatened to beat him and the woman who'd come through earlier and stab them with a skewer.

He watched from the outer edge, quickly looking for Samantha and found her next to the giant satellite piece at the centre of the crowd. Athien approached from behind and spoke quietly, not wanting to startle her.

"Sam, you okay?" Her eyes were glazed as she watched the last of the presenter's wrap up their speech, the great satellite the two of them stood next to.

"Athien, your father, he said things, in his speech, things about you and the night you were shot. A chip, memory enhancements…" She turned to him, voice trailing as her eyes searched for something within his own, she seemed to be on the verge of tears.

Athien attempted to reassure her, he'd heard his father talk about that night to many people before. Still, he had never actually told Samantha what had happened that night, mostly because he'd lost most of his memory of the events of that entire day.

"I'm sorry that I never told you about what happened, but, it wasn't entirely life-threatening, the doctors sowed me up easily enough." Samantha shook her head while Athien's mind exploded.

If it was more than that though, if it had been fatal, he would have stuck something in me…

"I think that he did put it in ,that you are his trial. That's why you've been able to do all you've done within the Order and now. As whatever you're calling yourself." She whispered, her voice exposed great care for him and sympathy for his thoughts.

Athien believed her, it made sense, why he was trained faster, could think more quickly than most he'd met. Even just after that night; in the hospital he'd woken in, his mind was already heightened.

Athien nodded slowly as the room exploded in the sound of claps from all around them, the introductions of the exhibits finished, it was then questioning time.

"I think you're right. It makes sense. What does Kali think about all of this?" Samantha wasn't surprised with how well he took the information in, and she relayed the information to Kali.

She responded with one, simple question that troubled Samantha and even Athien.

"Then why, is it not detected by metal detectors." Athien leaned against one of the poles that surrounded the satellite replica, he thought hard before he gave an answer.

"This is for Nathaniel, from Nicola. I was wondering if you could tell me what an entry bar thesis could be based on to specifically be applicable for M.A.K.E. Industries. Science division." Athien recognised that voice and realised it was Nicola Smite, who stood on the podium and had asked the question.

Athien smiled as he turned to Samantha, intense and focused expression.

"That's obvious, he hid it on purpose, him, or whoever put it there."

"Well, Nicola, "Nathanial said, beginning to answer her question. " That is a good question, and the best answer I can give you is that you should come talk to me after. Because this isn't the space or time to bore our audience with the in-depth things I'd need to cover. But don't worry, I'll be quick. I love your courage." Athien stared at the stage, past Samantha and Nathaniel, whose father stood behind him and begun to answer questions.

Athien stared directly at his father's face, not with anger, or sadness, just, questioningly.

I always knew my father was one to work to his goals with strength, and he has been secretive, about my mother, about his back story, but, why, what made him not tell me?"

8

Chapter 8 Confrontation

Athien enjoyed working at night. His brain was able to function to its fullest when he stood before an attack or altercation. Tonight, he'd driven all the way out to the convention centre from earlier, his mind set on ending Mordacai.

"Kali, Sam, are you both still there?" Athien talked through the radio on his chest, he'd donned The Sentinel uniform and watched from the darkened kitchen space as men carried gear to trucks outside.

"We're here, Sentinel, oh that's a cool name, Kali gave me a run through, and I'm currently looking at the cams of your area. It's a hellish night, with the rain and wind, not much like autumn at all." Athien struggled to count the workers in the night's low lighting, the moon was a sliver, clouds covering it entirely from view.

"There's not a lot I can see, without getting too close to them." Athien bent down, hidden from their view if anyone looked, and searched his belt, sure he'd put some night vision goggles somewhere.

"Well, surely you've got goggles for this kind of thing. Besides, from what I can see, there are at least, twelve, fifteen people, skulking around out there, in the darkness, with little more than tiny torches to light their way. Crazy he's not under arrest, the police didn't even show up, yet the kitchen definitely heard the shots." Athien found the goggles as Samantha continued to theorise over the day's events, he put them over his eyes and set the mask straight again, able to see more than before.

"Alright, their unarmed, which is interesting. Doubtless that Mordacai is overseeing it from inside his office, with guards, so if I stay around the truck and cars, I can use them for cover." Athien moved from behind the counters and approached the door, still unseen by the people that passed by every minute to make the trip back upstairs.

"Athien, be careful, there are a lot of them there." Athien thanked her for her concern, and rubbed his side, where the bruise was still healing, subconsciously. Then he walked briskly out of the kitchen door and into the open space before the vehicles.

Let's tango, Mordacai.

He reached the group before they realised he wasn't one of them. Two that carried boxes towards the cars saw him approach from the side, but they knew that toilets were through there, so it wasn't that strange to them both.

However, when one of them found a fist slammed into their face, they both realised what they'd just met.

"Mordacai!" The other yelled as they dropped the box they carried and started to run, moving towards the stairs as fast as their legs could carry them.

"Hey!" Athien followed with ease, his suit lifted up and down slightly as his legs rose and fell, catching the runner as they hit the stairs. Athien grabbed them from behind and threw them against the stair rails as they climbed. They fell from the first wring to the ground, landing heavily on their sides and scrawled back to their feet as Athien jumped quickly.

The others around the vehicles came to the aid of their comrade, surrounding them as Athien approached and they stood shakily, but with anger boiled on their face.

"It's that guy from the news, no way this is a plan from him," the closest worker shook his head with frustration at Mordacai's room and looked at Athien, his body rigid and fists clenched. "We got to take care of him before the boss kills us all." He sprayed the ground with water and saliva as he spoke, pushing his conviction out onto the others as he moved slowly towards Athien.

"I am Sentinel! You fight, you'll get fought, and I won't stop, until you fall, think about how much you want to use those legs." Athien yelled menacingly, he waited for one of them to attack, but they just circled him as he stood, waiting.

"I think you're in over your head." The henchmen all agreed with the main speaker.

"Nice tactics, surround me from all sides, then attack as one, overpower the weaker side. Except, once this circle breaks, you'll falter." Athien didn't let that sink in, as he launched himself straight towards the one he'd already downed, and the boss, both on his right and unprepared for his barge attack.

"Ah!" They both got caught as his arms came up by his sides, collided with their chests and collected them into his direction and threw them to the ground, flat on their backs as their heads hit the ground, hard. Athien dropped to one knee as the collided with the ground, he punched each in the face once with his right fist, then spun onto his back and rolled as he saw a leg coming at him from behind.

Athien stood and used the positions of the two downed men to control the other's actions, he moved around and kicked out as they all tried to come at him from one direction.

"I told you all that you would fall." He broke through the group, aimed back towards the vehicles and consciously aware he could hear footsteps on the stairs above them. His arms covered his head as he pushed and kicked through.

A man's arm snaked towards his face. As Athien arrived at the safety of the cars, he caught it, using three fingers to twist it over the man's head. Their arm locked behind their leader as he used them like a shield against the fast-approaching group.

"Stop!" Athien heard a shout from above him, Mordacai stepped onto the second level of the stairs, two gunmen pointed their weapons at him. Athien used the sudden appearance to his advantage, the others had stopped coming at him.

Athien pushed the man he held into the group, then stepped back and rolled behind the first car, unsure of what Mordacai would do with the gunmen.

"Do we shoot?" Athien heard one of his guards whisper to Mordacai. Athien unclipped his grapple gun and peeked through the tinted car's windows at the scene. The workers on the other side of the car looked up at Mordacai, and the gunmen at the vehicle, searching for Athien.

"No," Mordacai replied, his head shook as he pushed both guns downwards.

"Mordacai!" Athien yelled, his arm and body snapped over the top of the car as he stretched out his right arm and fired the grapple, aimed for Mordacai's shoulder.

Mordaci dodged, remarkably quick as he pulled the man to his left in place of him. Their body was propelled down the stairs, which Athien almost began to fall down, but managed to catch himself last minute.

Athien pulled the grapple back and the gunmen fell from the stairs, on top of the two that he'd dropped earlier.

"I told you to stop!" Mordacai shouted, he'd hurt himself on the rail of the stairs and ran down the last two wrings to get to the ground, the workers on the ground backed away from the car. The gunmen still up went down the stairs slowly, gun pointed over the rail and didn't let Athien out of his sight. Athien ducked back below the car windows and moved tongue back of the car, he wanted to be somewhere they weren't sure of, in case Mordacai changed his mind.

"He's the one the news keeps shouting out to, calls himself Sentinel." One of the workers talked for Athien to Mordacai, who disregarded the workers existence.

"Sentinel is it? my man won't shoot you unless you touch me." Mordacai stepped between his workers, guilded around a truck. Athien pointed his grapple gun at the corner.

"Stop! Don't come around the corner, I will shoot you." Mordacai stopped, and his snarl threw daggers at the gunmen.

"Throw the gun away! You saw what he did to those three, I won't have my merchandise destroyed again." The gunmen shrugged, and threw the gun across the ground towards the wall beneath the stairs. Athien watched from the windows and stood as everyone looked in his direction and waited.

"I want information, then you and your workers go to jail with you." Mordacai saw him and went around the side of the vehicle, he saw the grapple gun, pointed directly at his stomach, Athien's finger off the trigger.

"Look. We're obviously two smart people, who've come under a miss understanding, you want information on The Caretaker and Helm, I want to be kept out of prison. Surely we can work together." Athien's head cocked to the right as he thought over Mordacai's words.

"Who's Helm?" Athien watched as Mordacai took his glasses off and stared at him.

"What the hell are you doing in this game. You don't even, god, what the hell!" He stopped when Athien stepped forward and growled.

"Okay. This is what I mean, free of service, and in return for my way away, Barns and Annabelle both worked for, and with a man known only as Helm. He is devious, and strong and he hates being played with. I'm moving to save myself from him, he was a buyer, before today. Now I have to go to war with him, and The Caretaker." Athien shook his head and moved even closer, his arm came up as he hit his hand against the top of the car, the roof dinged slightly as he barked;

"You're lying. I talked to two different sources, both described you. With the name Mordacai." Athien saw the workers shy away slightly and the gunmen went for a walkie talkie in his belt.

"Now, that is true! My god, you're an intimidating type aren't you, like to threaten and make the mice run." Athien scoffed.

"You're worse than a mouse." Athien looked directly at the gunmen and clambered over the car, he heard the man speak into the radio.

"Yeah, it's going down, right now." He whispered and looked up from his talk, surprised to see a thundered up Sentinel sprinting the short distance to him in seconds.

"Who are you working for?!" Athien grabbed the man and pinned him straight to the ground, even with Mordacai's protest and proceeded to choke the man until he turned blue.

"You are a fool! You think just because you can choke me out and scare some other fools," The man was having trouble as he yelled without air, gestured towards the other workers as he did. "You won't be standing, so high, when," his throat almost out of air, Athien eased a little to allow him enough to talk. "When he takes care of you, you won't know what you wish you didn't. He will end you!" Athien had heard enough of his empty threats and dropped him, heaving in air, as Athien faced the others.

"Interesting way to blow off steam." Mordacai shrugged his shoulders, off-put by Athien's actions but unwilling to let the violence get the better of his deal.

I can use him and take down Helm, then Caretaker will lose his business. Athien thought as the two realised how much they could play off each other.

"Why didn't you stop me?" The workers beside Mordacai nodded, they all wondered why he'd allowed it as well, to both of the only people with guns.

"Because, I'm well aware that, without the guns and a sizeable distance, we'd have no way to stop you from beating us all into the ground." Mordacai realised an issue with his sentence, but figured the vigilante wouldn't catch it.

"I could kill you, not just beat you. With no weapons, you'd all be down before you knew it." Athien stood menacingly, his shoulders squared, and his head held high.

"Like I said, I have information, and I don't like killing useful people. I think you and I can help each other, and you'd easily get the bigger side of the stick."

89

"I am not an attack dog, you and I have different goals." Athien barked, acting insulted by Mordacai's words and watched the workers shy even further away, they had become unnerved by the confrontation and just wanted to leave. Two of them began to do so, before Mordacai screamed at them to stay put. He turned back to the vigilante, and composed himself, pulled his hands up and then down together in a short prayer.

"Please, let me sleep like a bear in winter tonight, no more minions either, please," He cleared his throat and took a step towards Athien.

"Look, we are both intelligent men, obviously both skilled in different areas. All I'm saying is, if you don't touch me, I'll give you everything I have and more, on the guys who jumped Barns, Helm, the Caretaker, everyone that I know in this whole city. I just, don't need the attention, and there is plenty to keep you busy out there." Mordacai emphasised the city by throwing his hands into the air as he finished. Athien nodded slowly as his arm sat around his waist, and the other rested under his chin.

"And, what do you get, a lead role in Caretaker's business, or the entire business?" Athien questioned, he was looking for some kind of untruth by Mordacai, but for what he could tell, the man was straight-faced, severe and, slightly afraid for his life.

It isn't like he has anything to lose from this, so what would he hope to gain? He thought there had to be some angle he was trying to grasp. Mordacai shook his head, seemingly upset by the question.

"Please," He moaned slightly as he began to speak. "I'm out to offset him, I've been building up against all the big players in this city, it's a battleground that not many ever get to see and appreciate." He sounded sad, as he recounted an obviously hurtful past.

So many years, wasted on these streets, no more.

"I'm my own man," he continued. "The people who attacked Barns, one of them shared the same name as me, that's why they said my name. The person who attacked him was dressed up to look like me, I know that, it was Helm, he planned to set me up to the cops, but Barn's didn't talk, then Helm threatened to kill him. Almost succeeded. You saved him. I, just want to end them and do my business." Mordacai, slightly out of breath, stopped talking and wished he'd brought a drink bottle with him on this venture.

Then again, I did think I'd be at my new place, by now.

"Okay." Mordacai's head snapped to attention at the one-word answer, the vigilante took down his arms and nodded, reassured that what he was about to do was the right thing.

"Okay, but where are you going? I don't want to have to track you down again." Athien walked right up to Mordacai, he stood over six inches taller than the criminal. However, Mordacai was bigger built with muscle and broad shoulders and a large gait.

"Have you got a phone? I can give you my number." Mordacai offered. Athien dropped his shoulders, annoyed by the prolonged conversation.

"I'll remember it." Mordacai listed the numbers and then answered the question.

"I'm moving, out of the CBD and hopefully away from my enemies, my place was disrupted. Then it was attacked by a vigilante, Helm will come for me after he finds out about his men and my empty office. Especially when that man,"

Mordacai pointed to the gunmen. "Wakes up." Athien was confused by something, why Mordacai was so important.

"Why?"

"Why will he come for me, simple, I'm one of the only people who know The Plan, and who and what he is?" Athien put out his arm, which Mordacai took, shook hard twice and let it fall.

"So, what's the plan?" This, caused Mordacai to smile.

"Now, that, is a good question. Did you mean the group of super-powered teens, or the city-wide plan to control all crime, all the time? Helm, is the man who runs everything. You want him, The Caretaker is the way to go."

"You can take me to him?" Athien hoped for a simple answer as he felt his eyes blink rapidly.

"To hell with that, but I can make sure he knows where you are and where the trap is that will end him."

Well, the day I work with a vigilante, the day I think I need a new expensive champagne glass for my drinks. Mordacai thought, putting on a very fake and very bitter looking smile as he watched the vigilante.

Athien stepped back and relaxed.

"You catch all that you two." He said into his radio as he turned away. Through the radio he heard Samantha answer and a slight snoring sound.

"Kali's asleep, but I recorded everything, well done, you're networking, smart." She slurred her words slightly, and Athien laughed internally at her optimism. He just hoped that he'd made the right decision to use Mordacai for the information he wanted.

9

Chapter 9 The holidays begin

Athien awoke late the next day, his torso aggravated by the fights the night before. He found a suit shirt, ordinary pants and a hoodie and ran to catch the next tram to the university.

Today I just need to hand in the USB with my projects on it, and I'm done here for a week, the perfect time to go all out on The Caretaker.

"Hey, Athien, imagine meeting you here, is it your last day too?" Athien stood in the tram and noticed the familiar voice behind him. He'd seen her as he entered the tram, but wasn't sure if she was busy on the phone she always on.

"Good afternoon, Nicola, yes it is, just got to hand in an assignment and I'm off for a week." Athien turned to face her and saw she'd dressed warmly, despite the decay in wind and rain the night before. She wore a giant soft jacket with fluff that bellowed from the hood.

"That's great, yeah I've got to pick up some things and then I'm off too." She hefted her bag over her shoulders and sat next to him as the tram emptied, people left, and more got on so they secured their spot.

"You showed a lot of strength, asking such an unorthodox question like that, by the way. I didn't know you were going to go to the convention." Athien prodded her for information, wondering what she wanted from work, if it was at M.A.K.E. or The Forge.

"Thanks, I suppose that's because you didn't ask, it was amazing," She closed off after that and looked to the floor as she remembered what else she'd learned at the expo. "I'm sorry about your accident all that time ago, I remember something being said on the news, but to be honest, it didn't stick in my head." She watched as Athien's face played through a series of expressions, finally coming to rest on a soft and slightly pained smile.

"I don't really remember the attack, I blacked out. There was a lot of pain, then I was in hospital." Athien rubbed the back of his neck and felt the sizable scar, hidden beneath his hairline on the nape of his neck.

"That's hard to think of, the world flashing before your eyes, unable to do anything. Did they find the shooter?" Athien's smile fell as he turned to the window and searched for an appropriate response to the complicated question.

I did, but nothing good came of it.

"No," He lied. "He was there for my father, but missed and got me, probably thought he could make some money from us. But whoever it was, I doubt that they stayed out of the light for long. Criminals don't usually."

They travelled the rest of the journey in near quiet, both watching as people left and entered the tram as they made their way through the city.

They moved around the university with quick strides. Nicola dropped her report into a teacher first. Then the duo made their way to Athien's teacher, who was in a lecture hall.

"You don't, have to understand my methods, Miss Zane, simply to understand that what I've said, is the common and best-understood model of the physical world. That is it, let's finish this up for today." They walked in as students piled out of the chairs and made their way out.

One student remained at the professors table, face red and hands shaking slightly as she gave him a paper and stalked away.

"Ah, Athien, your final assignment. I'm looking forward to reading this one. And who is your friend?" Athien stepped forward and shook the professor's hand as he placed the paper down on his desk and smiled appreciatively.

"Thank you, Mr Scot. This is Nicola, a Biology student." Athien let his hand fall and moved away, ready to leave but wanted to know why that women had barged him.

"Who was that student just now?" The professor sighed and picked up the papers on his desk, his bag open beside him as he placed them all in gently, he looked to the door as he did so. Nicola continued to look between the man and the student, as she disappeared around the door.

"Clara is a bright student, with too many ideas in her head. But I won't take up any more of your holiday time. It is a pleasure to meet you, Nicola. Always liked that name, granted, it's not as unique as Athien's here." Athien nodded, he'd heard the same thing before.

"I'm aware. Have a good holiday yourself, Mr Scot, if you get any." Athien smiled once more and stepped backwards, turning to the door with Nicola, who thanked the professor again as they left the room.

"Well, that's the events of my day's calendar finished, what do you have planned for the day? Going to go read a book or, build some technological achievement, that's what you genius types do, right?" Athien laughed at the joke and made one of his own.

"No! You've read the comics, you know what we rich genius's get up to with our spare time." She laughed as they moved into the main campus area, between two large buildings and a construction site.

"I have no idea, I've never been into comics, art, though sometimes beautiful, has never really spoken to me."

"That's fine, there are plenty of other arts, to fascinate yourself with. Writing, even your reports, that's an art." Athien shrugged, his offer to call her work art took her back for a second as they crossed the street, the CBD busy all around them.

"Thanks, Athien, that's a nice thing to say." Athien nodded and checked the next road, unsure of where they were going as he walked them down the busy Elizabeth road, towards Flinders Street Station. The shops they passed were mostly decorated restaurants and fast food shops. Fuel station stores on every corner shone brightly as people walked around, their mouths wrapped against the straws of dollar slurppies.

"Well, here we are, off for a week, both academically strong, with no worries in the world. Where do we go now?" He wondered aloud, thinking about whether or not he should call in Mordacai for any new information.

He flipped his phone around inside his pocket as he watched the giant crowds that travelled the road just ahead, the next intersection served as the second last before the station.

"Well, I guess that's up for the wind to decide, after all, I have no idea, I've lived here my whole life, I still know nothing about this city, or it's doing. What do people do here?" Nicola commented.

Athien followed an elderly couple to the side of the building as a large group of tourists marched down the street past them, cameras and phones flew left right and centre with them.

"Well, there's that. Fancy some sightseeing, I've heard the graffiti alleys and china town is meant to be pretty fantastic, night or day. Oh, and the market." Nicola feigned surprised and placed her hand under her throat as she dipped slightly, minding the elderly couple as they passed.

"My word, you've been here what, weeks, and you already know more about this city than I do." Athien scoffed as they crossed another street, coming up on Flinders and wades of people.

"That's nothing, this city might look big, but it's a pebble in comparison to Alazarath. I know a lot more about Melbourne than most, and some things weren't from good experience." He looked at her and wondered what she'd think of his out of school activities.

"Really, well I guess it is a city, so there's bound to be some, discrepancy's among the populous. But I'm surprised that you've seen them." The street became compressed and congested as they walked past the closed pub on their left, tourists passing in and around them as they crossed Graffiti Alley.

"This city can be cutthroat, those who don't thrive in it die. It's how this place works." Athien's voice became morbid as he thought about his father's betrayal. About the tasks he had still to complete. Evil on every corner he or the police hadn't checked.

"Well that got dark pretty quickly, cheer up, Athien, there's plenty of room for heroes to step up." They got to the end of the street, Flinders Street corner around the corner from them.

"You want something for lunch?" Athien offered, as he looked down Bourke Street.

"Do I hear sirens?" Nicola asked. They looked up the street seeing a police car as it raced down the tram lane at high speed, he couldn't see what it was after though.

Must be around the corner.

Athien heard the sound of a powerful engine as the sound echoed off the buildings of the street behind them. Hundreds of people begun to move as he saw the blacked-out compact vehicle drive towards them from behind.

"Nicola move!" Athien watched as Nicola acted, dragging her body around the corner as people ran across the street and into the alleys.

"Athien watch out!" He saw the police car skid to a halt behind the traffic. Then the officers' escaped their vehicles and ran down the street towards Athien and Nicola. The runaway car was blocked from leaving the main road, unless it turned into the street to it's left. The street Athien had just stepped into.

It came around the corner, as police moved to confront the driver, who panicked when they saw the street path, the hundred people who hadn't managed to get behind cover. They drove on, unable to stop and ignorant of the shots fired through the screen. Throwing the directional motion off with the glass in their face, the driver lost control.

Athien's eyes tried to match the motion, put his body at the point where he'd make the least impact, the tail end of the flailed vehicle, Nicola held his hand hard as they both tumbled.

What? As they fell, the car moving towards them at high speed, his brain was processing everything fast, he picked a foot off the sidewalk, pressed off with all the force he could muster, aiming his spinning body to hit the window of the vehicle as it passed. He pulled Nicola behind his back.

Then, his eyes adjusted to the speed of the vehicle, to the world around him. Then he felt heat all around.

The car slowed as Athien jumped.

This isn't a brain function thing, I'm fast, but this, this is insane.

He looked down at Nicola, who was just lifting off the sidewalk, the car now inching towards them at a crawl. She looked up at him with just as surprised of an expression as he felt, her face and mouth all smiles.

Nicola moved an arm experimentally, very much still terrified from the car that had almost ploughed through them. They both saw, something, an energy of sorts, stretch up the length of her arm and bounce across their bodies, changing from a pink colour through her and a grey colour as it left Athien.

"Athien!" He saw her yell, but he didn't hear it, as the world suddenly came spinning back all too fast, the car's back caught under Athien's foot and dropped him as it passed. A second later it smashed into the corner of Graffiti alley and bounced into the streetcars parked close by, the police raced to catch the criminal that had driven it.

"Athien, are you okay?" His brain overloaded with what it just processed, Athien lay, dazed, on his back on the road with Nicola standing over him. She seemed excited, overly so, completely energised as she waved in front of him and got him to stand.

"I'm, I'm fine," He was shaken, brain still hurling from the overload. "Nicola, what did, how did you just do that?" Athien asked, he was whispering, pupils undulating. Nicola's body shook as he held her shoulders to steady himself.

"Shh. I have no idea, hopefully no one else noticed, please, don't say anything about it. Oh, what a rush!" She let out a deep, shuttered breath and almost collapsed, as they were approached by an officer.

Athien felt something trickle down the nape of his neck. His hand frantically moved over his scar, relieved to find that there was only a slight cut above it, from where his head had hit the ground. He also felt his shoulders seize up from the contact with the ground.

"You've got it." He whispered as they turned to talk to the officer that approached.

They got checked up and wrote a short report for the officers of what they saw, the officers on the scene were surprised upon hearing his name.

"We hope you're safe and sound, Mr Dickens, heard about your accident when your father said, on the news. Sorry. You're lucky, we've had a few injuries here, but there hasn't been any deaths."

10

Chapter 10 The Caretaker's hand

"It was like nothing even I've ever seen, there was, this energy, and she was able to move way too fast, she's like Bolt, I just, need to figure out why." Athien sat, leaning back in his chair at the garage as he thought about the super-fast hero in Alazarath, Kali and Samantha sat behind him as he recounted the events. He'd watch a video of the interaction with the car, and to the naked eye and even security camera, it had seemed like luck, just a near hit.

It appears severely apparent now. Athien thought to himself, thinking of the disturbing news his father had given at the convention.

"Athien, you saw her, move at super-speed? That's amazing!" Samantha watched the video from over his shoulder, disappointed when Athien stopped it right when he'd explained the amazing event occurred, and she didn't see anything out of the ordinary.

"Well, it's clear that you were right, Sam, watch this," Athien played the video for a few seconds, the time it took the car to rage towards then and hit the wall. "Within a frame, of this time, I was able to see her move and the car stop to a halt, so fast, I'd have to slow it down to, a hundredth of a second, at least." Kali whooped as Samantha laughed.

"So, you do, have the chip in your head? But, that would mean, what happened to you, that night, then?" Athien shook his head, unsure.

"Well, it means, that, whatever happened that night, was most likely a lot worse than what we know, and that you, remember." Kali motioned over to Athien with her hands and rubbed her eyes, the long nights and short days were having a toll on her sleep patterns.

"That seems most likely, now I have to figure out that, and how to use this newfound brain power I thought was normal." Athien's head was slightly swamped as he thought about all the times his brain had kept him alive, how he'd noticed things usually overlooked.

My last job as The Shadow, Alazarath, someone, probably Hazard told the heroes what was happening, I remember.

He remembered, seeing Bolt, the super-speed Runner, seeing him through the scope of a sniper rifle. Bolt had dodged the bullet as if it had come from a hundred miles away. Athien moved, it wasn't the first time he'd fought supers, he ducked low behind the wall, abandoning he's rifle as he scrambled for a way to defeat his foe. Then, just like with Nicola, he'd gone into a focussed mode, just as Bolt came over the top of the building, able to run up the side like it was flat ground. Athien turned, limited the contact zone the other man had on him and grabbed Bolt's suit. He used it and the quick tensing of his fingers to throw Bolt from the roof. That trip had destroyed Bolt's ego and body long enough for Athien to escape.

"Athien! Athien!" He refocussed on the room, which was

brighter than he remembered. Samantha stood over him, her hands flew around his face wildly. He blinked. "Ah, there you are! Welcome back, I was just saying, I'm staying for the week, gonna go back for the practises to start next week."

"Good, something tells me we're going to be going into dark waters soon.

11

Chapter 11 Readying

Three days passed since the incident and in that time, Athien went about the city. His fortune diverted him, always getting back to the same problems, no matter who he broke or tied up, there was no new information on The Caretaker. His popularity as Sentinel grew, as he attempted to dismantle The Caretaker. It took the full three days, for anything to come to light, by which time he'd been working as Sentinel for a month and a week, when the name first circulated the media.

"And in other news, it seems the city has a real menace on their hands with this vigilante that stalks the streets of the CBD and southern suburbs. They're the talk of the criminal underworld, and today, we here at The Guardian interviewed some of the criminals that they've put away over the last month. Here's Ashley Partners reporting from Police headquarters."

"I talked with convicted criminal, Howard Lester, who was allegedly attacked by a vigilante, who goes by the name, Sentinel. This city has seen it's fair share of vigilantism. Still, Lester says that certain things make the police worried about public safety over the usual skirmishes. Here is a part of the interview." On the television he watched, it showed a man, slightly bruised and with dangly orange hair and buck teeth.

"Who attacked you, Mr Lester?" It showed his face contort slightly, a pained expression that crushed his fake smile and deadened his eyes.

"Call's himself, Sentinel," Lester said, mockingly. "a wack job with an ugly suit and strong voice, he came out of nowhere, not hiding, he just, appeared and came at us. Me and the others, he was a nasty piece of work, like a battering ram, we didn't stand a chance." The video cut out and the reporter appeared outside the headquarters again.

"Lester received multiple bruises to his head and body. Notably, his arm was dislocated, and he had a mild concussion, after a run-in with the supposed Sentinel early last week. Reports have been spamming the online forums over sightings of the masked vigilante. The question that everyone is asking, including police, who chose not to comment on this issue, is what does this vigilante want? So far his work has been mismatched, with various stories spiralling that he has been shot and almost killed many times. All we know for sure is he's out there, and the criminals, are running scared." News cycled over the web of this, the first notification of his name, over the day. Athien didn't see it until late, he'd been busy making repairs to his suit, a stray knife had collapsed the solidity of the strap on his hip, so he'd had to reinforce it.

"You should really opt for a better guard, if you're going to be doing this for a living, survival should become something you can't stop thinking about." Kali stepped into the room as Athien leant over his suit, splayed out over the counter he'd folded out to work on it. The computer showed the re-run of the newscast from earlier, and he was busy thinking of how he'd respond to being known, the best way.

I'd thought of this before. I'd hoped to have a little more time before they blasted my name throughout the entire city. There's so much more I have to do. My reputation isn't high enough for this coverage to work for me.

"Well, it's done, I'm officially a menace. They'll play with that a little while," Athien stretched and sat into his chair before the broadcast ended. "I know something, though," Athien said, he pointed back to the screen. He rewound the video and stopped it when the man they'd interrogated came up the first time, his face grimaced.

"What is it?" Kali asked, fully awake and functioning much better, now that Samantha had been taking the reins on her operations side of things.

"I never hurt this man, he's lying. I remember every person's face that I've come into contact with over the past month and a half, and he wasn't in the bank, until I saw this, just now." Athien tapped the screen, then rested back as Kali moved closer and examined the face.

"Then, what do you think happened, was this a setup, calling you out to correct the criminal you," she put up her hands and made quotation marks. "Beat on, or was this a ploy by the police?" Athien nodded a few times, his mind raced to collect his thoughts as his fingers swung the phone he'd dug from his pocket around like a pen.

"No, I think, that this was The Caretaker. Or Helm. Mordacai hasn't got back to me yet, but Helm is meant to be strong, and devious, more so than I am. Caretaker could be behind it though," Athien stood up and folded the uniform. "Well, he has a motive, I've been walloping him over the past week, he'd be the kind of person who'd beat his own man, send him to the cops with a story and have it fed to the media. I think it was, the Caretaker." Athien was sure, he crossed the room and placed the uniform back into its cupboard, the suns downward light approached from the west. Then he folded the table back up and crossed the room to Kali, who still stood by the door.

"It sounds to me that one is a bully, and the other is a crafty snake. What if they both work together? Or, what if they work, under someone else?" Kali asked as Athien turned back. He'd forgotten his phone. Just as he picked it up, a message came through.

Athien remembered the number and as he turned back to Kali, smiled.

This is going to be perfect.

"I don't think so," Athien said to Kali, he ignored the message as he talked to her first. "There is nothing that ties the two of them together yet, except that Helm hires men through Caretaker. If they worked together, then surely they wouldn't trade men and kill them." He finished and flicked the lock button to view the message.

"Who is it, that Mordacai?" Kali came over and stood by his side, her head angled up and over his shoulder so she could read the message.

"He says, that he's set a meeting, with the Caretaker himself, to hire men and resolve the spat they had last week." Athien paused, noting that Mordacai had never said he had had a spat, but that Helm had. "He's going to rectify his situation, then he wants to know if, The Sentinel can come in and destroy his," Athien passed a long string of curses. "Problem." Athien dropped the phone on the table and shouldered the wall, Kali took the opportunity to sit in his chair.

"Well, that sounds like the break you need, he's there, for the taking, after all." Athien nodded, his thoughts going over what he'd just read in his head.

It sounds too good to be true, a trap, set to undermine my strength after a grooming from the media.

"I think that it's a trap." Athien learnt over and picked up the phone, he's fingers whizzed over the button as he wrote back a short reply to Mordacai.

"So, you said you're going anyway." Kali laughed as Athien finished his written response and sent it to the reader.

"If it is a trap, I'll catch them both and the police can have Mordacai too. We'll have to be ready for anything, a secret code, something easily used, if I detect anything." Kali clapped her hands excited all of a sudden, her eyes flashing their dangerous spark again.

"I've got just the thing." Athien looked down as a small message beep sounded a new message. He clicked the button and found and address and time from Mordacai.

"He's headed to a park in Glenferrie, nine o'clock on the dot's the time for the meet. We'll have to be there early, scope out the area." Kali looked very happy at the thought of the meet, something devious Athien hadn't noticed in her business-savvy mind was being washed up.

"Well, I for one, can't wait to see these two criminals, in their rightful place, trap or not Athien, that suit and you are going places, isn't anything either of those two, or Helm, can do anything about that." She stepped up and towards the door, while Athien walked back over to the cupboard and found the key again, going for the lock as he heard the door open.

"You're not going now, Athien, you've got to have some

tea first." She walked into the house without having to wait, as Athien picked the suit back out, placed it on the desk of his computer with the belt and helmet and walked back into the house. Samantha sat at the kitchen table, hands already wrapped around a hot cup of tea as she watched a drama show.

She relaxed when she saw them both walk in, Kali, a little happier than usual. She watched as they set out on making their tea, the kettle bounced to life with bubbles, and Athien got milk from the fridge for Kali, himself intent on just having water.

Kali shook her head, playfully and watched him pour the boiling water into his mug, over the tea bag and start to swirl it.

"Really does amaze me, with all the things that you do, that you have no regard for your bone structure, trust me, when you're as old as me, that milk, you'll drink it for every meal." She poured her milk into the water-filled cup and begun to drink, she didn't even stop to pull out or swirl the teabag.

"Well, a flavour developed with time and care, is one better nurtured. You could think that way, with your criminal hunting." She did not explain as she sat down beside Samantha, shooing her feet away in the process as she drank.

Athien joined them a moment later, sitting heavily in his seat. His wound was less aggravated but still caused some pain when he moved in specific ways. Like jump from roofs or get punched.

He went over strategies for transport and then where he'd hide. Beside him, Samantha and Kali watched a T.V show, some explosions caught them in awe, but otherwise they nit-picked the characters and their actions. Something Kali, somehow knew a lot about.

109

"Athien, you can't take the car tonight, you know that, right?" Athien blinked, the show was over. Kali informed Samantha about the mission Athien was planned to go on, later that night.

"Thanks, Sam, I had thought of that, yes, though I could block cameras and park a way away to go unnoticed, it would be awful for my car to be seen leaving the scene as I do. No, better to leave this to public transport, a short train ride away as Glenferrie is, I'll have ample time to scout the area."

Athien passed through the train station at a smooth walk, hiss suit hidden inside a large backpack. He moved from the station and walked through the dark shopping alley and down onto the busy Glenferrie road. It was a busy street, plenty of people going for their dinner at the fast food, Asian and Indonesian cuisine that made up so much of the road.

The park was down at the end of the street and around the set of buildings that were there. Athien passed a hardware store and took the corner, the park clear in view, dark with the absence of the moon.

It was a clear night, nothing but stars and a slight breeze, perfect for a scout mission, as Athien wandered around the area, looking for somewhere that he could watch the entire space.

"That will do." He saw a building on the other side of the park, an old channel station with a broken satellite on the top and wired fence off this side. Athien walked over, checked the building for security cameras and threw his bag over the wall, nit seeing anything that could be monitoring him.

The building was an old brick one, two stories, with a dark facade and surrounded by structures, which he believed would help to obscure him from view when the meeting started.

"Kali, Samantha, can you read me?" He talked into his radio. Several cars passed the park as he did, but nobody stopped.

"Yes, Sentinel, loud and clear. We've checked what we can of the surrounding area. There are a few cameras, but nothing with a clear view of the park." Samantha talked through the radio, her voice severe and high pitched as she worked through checking all the sights for him.

"Thanks, Sam I need to make sure the place stays empty of civilians too, the problem is, if Mordacai comes, I mightn't see if it's him unless he goes under a light. And, he could be meeting anyone, there is no way for me to know if it is the Caretaker." Samantha made a sound that told him that was wrong, she clicked her lounge.

"You have an audio enhancer, you know." Samantha pointed out, as Athien reached into his belt and picked out the small device, which used a sensor to receive far noises and made them audible to the people who listen.

"Well, it's only early, so, now it's time to wait, and work on a strategy for getting this done." He turned off the radio and adjusted his helmet, the earbuds he wore fit snug inside the helmet.

12

Chapter 12 Stake out

The wait was tantalising. Athien walked the entire length of the building and scaled the service ladder several times, testing how fast he could act if he needed to.

Finally, it approached nine o'clock, and Athien watched the park with his eyes searching for any kind of disturbance.

"Athien, Mordacai is approaching the park, one of the cars he drove from the expo centre has just pulled into a park, a block from the park. The plates match." Athien heard Kali as she recounted the development.

So, this might actually be happening.

Athien moved to the closest corner of the building to the park, the audio device on and pointed towards the side to the park he'd enter from.

"Thanks, Kali I'll keep my ears open." Samantha turned to the other side of the screen she was watching and saw Mordacai turn into the park and leave the camera's line of sight.

"Good luck Sentinel, I'll keep an eye on your surroundings." Athien watched as a shadowed figure walked into the park, four others behind them, armed.

"Guys," Athien heard Mordacai's voice over the audio device, fed through his earpiece, as they entered. "Make sure no shots are fired this time, we're here to make the deal, and leave, no need to leave bodies. Don't look at The Caretaker, not his face, or feet. We're enemies, not friends." His men agreed with him, hands gripping their weapons firmly. Athien was just able to see their guns, as they walked into the park. Mordacai had donned his natural dark sunglasses, hair was tied back in a single wild ponytail.

"Good on you Mordacai, set yourself up for a defence, just in case." *As long as those guys aren't used against me, then this night should go well.*

Mordacai approached the centre of the park, his men stood behind him from a small distance as he stood below a lamp, to show his foe that he was there and ready.

"Athien, there's a car approaching from the left of you. They're headed for the park." Samantha said. Athien watched the car hit the sidewalk at speed and park just before it hit the poles that stopped vehicles from entering.

"I see it, looks like we're about to meet Caretaker." Athien's heartbeat a few beats faster and he breathed more quickly too, he'd soon see the man who'd caused a lot of people pain.

"Athien, he's there, two men with him, they're all wearing suits. One is carrying a black suitcase." Samantha reported.

Athien couldn't see the three near the vehicle, they'd all gotten out in the darkness.

Samantha, saw three well-dressed men that looked somewhat identical, except the leader was the only one who walked with an air of absence to his step. In contrast, the other two kept their heads on a swivel as they searched around.

"He seems confident and older than I thought he'd be." Athien looked questioningly at Mordacai's lit figure under the light as he wondered what was in the case.

"Does the case look heavy at all Kali?" Athien asked, only just able to make out the three bodies as they moved away from the car, which illuminated the three as the vehicle was locked.

"No, he isn't straining at all, but they've just left my view, you're on your own from now." Samantha stopped talking, and Athien was left to listen to the interaction by himself.

"His men will be armed so be careful, I'd rather not have any more dead assets, death is bad for business." Athien reasoned the two guards must have had concealed weapons as he still couldn't hear or see the bulk of a rifle on either of them. The one carrying the case was slightly larger than the other. Both were clean-faced and cautious with their movements as they closed on Mordacai. Athien readied and turned on the audio enhancer, immediately able to pick up the voices in the park.

"Hey, sir, what's you been up to recently? I've got to say, bit of a weird place to meet, what if there'd been children or a nice looking family, hey?" His voice was shaken slightly as he spoke, Athien wondered if he'd been on the wrong side of anyone before.

Hope Caretaker can't see it.

The voice that came from The Caretaker was indeed older than Athien had expected.

"Look, it seems you forgot that you've killed my assets, Mordacai, this is a business session, not a curtsy call." The voice was harsh and reminded Athien of the bark from a dog, dangerous and rude.

"Well, that's all well and good to say, but, your assets

destroyed a good portion of my business, I'd say I did you a favour." Mordacai stood with his back up against the pole of the lamp. His arms crossed over his stomach as he waited for the others to arrive. His men moved slightly closer and around him to get a better view of them.

Athien heard The Caretaker's lips smack as he stood just outside of the rim of the light. His guards took a step from either side of him, their sights set on Mordacai's men.

"Well that's too bad, cause I saw a loss of thousands of potential dollars in one week, millions in years to come. You've cost me too much already Mordacai, why, would I give you this now, when you've done so much damage?" Mordacai stepped forward, his body heaved forward as he stood straight and confronted the other man.

"You'll give it to me cause I'm paying for it, with extra," Mordacai motioned with his fingers together, he rubbed them together and continued. "And bonuses, how many times do you want me to apologise, half my stock, half my men, there's not a lot left for you to take from me." Mordacai talked evenly, his thoughts raced with wondering whether or not the vigilante had showed, he couldn't see him anywhere.

Athien saw the Caretaker step into the light, a bowler hat masked his lessening hair and grey stubble. Though his suit was an indication as well, an old mix of Italian materials and furs, grey and dark green two-piece didn't fit in with the guards and their black and white ones.

"I, am The Caretaker," Athien heard the hostility in the older man's voice and even Mordacai noticed the tenseness of the man's muscles in his neck. "I supply this city with its backbone on criminals. ANYONE hoping to make it in the big time faces my rank, my judgement, you'd be wise to remember

115

that." Athien watched as The Caretaker turned half around and waved his hand back and forth twice, his man with the briefcase, on the other side of his body, moved forward and handed him the case.

"Listen, I respect you, I know, who you are, believe me, it's nothing, bygones and such." Mordacai was good at lying, Athien felt, he kept his voice clean, closed off and sincere, while he waited for the vigilante he had no believable trust in.

Not yet, anyway.

To secure a partner and informer, Athien needed to deliver in this deal, he had to take down the Caretaker.

"That it will be, though the next few times you order with deals from my side, don't be dishonoured when the bill is more than you would usually expect, there is a price, to every death." Athien watched as Mordacai reached for the case as The Caretaker offered it. The object changed hands, and Athien found himself wondering what Mordacai had ordered.

"That's, fine," The case in hand, Mordacai relaxed slightly, eased on the success of his trickery and his buy. It had been a long time since he'd double-crossed someone. "My men will make good use of it the next time the police arrive, maybe even take a bank into shut down, who knows, in this city." He turned around, gave the box back to one of his guards, and faced The Caretaker again, who stood with hands together.

"Okay, I'm going to jump them at the car, let's take this guy down Mordacai," Athien spoke at a whisper, as he stood and leapt from the corner of the building and slide down the ladder, his feet landing firmly. However, the ground was slightly wet and left footprints deep in the slush. He went around the park and used the building for cover, before he dashed twenty meters behind the Caretaker's men and behind a tree, close to their car. Nothing suggested that Athien had been spotted, so he squatted down and prepared for their arrival, relaxing and flexing his arms and legs to get the blood flowing.

"Well," Athien continued to listen to the meeting as it entered the closing phase. "Thanks for the case, Mr Caretaker. My men, your men, will use it wisely and with great care." Mordacai took a few steps back, his face not turned at all as he continued to watch the older man.

Athien watched as the Caretaker turned to leave, his right hand reached into his pocket for a second, before it returned to his side.

"Oh, Mordacai," Athien turned away from the gang and hid himself as the Caretaker turned back around and saw Mordacai and his men still stood there, perfectly still. Mordacai stopped biting his lip. "There's a reason, that no one talks about me, why the cops, and certain, others, can make threats at me, but come to no avail. I'm The Caretaker, I," He clicked two fingers together, and Athien heard the sound of quick movements in the audio device. He looked around the tree again, and saw the Caretaker's men had drawn a small handgun each. "No one, no one, can be as calm and as withdrawn as you, Mordacai, and no one is as easy to read. The best part? while my men and I will look like the villains in this story, we'll be able to escape the confines of the cells that hold us." Athien heard the Caretaker's voice rise to a yell, so much so that he could listen to the man clearly from where he hid.

"That, is what true power gets you. I have a stake in this cities underworld. It takes care of me, not you. Snakes that wriggle in a lion's den become meals to the vultures that crave them." Athien watched as the two guards and Mordacai's men moved in front of their respective employers, Mordacai scrambled back behind his men. In contrast, The Caretaker remained where he stood.

"Hey wait the jokes on you here, I like living outside the hole, plus, I know the weight you carry, I know, that I'd be as good as dead if I entered a cell if you wanted it." Mordacai stopped moving away from the others when he was another two meters back, his thoughts remained calm as he was put on the defensive.

Athien witnessed this and was prepared to move. Though The Caretaker would hear if he came out.

Got to wait until the situation is back under control.

The Caretaker wasn't accepting any of Mordacai's rejections, something about his conviction to his thoughts made Athien intrigued and worried for his informant. The Caretaker stepped forward again, Mordacai's men responded by stepping one step back, their guns firmly aimed one each at each man.

"There's no reason for you three to be in on this death scene, I know you're paid but, you don't all wish to die painful deaths." The Caretaker brought his arms up and carried them up and in an arch, as if he was trying to hug all three of Mordacai's men, without touching them. One of Mordacai's men, the one in the middle, which had held the suitcase, stepped forward slightly and snarled at him.

"We work for Mordacai, he pays us better and, frankly, you're an old man, who will be in a casket, probably before the summer." Athien winced as The Caretaker roared, Mordacai put a hand on his guard's shoulder and pulled him back again, himself still staying behind.

"There's so much that can still be earned from our relationship, Caretaker," Mordacai talked between closed teeth. "What grounds do you have besides a man who's happy he got what he wanted from a deal from a man as notorious as yourself? Other than my apparent awkwardness, which I'll admit, I always portray." Mordacai flapped one arm around as he talked. At the same time, his other held the suitcase.

"See, that's your problem, too much of who you are relays on others not noticing what you're doing. You've been waiting this whole time for something, other than me, it's so obvious, and what's worse is that your men know nothing about it. Loyalty is earned, not simply bought, like you have tried." Athien heard a phone cell ring and saw The Caretaker take a small flip phone from his left pocket and put it to his ear.

"Athien, I've picked up a call from the centre of the park, Kali is cracking it as we speak." Samantha broke the tension with her interjection, and Athien watched The Caretaker as he began to speak to the phone and turned away from Mordacai. Mordacai looked frustrated.

"Hurry Kali, who is he talking to?" Athien backed behind the tree again to be sure he wasn't seen.

"Look, can I go now, if you're too busy to talk…" Mordacai offered hopefully, to which The Caretaker responded by waving the thought away with his hand, undisturbed.

"Almost there, Athien, one more second." Samantha ran her hands against the desk, creating a drum sound as Kali worked on the crack.

"Come on," Athien muttered, his hand, which held the side of a tree root, snapped the small bind and he flinched, unsure if it had been loud enough to be heard.

"Patching you through now." Kali's said over the radio as Athien heard an unknown voice emit from the earpiece.

119

"You better know what you're doing then. Otherwise, this will be the last favour you owe me." The mysterious voice said. Athien's eye's widened as he figured what was going on.

"I would never waste such a good time, officer." The Caretaker's voice, smooth and almost silk laden as he spoke to the supposed police officer.

"You're lucky we're in the neighbourhood, coming up to the park, now." Athien heard the call end, simultaneously he heard sirens go off down the street, a block from the park.

Ahh, why did he have to do that? Mordacai heard the sirens too, and he made to leave, his guards followed behind him for a fees steps, as Caretaker's guards were also distracted.

"Hold it, Mordacai." Athien heard the gunshot, saw one of Caretaker's men shoot at Mordacai's, the one who'd held the briefcase fell, with a straight-through hole bullet wound in his right leg, just below the knee cap.

"That's the difference between us, Mordacai, your men, are always, always going to be the second tire. So, this one will keep his leg, if you tell me who or what cops or a small army, that you have waiting to spring out at me the minute you get clear." Caretaker pushed his men aside as he revealed a gun from the side of his hip and pointed it at the other man's head. Mordacai dropped his weapon and attempted to scramble away before feeling the sound of cold metal against his head.

The other two guards put their guns right up to Caretaker, whose own guards threatened them and Mordacai found himself without a weapon, and no firearm faced him. It was a standstill.

Athien heard the police car as it got closer, and stepped out from behind the tree, with everyone's attention diverted to the situation, he was able to close the gap without so much as a noise.

Mordacai smiled at The Caretaker and ran. His men saw Sentinel walk up behind The Caretaker, and the two that still stood swivelled in their attempts to shoot the guards.

Gunfire erupted in the night as the five gun-shots sounded. Athien saw Mordacai's two men both drop, and The Caretaker dodged the attack. Then his men chased Mordacai. The Caretaker stood and simply watched.

A police car appeared at the park's entry seconds later.

Athien grabbed Caretaker's arm as he pulled the trigger at the third man, threatening to kill all three of them in response to their false loyalty.

"What the." Athien pulled the arm back and into the Caretaker's body, which threw him off balance as he stumbled hit the ground, from which he rolled to recover.

"Caretaker, isn't it. Time you answered to someone for a change." Athien came at the Caretaker, who didn't seem at home in the brawl.

Caretaker stepped away and stood with his legs and arms tucked in, his eyes looking straight towards where Athien's eye covers were, unblinkingly.

"I knew he had someone he was waiting for, might as well have been the one responsible for destroying part of his crop. You're just a vermin on this city's streets, that cop that's about to come, he's on my side, like the others." Athien matched his stance, he had no idea what he was about to walk into.

"It's not my place to say who means what to this city, but, you don't mean anything to me, or the people you solicited to a life of crime." Athien attacked, weaving into Caretaker's path and punching first his arm, them his side and head. The Caretaker blocked the first two but spun as Athien's fist collided with his face, almost falling.

Steadied, Caretaker came at Athien with rage behind his fists as he punched a sequence of times at Athien's chest, shoulders and back, as they circled each other. Their blows traded with even hits on both sides, but Athien could tell his opponent weakened with every jab, kick and punch he threw at him.

"You don't have long," Athien grabbed him and pushed The Caretaker against the tree closest to them; meanwhile, the officer had entered the park and stood directly behind the trees. He could hear the sound of a fight and saw downed bodies under a lamppost ahead. "Tell me about Helm, tell me," Athien was pushed off Caretaker, who kneed his stomach and chopped at his neck with a hand he wriggled free. "Where I can find Helm." They both heard the leaves and twigs snap in the damp undergrowth of the trees as the officer ran past the tree, he couldn't tell where the fight was so he went straight for the injured.

"I think, that it is you, who doesn't have a lot of time. Unless you feel like attacking an officer now, Sentinel?" Athien watched as the officer rolled the bodies, the men were beside themselves with pain. Still, one was already beginning to stand, his arm over a shoulder wound. "Officer you fool, there's a…" He started to yell, as Athien took the distraction to punch him straight in the throat, his voice drowned he dropped to the ground, rubbing his neck furiously.

The officer saw Caretaker go down, and held his gun quickly before him, finger already on the trigger as Athien stayed turned around. He then kicked The Caretaker in the chest and looked at the officer.

"You're a snake in the grass, officer, call it in and get these men arrested, you'd be taking down the man who sells criminals to the city, our city." Athien faced the officer, his hands in the air, as he watched Mordacai's car drive past the park from the other side.

The officer, his badge not displayed, watched Athien closely, a muscular person, Athien knew, if it came to a fistfight, this man would be well trained. Unlike the criminals he'd faced over the last month.

"You know what? I'm gonna do that. Then, I'm going to put in my report, that a strong-armed vigilante, shot three guys and bashed in a wanted criminal's throat." The sarcasm dripped from his voice, he spoke with a western accent, but it seemed artificial to Athien, like he put it on for show. Though he's size did make him out to be very American looking, since Athien had lived there for over half his life, he knew what people looked like.

"They'll run tests, whatever lies you pull, they'll know, and then you'll be charged, and I'll never see your face on these streets again." Athien took a step forward, then another, as the officer continued to point his gun forward, albeit, it lowered slightly.

"Be that as it may, you are a fugitive," Athien searched the officer's body while he stood there, he wanted to make sure there wasn't a camera on him.

Can't have people seeing me yet, not until the new suit is finished at least.

"Listen, officer," Athien put down his hands and left them by his side, his voice remained a grizzle, but he let go of the menace behind it. "There's only one way this goes, you call it in, and these four get arrested. You leave out my involvement and he," Athien nodded down at Caretaker, who still lay behind him, he breathed deeply. "Tell them he fought me, if he gives you up, you'll be fired, most likely he won't, because you'll break him out before he does." The officer feigned ignorance as he gasped and waved his gun at the criminals behind him and then at Caretaker.

"You think that I'm with, these criminals!" Athien stepped another step forward, he was within a metre of the officer, who he could see was beginning to sweat, even in the cold.

"I have a recording of that phone call you just made with him. You do what I just said, get him out, or fight over his word and yours. But if I hear any news about me other than what they already know, you'll wish I attacked officers. The officer nodded and gulped several times.

"So, you don't, kill officers. Good to know." Athien lunged as he dropped his guard and grabbed the weapon from the officer, he threw it across the ground and took the officer by the neck of his jacket, green vest shining.

"I haven't, you and I have different goals, that doesn't mean that we can't work together to stem out the criminals that seem to besmirch us. You are one of them too, I'll come for you, if what I've said isn't done." Athien held him by his toes and didn't let go.

"Okay, okay, I'll do it. What is it you want anyway? If you don't fight cops, there's got to be a nobility in you; otherwise, we'll be a larger hindrance than most criminals you fight." Athien let him down, slowly and stepped back.

"It has nothing to do with nobility or morals. I don't kill. And we do the same thing, I put away the ones that matter, make sure they think twice about leading the next arms race against the city, you put away the ones that will stick and the small fry. I'll hand the ones I fight right to you. That's how this works." Athien turned around and kicked the officer's gun further away. "we'll still fight, you'll chase me, I'll get away. But I don't care if Caretaker, or whoever else gets out again, the law isn't perfect for everyone, I'll just keep him from doing something that hurts others." He walked away, the officer ran for his gun even as he saw the vigilante run off into the trees, east and away from either of the main exits.

"That's one strange dude you pissed off there." The officer knelt as he handcuffed Caretaker and grabbed his radio from his hip.

"Oh, and officer," He started, as Athien appeared behind him again." Don't forget our bargain, or I will find your name, and you'll get what he got." Athien ran from the scene.

The officer called in others, his brow wet with sweat as he recovered from the bizarre night he'd been through.

"Come here, ratbag, we've got a nice cell, just waiting for you and I think you're going to enjoy the stay you thought, would be a lot less than I believe it will be." Caretaker offered little resistance as more officers showed up and a van took him and Mordacai's men away to the inner CBD's prison.

Athien watched over the transaction, his hands holding the suitcase that Mordacai had left behind, opened and empty, with a foam cut out inserted inside it.

"Kali, I might need your help with this," Athien noted the bowl-like shape, a sphere cut out of the box. He closed it and turned his back to the park, and made his way back to the train.

13

Chapter 13 A visit

A day and a half later, Athien sat at the kitchen table. He was listening to the news, as he thought about how to improve his suit. It was slow in progress, the material he wanted to use was hard to find, he believed he was the only one who even knew it existed…

The container from the night before sat on the table in front of him, closed. Kali hadn't been able to find a single lead on what it could have contained.

"What is that?" Athien bolted upright. He watched the window he'd been staring at, when a gust of wind had ripped past the house and then stopped again. He could even see whiplash, the trees down the street threw leaves all over the road and house lawns as they were pulled right and back again.

Athien looked away again, the T.V. showed a reluctant head covered man being escorted into police headquarters, the reporter said;

"Police tell us they've caught a high-value target, as of last night, and apparently they'll prove of great use to eliminate the two hundred per cent rise in crime in the last year." Athien heard another massive clap of wind as he turned the T.V. off and sat again, the trees wiped side's ways even more powerfully. "It's not Bolt. But it might be…" He saw the gush happen again and stood, he's body moved quickly around the kitchen, through the hallway and left at the front door. He went out onto the street and saw a little blur at the end of the road.

"Nicola." He'd seen, just as the body of his college friend ran past the house for the third time. *She has to be looking for me.* He thought, it was the only thing be knew that would draw her down this specific street, which otherwise had nothing of interest.

If it was her, he had to make sure she didn't go into the garage or the kitchen. Otherwise she'd see the plans for the new suit on the table.

"What is she doing?" Athien could just make her out, at the corner of the street, as she stood at another house and waved her hands around as she pointed down the road.

Briiiiing. Athien heard his phone ring and the small device vibrated in the left leg pocket of his jeans. He lifted it out, saw Mordacai's number on the screen and pressed enter.

"Sentinel, there's a club in the suburbs that's attacking Helm's business, you should look into it." Athien saw a blur move in his direction, a neighbour had given her something. He saw an address at the end of the message and closed it, just as Nicola crashed into the ground and rolled several meters past him. Athien winced as he pocketed the device and waited for her to move.

"Hey there, Athien. Fancy, meeting you here." Her voice box rattled when she spoke, a side effect to moving so fast. Athien helped her stand again, hit by static shock multiple times from the strange static-electric energy she created, like an aura.

"So, you can, what, accelerate yourself, move fast? Static-electric runs through you like a battery." He said quickly as she straightened herself.

She stood shakily and used Athien's body to keep her own from toppling over as she laughed.

"Yeah, all, of the above," She swung her arm up. "It's so, thrilling." Athien watched her eyes flutter she breathed heavily, ragged huffs and puffs as he began to drag her slightly towards the house.

"You really shouldn't be running around the streets in common wear, if anyone notices you, there would be some extreme questions." They made it to the front door he'd left open, he was tempted to laugh at the ridiculousness of her situation. Her hair was all over the place, the broken half of two hair ties still stuck in the wild mess that had been a perfect bun or ponytail every other time he'd seen her. Like Athien, she wore light blue jeans, but also a bright blue plain shirt, whereas Athien wore a black one.

"Wow, I didn't take you for the old tea cosy types, Athien." She giggled as they came onto the kitchen, Athien lead her to the seat furthest from the window, under the T.V., and sat her down as gently as he could. Nicola was instantly intrigued by the house. Her eyes roamed everywhere as Athien took his notes and placed them inside a closet in his room, catching the documents on the table in an off-handed way.

He came back and heard a thump as she broke a cupboard door, she'd sped from her seat and slammed straight into it in an attempt to find a cup or glass.

"I'm still getting used to it." Athien put his hands to his ears as she talked, the sound that came out was deep and deafening, a throbbing boom that throbbed through Athien's body.

"Don't speak." He yelled slightly, helping her with the tap and then they moved back to the table.

Nicola calmed down after she drank the water, her hands stilled. As she talked, the vibration left her voice. Athien get her another one, before he asked her his questions.

"So, how did you get these powers?" He waited while she drank again, not bothering to ask why she'd sought him out.

I was there, and I'm the only one who witnessed it, makes sense that she'd talk to me. Though Athien was slightly worried what would happen, once everyone knew she had powers, and what that could lead to for him, having been seen with her by a few neighbours today.

"Athien, it's so amazing, I have no idea why, or how this had happened, but, it's so weird, it just occasionally happens. Like, yesterday morning, I went to leave my room, back at home and zipped right past mum in a heartbeat. She didn't even see the energy, or feel it, but the shout I made later," Nicola rubbed her head, Athien could see there was a slight red mark on the top of her forehead. "She heard that. I hit the roof as I tried to jump my cat, Boris. I was out for hours." She bowed her head as she recounted the event to him.

"So you have no idea?" He asked again, probing her slightly to jog her overactive brain to try to think. She shook her head.

"Nope, none at all." Athien thought of a quip he could play against her, instead of drilling her out of the great mood she was in.

"Well, now you could get into M.A.K.E. Industries as a science experiment of your own, you could be the topic of your science thesis." Nicola smiled, then noticed the trees outside the window, sticks and leaves thrown all over the place from her venture.

"Whelp, I found you. Sorry about the view though, I'm still getting used to this whole, super speed thing. Apparently there are different repercussions for the speed, depending on where I am, what I run on and how fast I go." Athien leaned forward, intrigued.

"Go on." He said, the research could wait a while. Samantha pulled herself together, her mind finally slowed down from having to read and gather information as fast as it had.

"Well, the day after our incident with that driver, I woke up and thought that it was a dream. But, then I realised I was in an alley on the other side of the city, clad in my jacket and pants I'd worn that day before. It wasn't something that I did willingly. What was weird, I couldn't make it happen on purpose, but managed to walk to my mum's workplace, which was closest." Then it happened again when I stepped into my room at home. The wall of my room now needs new plaster. I told them it was a chair I'd used to reach the light." Athien was trying to put this in order of the events in his mind, for categorising later. *I'm not using her, but it will be helpful to test and see how close to Bolt she is, just in case.* "It appeared that places I knew well, made it happen, and I kept viewing events in slow motion, dinner that night was the worst!" She continued. "I ran here this morning, after having a dream that I took to heart. Basically, I thought about the powers and then, they worked." Athien looked questioningly at her, that whole sentence set off warning bells in his head like fireworks.

"So, you can't run fast, unless you think about the power, it is, not the actual action, interesting. Probably a side effect of your brain trying to handle all the information, it would act like a key." Nicola nodded, and he saw her fight to not stand from her chair, exhilarated again.

"Yeah, it's something I'll have to work on, but I'm getting ideas and am going to run some tests on myself, speeds and what happens around me. Whatever that energy is that only we can see." Athien rubbed the back of his neck as he thought about the chip that inevitably made it so he could do so.

"Wow, yeah. There's that, so you're sure, no one else can see the sparks that fly off you, or around you?" He asked, to which Nicola nodded again and whipped her arm up and down at speed, her finger nicked the table as it came down and Athien grinned as she winced and rubbed it.

"Yeah, see, I got breakfast this morning and ate with my dad, before he went to work. He saw some paper move, but our house is breezy. If he'd seen them, it would have made him react in some way." Athien remembered when he'd touched her outside of the house.

"Well, those sparks can really hurt, felt like someone had put a thousand little Tasers into my body from all different directions. You'll have to test that, they don't seem to just come from you, more like you can conduct it, like a battery." Athien's phone rung as Nicola lept from her chair, her own phone ringing with the sound of a slow melody, Athien's a simple bleeping.

"Hi mum," Nicola said, as Athien turned away, his face an iron mask as he answered his call.

"I told you before, Mordacai, I'm not your attack dog." He whispered harshly, careful to ensure that his voice didn't carry over to Nicola. The voice over the phone was slightly squeaky, shaken. Athien could clearly make out the ever defiant voice of Mordacai.

"It's not like that. The guy who owns that place is just terrible and, he's defiant of Helm. He might be able to give you some information, unlike me, because I got nothing on him over the last four days." Athien sighed deeply, his eyes diverted quickly from the lawn, he saw Nicola stood next to the T.V., her back turned to him.

"Yeah, mum, I can meet her there, you know, it's not that far from where I am now, so I'll just change and be off," Nicola lied, but she wanted the excuse to have to run again, even though it meant she'd have to leave Athien earlier than she'd wanted to.

At least I know where he lives now, just got to get his number, make it a little less random next time.

That's the place that was called in by the police. Athien remembered when he was off to see Barns at the hospital, the address Mordacai had given him was to The Vampire's Drool. Athien moved from the window and around the kitchen calendar which sat magnetised to the fridge. On it, he saw Kali's schedule had her not home that night for over five hours, pulling a late night at her nurse job in the CBD.

"Look, Mordacai, if this one can't give me anything, I'm going to start poaching the customers you have near the ports, and your old office." Athien threatened, he didn't want to, but wasn't prepared to let the criminal off with an ok, after he took the mission. *Have to remain on top of those you use, or become the used.*

"That's fair. Just, make sure not to destroy the place, he still works in Helm's territory and mine. If you destroy him we all lose, you included when they all bank the goods that they ship. Your advantage only works as long as they remain confident in your efforts to be against the weak." Mordacai shuddered as he spoke. Athien heard him make the suggestion, and thought on it, as he heard Nicola talk with her mother, their conversation was near to its close.

"Yeah, I know, I'm always careful." Nicola cooed her mother while she reprimanded herself mentally. Athien went to the sink and poured himself another drink of water.

"Ok, Mordacai, I'll go, I'm not sure when, but it won't be tonight, there's somewhere else I need to be." Athien ended the call, he knew that his lie would stick, it was the only thing he and Mordacai had in common.

We both lie to survive, letting him believe I'd be there tonight would put me up for a trap, safer to set my own time, without him.

Nicola put her phone back into her pocket, just as Athien did the same. They both stared at each other for a moment, before Nicola smiled and ran her hands up through her hair a few times and took out the broken hair tie pieces. She pulled most of her hair into the shape of a ponytail expertly and held it.

"Wouldn't happen to have any hair ties?" She asked jokingly, to which Athien nodded, surprising her as he learnt over the kitchen counter from the sink and grabbed two new ones from Samantha's half secret collection. She kept forgetting it was there.

"Yeah, my cousin's staying for a while, so I do, not for me of course." Athien ran his left hand through his short blond hair, eyes closed for a moment as he remembered when it had been long, not two months ago.

"Wow, I can't imagine you having long hair, so that's fair enough. What's her name?" Nicola asked as she did up her hair.

"Samantha, she, came over with Prometheus to the expo last week, she aims to act in a show in a week. It's a new drama some channel is starting to film." Athien took her cup and placed both of them upside down on the sink bench, ready to be washed when he got back from the club.

"That's amazing, it was a plan of mine, when I was a little girl, so much fun to impersonate my brothers and sisters." She hopped from foot to foot and Athien remembered her phone call.

"You need to leave, that's ok, there's somewhere that I need to be as well." She looked relieved, but her face also fell at the same time as she moved towards the hallway.

"Thanks, yeah, ah, can I have your number, before I go rushing off again? So we can talk about, well, me again? It's nice to have someone who knows I'm not crazy." She wasn't shy to ask, Athien noted the necessity that she had for his company. They were alike in that matter.

We've both got something unexplained about us.

"Sure." Athien pulled out the phone he'd used before, and put it back. His head shook as he grabbed the newer flat phone that had been off for the past five days. Nicola looked questioningly at him as he stood there, waiting for it to turn on.

"You seem to be completely oblivious to how strange it is, for you to have an old and new phone." Athien quickly came up for a reasoning that he thought would be acceptable and throw her off fastest.

"This is the family and friend phone, personal, the smaller one is for work." He gave it to her to put in her number.

"So I'm family and friend worthy, noted. You're cousin and father's are the only numbers on here, under family, there are no friends?" She handed the phone back to him, and Athien pocketed it quickly, smirking slightly.

Athien grimiced.

"There is now." He smiled at her and then led her to the door.

Nicola thanked him again and walked onto the street. Athien watched as she saluted him and knelt like she was a sprinter.

"See you next time, Athien, turn that phone on more often, or I'll whiplash your trees again. He stepped down to the fence and learnt on it.

"I'm sure you'll be back, in a heartbeat even." He saluted her in return as she stepped away. Athien's eyes auto-focused. He watched her run until she became a blur on the horizon.

"Guess I'm at this solo tonight." Athien wandered about the front yard for five minutes, as he cleaned the place of the broken twigs and leaves, before he prepared to make the drive for the club.

14

Chapter 14 Exertion

The drive took him near to the hospital that Barns had been held in the week earlier and the club appeared on his right moments later.

It was an old building, half brick on the upper floors and concrete on the bottom half, something that caught Athien's attention as he thought of entry points. The service entrance was at the side of the building, but several guards were there, heavy set security. The front door was a giant glass slide door, plenty big enough that Athien could see almost the entirety of the ground floor. He drove past and watched as several groups of three and four people walked from all sides of the road to get to the club, the night just beginning.

Athien itched the side of his hands as he turned the car down two lanes and passed others as they walked among the side streets for dinners or just for walks, dogs often dragged behind as they moved in the silent place.

There's got to be somewhere close that I can get in, without drawing too much notice to myself.

He locked the car, his duffle bag hefted over his shoulders.

Not having a tech guide could come to haunt him if the sting went south. He walked around onto the main street of the club.

Athien felt overly secure, with his two-piece black suit and loose tie, as he walked with another group, two women and a man. The lights from the building painted the sidewalk and front facade in bright neon pinks and purples as the crowd gathered in, bleak sunlight just exiting along the horizon and night falling fast.

It's getting cold already. Athien could feel the first bite to the air as he took a breath, the group outpaced him, and he was left to continue to wonder on the point of entry. In his bag, Athien had put jamming devices and the suit, with some infrared light goggles to boost so he could see among the bright lights, without being blinded by sudden bursts of colour.

He walked up to the front, stuffed the sides of the bag into the inside to make it smaller and wrapped the bag handles around his wrist as he pulled out I.D.

"I.D." Said the doorman, another large man with a bald head and dark brown skin, eyebrows as brushy as a tree. His voice was flat and uninterested as he took Athien's I.D., checked the old photo compared to Athien's face and gave it back, beckoning inside the slide door. It remained open while the large groups of people came in, but closed as it got darker, a smaller side door next to the first was then used, Athien noticed.

Athien entered the club, his eyes immediately darted for the walls and roofs, security cameras were set in place all over and were well distributed across the spaces. He was knocked into several times as he made his way to the couch seats, three of them in the right corner, where only one other person sat.

There are five security cameras here, only two I need to worry about, the one to the bathroom, which caught my face, and the one that I have to go past to get in front of the toilets next.

Athien got up, his bag switched from his left shoulder to the right as he left the couches and entered the lounge area. His bag went up as he passed, covering his face as he walked. He pretending to stretch his arms, body turning in a loop as he looked up to the bar tops, his back against the camera in front of the toilet.

Athien turned around as a group of three women, all who wore matching jeans and tie-dyed shirts, followed him as he entered the toilet corridor. He stood straight again as he entered the small hall and saw the doors that faced him. Athien reached up the wall and positioned a signal jammer under the security camera, scattering the feeds.

"Service toilets." Athien read as he turned to the door to his right. The hallway seemed older than the club space, darker and more worn down.

Time to change. The toilets were the same as usual, but in addition to having the sinks and cubicles, they also had small storage cupboards for the workers' belongings. Athien got an idea for how he'd hide himself inside the bar.

He quickly went through the bags lightly, the cheap brown cupboard moved slightly as he looked for someone with similar clothes to his own.

He found some after the third bag, the manager of the space wore a casual suit shirt and pants, alike to Athien's, but cheaper quality. Athien stripped down and changed into his suit, the clothes he wore he placed inside the other man's bag as he took the others and put them in his own bag. He left it in another empty box, closed the door and exited via the service doors, at the back of the room. His suit decked out with the infrared light goggles and the jammers in his belt, ready to scramble the security network if he needed to.

He entered another hallway, this one was brick, closed off from natural light. Only three small lights covered the space he travelled, and the end of the hall was locked off by a closed and padlocked door. Athien approached a window next to it.

Outside, he managed to see the deranged owner, a man with bad curly, black hair and small brows with his gait tucked and muscular. He disappeared from view a moment later, Athien ducked down below the door as he saw him. It was irregular for the owner to be meddling in the simple affairs of suppliers, especially at night, Athien thought.

Unless, it's not regular. Athien opened the door, slowly, he's eyes scanned the ground and looked for feet, while he's ears listened to the shouts and scattered feet he could hear behind the pallets the owner had gone behind. The loading zone was packed with pallets of alcohol, all boxed in large sizes, the pressing concern was what he heard around the side of the pallets he stood behind. He could see the alley well and was enclosed in darkness.

"How could you get an entire truckload, wrong? I haven't got time for this, my customers expect the best from me, so you understand what that means?!" He heard the screaming voice, around the pallets and a quick succession of thuds as a fist collided with someone's body.

The Vampire, Myles Drool. Extreme perfectionist when it comes to business and severe anger management issues. If I'm right, it's because he's crazy and violent. Athien stood, sensing the danger the man who was getting beat on was in and jumped across the pallets, his body skidding over the pile that was slightly taller than him.

"Myles!" He crashed into the bodies on the other side, Myles had been sitting on the supplier's chest, he's fists dripped small droplets of blood from the victims bloodied, bashed. Athien pushed him off as he rolled over and Myles sprawled across the ground, dazed. As Athien picked up the supplier from the arms and brought him to his feet, pointed towards the door, he'd left open.

"Oh, why, you're finally here!" Athien was taken aback as he closed the door to the club and found Myles was not only standing, but stood with his arms open wide. Myles's hair flopped around as he watched Athien, who stood clear, he'd already seen those fists could kill easily.

Myles Drool! I need answers!" Athien came at the criminal, who stood perfectly still for as long as he could, before he sprang into action.

"It's such a long and boring name, though! Call me, Vamp!" he lunged at Athien and grabbed hold of the vest he wore, knees and elbows launched out from the sides as he attempted to take him to the floor.

Athien let himself be carried forwards as Myles ran out of the room. His attacks found no hold on Athien, who held onto the other mans' arms and raised his knees in tune with Myles, to stop his legs from attacking.

Athien slammed Vamp against the wall he'd backed himself into. Finally relieved of his grip Athien barged down into a spread, bent leg stance and threw five quick, strong punches into Myles's stomach and clipped his head with a final jab which sent Myles flailing.

"You will answer to me!"

An hour ago

Nicola had run, haphazardly, from Athien's house straight to her parent's house, both still at work until late that night, at a local eatery. She'd been told by her mother, that there was a friend's birthday party she had forgotten she was attending. It was in Hawthorn, a place she knew next to nothing about, though she'd been there many times.

She slammed into the front door, head throbbing slightly but she felt better than she had when she'd almost fainted at Athien's earlier.

"What am I going to wear?" She asked herself as she stumbled into her room. Not a fan of tight skirts or fancy dresses, Nicola went with black buckled jeans and a brown belt for the bottom half, and her favourite top, a white and blue sleeved shirt with a crisscrossed fabric pattern over the neck.

She did her hair up into a tight braid as her phone chimed, her mother asked her if she was there yet or not. Nicola dropped her shoulders, one hand holding her braid as the other texted back.

"I'm not yet, trains are running slowly right now." She threw the phone onto her queen size bed, covered with a princess warrior from her favourite book series and finished the braid, her head stung slightly as she let it fall, her head felt tight at the fringe.

I wonder if...

Nicola felt a buzz begin in her brain as she thought about running to the club. She wiggled her finger experimentally and saw it move quicker than she could register.

"Cool." She ran, instantly happy as she always had felt since discovering her abilities. When the car had come to hit them,

141

she hadn't been focused on that. Still, by the simple acts of heroism that Athien had expressed in shielding her from the attack, she was happy to have someone do that for her, as she always had for others.

The house fell away as Nicola raced to the party, her body was streamlined and unaffected by the air that seemed to cause havoc when she ran too fast in certain places. Just as it had on Athien's street.

She past cars and trucks, people on the street as they walked about the busy afternoon, her house was only six blocks from Athien's and the club her friends were going to meet up at was in the CBD, but that wouldn't take her that long. To the people around, there was a slither of white that passed them, followed by a sizable breeze that caught them by surprise, but she ran slower than before, so there wasn't any whiplash.

Nicola passed a train as it sped towards Flinders Street Station, her reflection visible to her on the side of the shiny, blue metropolitan train. She stopped inside a public toilet. The wind buffered around inside and threw her into the wall with a loud thump.

"Oh. So stopping, still an issue." She muttered. She fixed her hair and put on some warm pink lipstick, her bag had almost flown from her hand as she'd escaped the run and her head swam slightly as she stayed still to let the room spin before she left.

Nicola took stock of her bearings as she stepped back into the street. The club was just a little way down the road. She walked up at an average pace.

"Hey, brainy Nicky! Thanks for coming!" Nicola stepped into the near-empty bar zone of the club, her friends shouted the second she did so, it had been months since she'd last seen

142

any of them.

"Hey, Fallen, Crane, Brianna, how are you all?" They moved aside, and she was able to see them all more clearly as she sat with them. Fallen, the leader and planner of the group, was a sports enthusiast and was in her first year of Sports science. She wore a long-sleeved T and jeans. Crane, an elegant dinner and most opulent of the group, had just started her own studio for art and animation and wore a suit. Brianna followed a little on both of their worlds, being Crane's slightly younger yet, much more mature sibling and sporting suit pants and a turtle neck top. Brianna had wild blond hair, unlike Crane's kept short hair.

"You all look amazing! How's life? Where are you all at at the moment?" Nicola bombarded them with questions as a drink, was skidded across the table towards her. She drank from it greedily, noticing that her throat wash parched from her running all day.

Their babble went for an hour or so, each person saying what they'd been up to. Then they ordered food and the club became alive with colourful music and rocking tunes that had nearly everyone dancing within minutes.

"Yeah, I've been helping Crane with her studio and studying her school work." Brianna bolstered her chirpy face up as she smiled, the ends of her lips reached each ear on the sides of her face as she beamed.

The others chortled into their new drinks, amused as their smallest member had to yell to be heard over the ear-drum-d estructive music.

"You know, this is a really nice place," Nicola began to say, then realised that no one could hear her as they watched the dancers on the club floor. "Maybe we should go somewhere a little less noisy." Nicola liked music, but when it came to ear-splittingly loud; the kind that made people on the actual dance floor dead for a time afterwards? She tended to lose the beat within the noise and it became detestable.

My mother suggested this place, but it's too rowdy, and there aren't enough people, even though it's nearing night time. Fallen thought, trying to think of a new place that they could go instead.

"We could go to Drool's, it's meant to have decent people on Sundays, but it's a little way away, there's probably a line." The other three winced as her voice rose above the music as the songs switched and she stopped herself from continuing.

Nicola nodded her head, eager now as she felt the first throb of a headache lurked behind her eyes.

"Well, then it's settled." Fallen stood and the other three followed as they cancelled the sides and left the club, half jogging and half at a walk as they charged for the closest train time. Nicola put a hand to her head and felt a lot of heat behind her fingers, something wasn't agreeing with her.

Present

Athien kicked off of Myles as he thrust back, his face bled slightly. Athien marvelled at Myles' ability to ignore the bruises that must have begun to form all over his body. Their first struggle had moved into the hallway as Athien had been attacked by some workers of the owner. Myles kept his attacks wide and fast, but occasionally skipped and simply tried to tackle the vigilante to the ground. So far, Athien had been able to avoid it, but the small space was proving slightly challenging to work with.

The militant group breached into the toilets for employees

and Athien used his brief time, being first through the door, to come up with a plan. He directed the five workers that remained through the doorway as best he could, his grip managing to find one man's neck and another's wrist as he propelled them backwards. They fell into each other on the floor.

Then he saw a woman come at him at a sprint, she pushed by Myles and the others to get enough speed to drive the sledgehammer she wielded with enough force to destroy his skull, if it hit.

"Wow!" Athien broke the run by catching the hammer as she swung it sideways into the room, the attack clipped one man's face from behind her and landed into another's back as Athien redirected her into them with one swipe of his arm and a jab to her elbow, which fell limp with the weapon.

Athien felt something cut into his shoulder as he watched her drop and kicked at one of the men on the floor. He felt the handle of the knife now wedged into the side of his arm's muscle. Luckily, the suit was strong enough to take most of the hit, and Athien took out the blade. Myles stood proudly as he entered the room, wielding two more throwing knives and closely followed by other workers.

Myles lifted another knife to throw and Athien rolled towards the door on his right side. Myles threw the knife he held at Athien's general direction. The thud of the weapon against skin told Athien Myles' had hit someone else. Athien was preoccupied with Myles' other knife and didn't look back as something landed right between he's closed fist and the door.

He left the room and entered the hall, closer to the club's dancing disco then he'd ever planned to be while in the suit.

"Come here, Sentinel! We're not done playing! Hurry, get after him, can't have guests being disturbed now!" Athien heard Myles' near screams of supposed delight at the chase, as he saw two human shadows etch into the wall at his side. He scrambled up and towards the club hall.

"This is going to get messy." He saw the two fresh workers, both advanced with a knife in their right and left hands. The hammer wielder was back, hair wild and eyes in fury as they all came at him. Myles didn't come through the door as Athien backed up right before the male and female bathroom doors, aware that in a few more steps, he could have more than just a few people to deal with.

I could make them run, but most likely there'd already be some drunk ones out there and I have no idea how they'll react to seeing a combat suit-wearing bad guy fighting workers and the owner.

Athien met them halfway, he's body snaked around the first two and sick kicked the hammer women backwards and into the floor, so he could have some time to deal with the weaker links.

He faced the other two, back faced towards the door they'd just come through as he thrust out with a punch at the one to his right, a stoic, fast-moving man with a short stature but the strength behind his grip. He took hold of Athien's arm and, as he did, started to kick furiously at the vigilante's knees and feet while he tried to pry him off.

The other attacker was taller, broader and less hands-on. His arm went straight back and nearly hit the wall as he drew the knife and plunged it at Athien as the vigilante fought off the smaller man.

Athien dropped, aware of the knife and he's inability of escaping the other's iron grasp. His knees hit the floor, and he tumbled forward with the wrestler, who'd been pulling him so hard that the force of his drop sent them spiralling across the floor. The knife that had threatened to kill Athien stuck into the small of his back and bruised him, but he couldn't feel any broken skin immediately as the bigger man followed them down the hall.

"Get off of me," Athien had enough of grappling the man and punched him in the eye, his knuckles purposely missing the soft fleshy centre and instead hit the side.

"Weakling!" The man yelled, throwing Athien off as another caught him from behind. Athien was charged into a wall and then was pushed out into the bar.

Athien brought he's arms back, caught the scruff of the man's shirt and yanked as hard as he could, which caused the man to tumble forward and fall flat onto his face as Athien slid under his falling grasp.

They rolled into the club room. The noise fell away from Athien's ears as they stopped, right in the middle of a group of people, and who all froze. Athien carried the other two over him and barged them into the bar, he was surrounded, and the room suddenly felt a lot smaller.

"Everybody clear the room!" He yelled, aware of the hammer that had slipped through the doorway and was about to snap his back. The room launched into chaos.

Athien took a hammer to his side. He rolled across the floor and past a group of people who ran for the door.

He felt he's arms deaden as he rolled, some people jumped over him and Athien could hear shouts and screams as he was hit again.

"Ready to die, vigilante!?" Athien stood, his plan to block the attack and dislodge the weapon from her hands. She attacked,

147

the hammer came down from as high as her arms could reach. Athien caught the weapon with both hands and pushed it down and through the wooden flooring.

"No." He spoke directly to her face and swung his right fist into her shoulder. She dropped the hammer as others passed by them, Athien dodged backwards through the crowd as he saw the gap behind.

Got to get her away from the civilians. He pressed on, thumping and pushing by people as they thinned out. He was able to turn around and climb the stairs to the higher balcony level, the hammer wielder took time to get her weapon out of the cracked floor, seconds behind him.

Athien kicked backwards, his foot landing into the handle of the hammer and caused her to fall sideways against the wall. He took the hammer and threw it down the stairs, then punched her into the wall. She dropped, energy gone as she gripped her face.

Athien came back down the stairs, searching for Myles. The club room was mostly empty, people lined the street outside, and he could see the lights of phones as they attempted to catch him on camera, hidden in shadows. Athien's head ached, but he was intent on getting information from Myles, so he ran from the scene, back down the toilet room hallway and straight into the worker room.

Ha! You thought it would be that easy to take me out! Hey, Sentinel!" He turned and briefly glimpsed the glimmer of another knife as it passed through the doorway, Myles stood halfway down the hall. Athien began to step sideways as his right arm came up in a sweeping arch, the knife cut the inside edge of the suit but span off and away from him.

Too close.

148

Athien charged down the hallway with a battle cry that sent Myles at a run to cross the gap and get outside before he was caught by the angered vigilante. They both exited the door seconds apart.

Athien was taken aback as he saw the loading area. It was full of people, over twenty ruggedly dressed and uncoordinatedly organised people, half with guns.

Myles sniggered and stepped into the group as Athien took everyone in. They were all tense, doubtless ready to protect their boss and secure his business.

"I got you good! Ha, you're so surprised," Athien snarled as Myles jumped up and down with glee, then disappeared from view as the group got closer to him.

"I will take you down, Myles, after your goons here, I'll end you." Athien moved, he's legs balancing his weight, bent arms covering the front of his body as he watched all sides for the first attack.

"It's funny how you think there'll be an, after this, when my guys are done with you." He heard Myles cry between cackles. The group launched at him from all sides at once, he was outnumbered, but still sure of his victory.

I'm going to take some hits, just got to ensure that I make them the right ones. Athien remembered a martial artist had once told him that, back when he was first starting out.

"Uhhhh!" He yelled, a shout from the centre of his being that riled every fibre of his being to fight for everything he had and would achieve. The first person hit him from the side, and Athien was already among the others and used the proximity to his advantage, attempting to get out of the circle of doom.

"Not going to happen." He was caught by one arm as his

other punched a man in the face, a tooth flew from it as they fell away, but another caught his arm and slammed an elbow into Athien's face.

Athien's head snapped back, dazed, he head-butted one man who had grabbed him and kneed the other's elbow. Then something collided with his back. He fell forward into the mass of bodies that surrounded him spinning into near unconsciousness.

What's going on? For the first time, Athien awoke to a place unfamiliar to him, in the short seconds of falling he'd been kicked numerous times, he couldn't hear anything.

"Listen, love, either you leave, or you'll end up way worse than this fool." He made out Myles's odd voice as it spoke harshly to someone that he couldn't see. His eyes opened to reveal many feet, all pointed away from him as he turned his head slowly, finding the source of the voice.

"He's probably got a good reason to be here, but killing him won't get you all in the clear just as easy as him killing you would." He heard a familiar feminine voice come from behind him, and shuffled footsteps fell beside him as a pair of white flat suit shoes stepped into view and moved behind him.

"Just, get lost girly. My vulnerabilities are not up for debate here, or my setbacks, you just make sure that no one hears about these here happenings, okay?" He saw the shoes stop before another pair, white heels, shorter than the ones he usually saw around.

"I'm sorry, but this is a human being, and whatever right or wrongs he did to you all, everyone here's still alive. Not like he's going to be if I step away," Athien remembered that voice and leant up onto his side to get a look at the situation.

Nicola! His screamed internally as he saw her there, in

clubbing clothes as she confronted the criminals to protect him. *But she doesn't know who I am, yet.*

"I'll give you one last chance," Nicola continued, her eyes looked from between Athien's, to Myles's, who stood right in front of her, hands twitching silently at his sides." Before I give you one hell of a surprise." Athien reached into his belt and flicked the security scanner towards the hallway, between the legs of everyone around. The signal sent a corrupt hack to the rest of the building.

"That's that then, we deal with people in, extreme measures, you were warned," Myles spoke in a matter of fact tone and moved to put his right hand over Nicola's shoulder. Athien pushed himself off the ground by his shoulders and reached for Myles's foot. At the same time, the rest of the gang realised his alertness and began to split, the ones behind moved towards Athien, the others to Nicola.

The world slowed down. Athien watched as Nicola moved, faster than before, more erratic. Her movement almost too fast for even him to see. She begun to push each person with her heightened speed, and they all moved as she touched them, but stopped as soon as she let them go. Athien marvelled at how composed she moved. She expressed fear, wincing every time she touched a body. Athien also thought he saw a tad of sorrow as her eyebrows furrowed downwards.

Athien stood as Nicola sped up to him, everyone but Myles was in the motion of being pushed away from the scene. She let go, and Athien took hold of his grapple unlatching it as his body slowed again.

Time sped back up. The storage zone became a cacophony as gargled, surprised shouts erupted all at once.

Myles turned around and met Athien and the Nicola,

Athien's grapple gun already punched past him and recurved off the wall. It went around Myles. He was trapped.

What, what just happened! Myles threw his arms up and almost tripped over the thick wire that pulled into the centre of his knees and threatened to buckle him forward.

"How? What are you?" He swung his arms around in a broad sweep as he took in the sight of all his downed workers, then begun to smile and snigger. "You, you're a quick one," his body shook, slightly but more violently with every glance he took around the space. "Like that fool, over there. Ohh, I'm going to enjoy filleting you." Athien pulled on the wire and Myles fell from his awkward stance and wriggled around on the floor as Athien wound up the grapple again.

"You'll do nothing, to anyone, Vamp." Athien stepped over him and took a handful of his coat in his grip and yanked him around, he found the body heavier than he anticipated and dropped him half over.

A knife sliced out at his hands as Athien reared back, feeling Nicola tense nearby as the weapon came forward. He dodged it, and Myles instantly regretted his decision as the vigilante took a moment to kick him square in the ribs.

"Ooh!" Myles shouted, he coughed as Athien turned away and faced Nicola, who had walked a little away and into the open sky of the alley road, she sat on an old box at the gate.

"You need to leave, before the police show." His voice was softened slightly, but not enough to make it sound suspicious. She watched him and kept her eye on Myles at the same time, worried he might try something again.

"It's not my fault I wanted to help." She stood, unsure of what she wanted to think about the vigilante that stood over her, he'd just beaten people that had attacked him too.

Athien grabbed her shoulder and shook it slightly, sure the police would be there soon. She blinked rapidly, and heard the sound of sirens in the near distance.

"You need to leave." She disagreed, without even knowing it, she realised what would happen if she left.

"You need me, there's a lot of bad people, and if I go, you won't get anything from him before the police get here and shoot you. as they will, on the spot." She walked away from him and towards Myles, as Athien attempted to protest.

"You can't, there's cameras, evidence and, not to mention, I doubt you can carry him and run like that. You'll overtax yourself." His voice back to being gruff and slightly angry, he wanted her out, but was desperately realising how useful she could be if she could do it. Nicola stopped short of Myles, her heart skipped a beat as she realised what it was she was thinking of doing.

This is illegal, this, I'd be helping a random potential killer. She had no idea who he was, or what he wanted from the man, or if it was even real. *He could just be beating on the owner for protection money, like an overly dressed mugger.*

"Actually, I don't think I should be here," Myles groaned as he faced them both, recovering from the kick he'd been dished and wishing some of his workers weren't weak and as scared as kittens in storms. "I won't say anything, but don't hurt him anymore, you've done enough to them already." She smiled and wished she could stay, if not to protect the man then the others or even the vigilante himself.

"That's a good decision. Leave." Athien, slightly crestfallen and happy at the same time, passed her as he went to finally interrogate Myles. He felt a slight adjustment in the atmosphere and temperature as she left the storage sight. He directed all of his attention to the knife thrower, Myles, once more. Myles had almost made it to his feet.

"Girl's right. You hurt me, and you get nothing. Cops come, at best you're shot, at worst, we both do." Athien shook his head and sighed, he was done with all of the talk this man kept pushing out of his fat, pursed lips.

"I know about Helm, tell me where he is, then I leave. That, is how this works." He stood right in front of Myles and even with the eye covers, he could see what such a proximity was causing to Myles's brain, he couldn't take his eyes from Sentinel's eye masks.

"Wait, what? Why do you, what. The hell you put up with in this world isn't enough? You want to go fight with the devil?" Myles talked sarcastically, but Athien could see the fear that spewed from his eyes as he'd mentioned the name.

"The only hell you need to worry about is your own, and how comfortable it's going to be." Athien pressed, he shoved the smaller man, slightly, but enough to let him know that their fight wasn't forgotten on him.

"You are insane, there's no way you can take him on. He's strong, fast and smart, he'll crush you."

"So I've heard, give me something, before I, crush you," Athien heard at least one car stop on the other side of the building, his patience wore thin as he figured escape routes in his head. At the same time, Myles took his time to answer. "Now!" He grabbed Myles again and shook him violently.

Myles pushed off of him and stood, away from the doorway, now fully aware that he wouldn't be getting apart from the fight without trouble.

"He's good, he's one of the dock masters, like, legitimately, and the only other thing I know for sure about the man is." He gulped. "He's got enough firepower to take a decent stab at war in this city. I've stopped supplies in weapons. Drug money, phone calls and radio channels to most organisations in this city at some point. He won't have anything but my eternal destruction." Athien heard boots down the hallway into the club, and he moved away from the door. He stopped at the back of the storage zone, a wired, high fence with multiple trucks positioned on the other side and a clear view of the main road in and out of the suburb.

"Is that it, he's a big bad, and nobody deals with him in the usual organised criminal groups. Then who supplies him? Who gave him weight against others? Why does he push the others out of the woodwork?" Athien grabbed the fence as he saw the light appear at the other side of the hallway, he ducked, and Myles followed as they both watched.

"That's the thing, nobody knows him, and no one knows how he knows so much, but it's like, like he has holes in everyone pockets, like he cuts them there himself." Athien saw the genuine concern in Myles still crazy looking face and checked if he had the foot holes to scale the wall.

"You'll pay for your actions soon, Myles, but I've got other places to be as of three minutes ago." Athien aimed for the third wring of the fence and jumped onto it, using a quick succession of jumps to scale the fence. His feet landed firmly underneath him, as police officers entered the storage yard, immediately arresting the workers, who had been waiting for their boss's words to continue work.

"Sentinel, don't let that devil kill you, I'd like the pleasure fighting you in my peak form and you in yours." Athien ducked down and jumped from the roof, he used the pull-up pipe on the side of the doors to fall safely and then stepped into the shadows.

"Myles that will never happen. I've beaten your workers and you, leave this city, before this war begins and your peaceful club is put in the centre of something it never should have been a part of." Athien left, as police saw Myles stand from behind the crates, they'd hidden behind and surrounded him.

It's a pity that they won't find any security footage of what happened, I might have gotten him put away for good, but, protecting Nicola was worth it.

Athien took off his mask as he entered the enclosed space of his car and drove from the scene, he's mind raced with the contents of the night still fresh. He had to rely all of the information to Kali, then to his computers, nothing could be forgotten, about his encounter with Myles.

15

Chapter 15 Helm

Athien drove back to the house as fast as he could, head whirling from the night's events. He almost forgot to turn the loop on the sets of cameras he passed in his neighbourhood to get there. His suit lay in the back seat, half stowed away in the bag and half against the seats.

"Kali, you there? I'm pulling into the street now." Athien said, turning smoothly into their street, which was almost devoid of lights or cars.

"I'm here," Samantha called over the radio, while she monitored the web for police calls and him drive towards the house. "What happens next?" She leant into the chair and saw a car pull in behind Athien at the start of the street.

He stopped the car inside the driveway, seeing the car pull into the street himself and another right behind it. *Something's not right here.* Athien heard more wheels from the other side of the street as he exited the vehicle.

"Athien! They're coming for…" Athien closed the door of the car, and his head snapped back for a moment as his hands brought the helmet back over his head. He backed between the left side of the car and the wall of the property.

The three cars roared towards the house, their wheels screeching across the road. Three vehicles came into the driveway.

Athien hid behind his vehicle, his feet squared, head bent low as he watched people exit the other cars. Stacked to the teeth with guns and ammunition, visors hiding their faces, it was apparent what was going on.

They followed me. Athien backed around the side of the car, cautious about being silent as he heard a man's voice shout orders into the darkness.

"He's here, no way has he made it to the house. Sentinel! I've been watching you since that attack on my warehouse." He yelled. Athien heard the footsteps of soldiers surround the car, guns aimed at the wall. He was surrounded, between the car and the tall brick wall on the side of the property.

"There's no point to a standout fight here, you'd have the advantage of knowing the terrain. So I decided to catch you unaware. I apologise that it had to end like this." Athien, shook violently as he thought frantically for a way out of the situation.

"Light it up." Athien heard the leader shout. He reacted before the guns fired to his sides, but felt their impact as bullets punched through the side of the car. Windows smashed as he jumped up and onto the roof of the vehicle. His body skidded across the top as the shooters on the other side aimed upwards, their fingers didn't even lift from the triggers as he moved.

Behind them, not two meters away, Athien saw a man, dressed in a suit, jet black, dyed hair stuck in a spiky mess on his head and no stubble what so ever. Over his eyes, a dark tinted pair of shades and across his knuckles, Athien caught a glint of light, metal knuckle busters.

Athien dropped as he heard the others turn to face him. He grabbed two soldiers closest as shields as he ran forward, his body dragged back slightly by the weight. He went straight for the leader.

"Helm!" He came forward, the men behind him stood back, their guns pointed at him from all sides. They didn't shoot as Athien grabbed Helm and pushed him back onto the lawn of their yard, dropping the two others he'd held. Athien could see lights as the neighbours hurriedly attempted to find out what was going on.

"So, there is, a man under that mask, and he's currently angry with me, right?" Athien pulled his arm back and punched his blade towards Helm's chest, who matched the move with his punch, his other arm dropped and blocked Athien's dagger as the two hit each other and staggered back.

"Maybe!" Athien lunged forward, tricking Helm into moving into a defensive stance as he prepared for another attack. Athien sidestepped passed him, his blade found a gap under the closest henchman's armour and struck his soft flesh as Athien dashed past.

I've got to lure him around the back, if Kali has heard anything, she'll take Samantha and go into phase two. Athien had been worried that one day he'd be attacked, it was always safe to prepare for such an event, but he was angry that it had taken so little time to happen.

Guns fired towards him as Athien made it to the corner of the house, around the side. He was narrowly missed by a few stray shots that fired through the wall and past his helmet. Helm shouted something, as the sound of footfalls came from behind, signalling he had seconds before more guns would fire at him.

Taking a quick look through the kitchen window as he passed the halfway point of the house, Athien saw that the light was on. The television was off, Kali could still be asleep. He doubted that. Athien slid across the ground as the first body came around the side of the house and looked for him. He moved behind the small, meter alcove that was created by the shortened house back and proceeded to check his pockets for another set of knives.

Then, his arms locked and loaded, Athien breached the cover he'd been given and threw the two blades towards the soldiers at the other end of the path. Their aim angled towards him immediately as the knives found their mark in the attacker closest to the wall of the house. The second furthered into the centre of the group catching the face of another. Then the others fired seconds later. Athien rolled across the ground, behind a tree positioned next to a wall, and passed the side of the house.

Made it, let's hope that Kali knows what she's doing. It was then that he heard the gun fire stop, as the tree was close to being ripped to shreds. Bullets hit the roots and the taller branches in an attempt to reach him.

"You better not be shooting up my aunts' garden you jerks." He heard Samantha angrily whisper as she moved around the back door and into the garden, she stopped and ducked low behind the little veranda. She saw Athien, clad in simple pants and a suit shirt, with his helmet barely obscuring his identity from her.

"Why did they stop?" Athien asked as he poked his head around the side of the tree and looked for the gunmen. The path was still full of soldiers, but they had gotten the injured two out of the mix, and that left the other four, who had their guns pointed out, but seemed to be awaiting some kind of order. Their aim was still on Athien as he hid behind the tree, they knew he was there.

"I don't know, but I saw Kali running off to the front room as I saw you run down the side passage. Why are there soldiers at our door Athien?!" Samantha whispered harshly, motioning for Athien to roll across the gap while the gunfire had seized. He got the message, deciding not to answer the question until he crossed the gap, without giving the soldiers even a second to shoot at him. He ducked as low as he possibly could.

The soldier's guns trailed him as Athien's body passed by, before he hit the safety of the other side and squatted with Samantha.

"Good. Look, Kali and I have this covered, right now, you need to not be here when the police show up, like, at all." Athien said seriously, his eyes staring intensely straight into hers. Samantha begun to turn her head quizzically, but instead nodded gravely, standing slowly as she began to back towards the house.

"Well, in that case, I bet I should be leaving now, then." She climbed the stairs, Athien agreeing with her as they both cut back into the house, fast and low, as they heard shouting at the front.

"Don't go up the front, just get to your room." Athien guided Samantha around. Instead of taking her directly through the lounge they came into the front hallway, the door ahead open, with Kali's short frame taking up next to none of the space. They ducked into her room, and Athien helped her quickly gather clothing, while there was a loud report that sounded from the front of the house.

"Please let this plan work." Athien almost jumped as Samantha came to the door and turned the light off, he'd gone into a slight lapse of time.

"Come on, we've got to move, don't we?" Athien nodded again, and they both jogged back through the house, looking through the side windows and around the side corners as they made for the back fence. It led into a side alley that would take her off the street and two blocks west of the house.

Athien bopped down next to the fence, his hands latched together tightly as he readied to propel Samantha over the wall. She paused, however, and caught a breath at the fence, looking back at the house.

"Why do I have to leave? And what did you give to Kali to scare seven soldiers?" Athien huffed and looked at his wrist, thinking about the little time they had to get the soldiers off the street, before there was serious influence from the police force.

"Look, I can explain this later, just, it's easier to explain this to the police with less variables and, the plan might not work." Athien shook his hands, gesturing for Samantha to take the climb, her bag, only hanging just tight enough to show weight, wouldn't hinder her jump.

"Okay." She took hold of the top of the fence and put a foot on in his hands.

"And don't you worry about Kali, she's tough." Athien pulled up as Samantha, looking even more confused than before, pulled herself over the high wooden fence and landed on the ground over the other side a second later.

"Thanks, I'll catch back up with you before I have to fly home, Athien, please, be careful." Athien smiled under the mask and walked away.

She'll be safe, if Kali wasn't able to scare them away with that gun, then I'll probably be walking into a hostage situation, but...

His thoughts were broken mid-sentence as he heard a mini-explosion from out front of the house, and the sound of an engine starting took place as Athien ran up the house side path.

"And don't come back, you hooligans!" Athien rounded the corner, his hands going for the helmet over his face as he saw the neighbours all down the street looking through cracked windows and doors.

He dropped it by the house side, as he rounded on Kali, who was standing still, on the front veranda and shaking her fists at nothing, the car already speeding down the street. There were sounds of sirens almost masked by its screeching tyres.

"Kali, how are you? Did the plan work fully?" Athien took her shoulder and saw the blast streak on the lawn, where Helms car had parked. Kali stood there with a small, makeshift grenade launcher.

"I'm fine, Athien, it's not like I've never shot fireworks at someone before, but, to be honest, I thought their boss might take a second glance at this baby." Kali hefted up the fake weapon, and Athien noted the finger she still had wrapped around the trigger as she showed him the inside barrel. A pointed firework sat inside, ready to be shot.

"You've fired, fireworks at people?" Athien took the launcher, content to be rid of it before the police came up.

He walked into the house, mind pumping out thoughts of what he had to be sure to hide, to not let them see, like his giant surveillance computer and the spare suit he'd hidden in the toolbox.

"Yep, was good fun too. Getting to watch their clothes catch on fire as the police, at the time, watched and laughed at our stupidity." Athien rounded the corner and opened the door into the garage, sure to turn off and tarp the computer, while his other hand and Kali locked the tool draws and cleaned the space somewhat.

"That sounds exciting." He heard sirens out the front, could see the lights ebbing through the slight gap between the garage door and the concrete beneath it. Athien wiped some dust off his hands and onto his pants, only just remembering the helmet he'd left at the corner of the house.

Shoot. As Athien heard the knock at the door, he motioned for Kali to answer it, himself running for the side window of the house. He slammed it open, checking for any policemen who had decided to go around the house.

He was luckily, Athien managed to lean out the window and grab the helmet without being seen, and hid it in the cabinet in the lounge that adjoined the kitchen. He made his way back to the door, Kali was already busy giving the police officer all the details.

"Good morning, young man, already dressed I see, good to see you're both doing, well, after this unfortunate event." Athien met the eyes of the tall women that stood in the doorway, her silver police badge shining light across his face as it reflected light from the house. The jacket was a black one, and she wore a coloured fluoro vest of green over the top of it.

"Hello officer, thank you for coming so quickly." Athien stood to the side of the doorway, with Kali leaning on the wall across from him, and the officer taking notes ahead, seemingly unshaken from the bullet holes in the woodwork or the ground around the house.

Athien took a glance around the yard. He was unsurprised that there was only one car at the scene so far, no doubt, after an initial report, the house would be swarming with the police department.

"Can you tell me what you saw here this morning, or heard? Would help the investigation a lot if we could get a picture of," She gestured around the front yard. Pointed at the blast pattern, the bullet holes and then looked Athien directly in the eyes. "Why and how this all came to happen?" She finished with a puff that let out a cloud of air.

"Yeah, well, you see, officer, we were attacked, by a gang of violent youths, dressed up as commandos." Athien turned his back against the wall and pulled an arm backwards, pointing down the hall. "Please come in, and we'll tell you all about it." He sounded tired, his voice was stalled. Athien drooped his eyes low.

Have to get her inside. The officer hesitated, and Athien continued to stand there, waiting for her to back down and enter the house. Her hands still held the pen and paper, as if she was deciding if a gang had attacked the house, or the house had attacked them.

"Come on in officer, Bridget," Kali said calmingly, her old hand rose and grabbed a firm hold of the officer. She pulled them gently into the room, leaving Athien behind for a moment as he briefly looked outside, awaiting the sound of footsteps entering either the lounge or the kitchen space.

His feet moving quickly, Athien took to the veranda as he shot for the car, his combat suit still sitting in the back seat, in plain view to others that looked through the glass. Athien unlocked the vehicle and quickly took the bag, his eyes trained on the garage side door. Before he'd even taken another step, however, he heard the police car as it drove up to the house, lights off and at a snail's pace.

Athien threw the bag, under-armed, towards the side door, at the left corner of the shed's sliding door and out of sight. However, his arm was still coming down again when the officer's lights cornered him in the middle of the very awkward scene.

"Hey, kid? What are you doing up at this time in the morning?" The car stopped mid-way in the driveway, and Athien dropped his arm as the officer climbed out of his car. Their eyes wide and badge gleaming as they pressed his oversized gait into a flexed form and approached.

"Nothing officer," Athien lied, thinking quickly to ease his questioning glare as soon as possible." I was just checking the car after the attack that has only just ended half an hour ago." Athien spoke shortly, his eyes narrowed, and he curled the left side of his lip up as he watched the officer, whose gaze instantly left his.

"There's nothing wrong with asking, is there, where is your aunt?" *Marrow,* his name tag read, Athien took the seconds he had to edge slightly closer to the garage.

"Well, that's subjective, but, on to your job, detective Morrow, my aunt is most probably in the kitchen, with another officer. They've just started the interview." Athien waved his hand at the front door and then turned away from the officer, who positioned himself towards the door.

"Well, thanks for that, may I take your name? Before you, what is it that you're doing now anyway? Shouldn't you be with your aunt?" Marrow stopped moving and awaited Athien's answer, one hand on his radio, the other sat limply beside his firearm.

This is one withdrawn nephew, and he was doing something before I turned up. Morrow thought he'd come across something that might link the attack to this half-suit wearing boy, but he wasn't sure what it was, yet.

"I'll be in there in a moment, trust me, and if you need to look up my rap sheet, my name is Athien Dickens." Athien kept walking and didn't stop as he passed the corner and kicked the bag into the garage without breaking his stride. Officer Marrow, after looking after Athien for a moment longer, moved across the veranda and entered the house, knocking as he went.

Athien entered the garage, letting go of a deep sigh as he stooped down, picking up the bag and took it to the tool carrier. He rechecked the keys, hid them in the roof and then turned off the computer. He returned to the kitchen area and helped to weave the cover story he and Kali had conceived long before the attack.

Athien awoke sore the following day, after bruising some muscles and staying up to the earliest hours of the new day, he had been well past weary. The house was now devoid of officers and their probing lights and questions, after they'd taken all the evidence they could and wrapped the tree and side path of the house in police tape.

He walked into the kitchen, set on water as he collected a glass and drew some from the sink. He saw a familiar face sitting at the dining table.

"Morning, Samantha." Athien leant against the bench and smiled as she turned to look at him, beaming, but, with a concerned look across her brow as her eyes clenched closer to each other, she looked him over twice.

"Well, you look fine, at least, but I hear Kali has a fine for a fireworks launcher? The news is going crazy over the rich American genius whose home was attacked by a gang." She gestured at the screen and Sentinel saw footage of the house from the street. The neighbour right across the street had videoed it up to that point.

Athien nodded and came forward, seating himself down beside her so that he could easily watch and hear the rest of the coverage.

"Police also reportedly stated that they already know the name of the gang leader, thanks to victim Athien Dickens, famed son of the genius technological leader Prometheus. Helm, was reportedly what the soldiers dressed in the video called the middle man," the reporter showed Helm on screen. It was a blurred image of him as the group ran to the car to escape Kali. " Helm, by name or secret identity we are yet to be informed. The police believe this gang to be highly dangerous, trained and heavily geared, so all effort should be taken to stay away from their members." Athien smiled to himself, convinced that their plan of blaming a gang and throwing Helm's name out there would raise the awareness of whatever he was up to.

"Hopefully this makes people look for him, then we'll be seeing more of his goons."

Athien moved about the house for hours, cleaning the garage, fixing his PC and awaiting the arrival of the next police van that would be coming to collect the forensic data.

"Hello Kali, how are you?" Athien was partway done cleaning the counter in the kitchen and stopped when he saw his aunt coming in, hair done up in its grey bun and eyes open wide. She wavered slightly as she stepped into the brightly lit space, and shielded her eyes, now squinting.

"Good morning Athien, suppose we should probably step into the next phase of this mission of yours. After all, it will be suspect if a villain comes running around our house for a second time." She spoke with optimism, her voice uplifted, though the matter would seem quite dark and dangerous for most. Athien leant against the kitchen counter deeply, bending backwards into an arch as he thought of a response for a statement he'd spent the hours since waiting thinking about.

"I've been thinking on this, our plan still works, to leave and move closer to the action, we've just got to get the garage running, then we'll be able to run all our operations out of a secure place." Athien almost laughed as Kali scoffed, moving close into the kitchen as she nodded.

"Ha, you mean your operations, I might have an interest in killing the men and women who kept you as a murderous slave for over a year. But I didn't sign up to shooting people with rocket launchers every other week. Besides, what kind of name is The Garage?" She sat down at the counter and grabbed the cloth that Athien had been using, using it to scrub off the last of the grime that had been collected over the week.

"Wait, does there have to be a name? Anyway," Athien stopped and shook his head at the absurdness of the sentence. "I know I didn't, I didn't see him coming. I have no idea how he found me." Athien's eyes narrowed as he began to question that again. How had Helm managed to get a hold of his location?

"Well, you'd better fix that, because he did, and you, for the first time probably, hadn't known an attack was coming. What evil gangs have you actually annoyed enough that haven't got the message that you're a bad deal anyway?"

"Besides whoever Helm's undoubtedly with? The Caretaker's network is still running, maybe someone took it over from him?" Athien felt ideas spinning in his head as he ran through a list of people who could have connected to both the individuals.

"Didn't you work with, that Mordacai guy?" Kali remembered briefly the day she'd been told about the expo day scene and how close Samantha had been into the darkness.

"No, Mordacai is working with me to take down Helm…" Athien trailed off as he thought about the screaming businessman he'd been shaking-ly working with.

Is he capable of that?

"But, if I was dead, then Helm would just continue to work and pay him, Mordacai really did just want the business, it makes sense." Athien stepped away from the counter, fists clenched.

"That was a risky plan for Mordacai, he truly believed that Helm could kill you." Kali's voice was morbid and quiet.

"He could," Athien let the sentence set in as he thought about the fight. "Helm was on the upper edge that whole fight, but his too brick layered, it's like I'm fighting a soldier, who feeds off failure, every hit he missed his next was stronger, faster. If he aimed a little, then I would have come off a lot worse than some chest bruises and an aggravated stab wound." Athien tentatively touched his stab wound as he talked about it.

Kali stood up, her lips pursed like she was going to pierce him with words.

"Well, there's a first for everything, I think you can beat some military brute he ran away from me soon enough, one hit at the ground and another at the car and he ran for the hills. His goons though, they are loyal, wouldn't run until he did."

Athien shook his head and bowed slightly as he stepped away from the kitchen, looking for benchmarks on the counter.

"The goons aren't too tough, it's like his gang is a bunch of new mercenaries, when he was a decorated soldier. I'll need to do some work on finding his name, Helm, I'm sure that's a last name." *Just from the way he dresses professionally, and the quiet and quick sentences. It figures that an army man would use just his last name as a title.* Athien thought to himself, as he began to stalk the kitchen and around the dining table.

"So, get a new place, a new informant and go rad out Mordacai, getting some more information on Helm in the process, something tells me that man doesn't work for free." Athien stopped under where the TV screen was positioned and leaned on the chair there.

"Oh, and don't forget to name the place, we'll need a nice name to fall on when we mention it in public." Kali smiled for a moment.

Again, despite the dark undertone of the conversation, she remains, calm and steady, where, did she get this from? Athien mused.

"How long until Samantha goes back, 2 days, right?" Athien wondered aloud, unsure of the exact date Samantha had briefly said sometime in the morning.

"Yes, why?" Kali looked confusedly at Athien, her brows furrowed.

"Because," Athien's voice became guttural, deeper. "I'm going to need her help to collect data on Helm, while I visit Mordacai."

16

Chapter 16 Caretaking

"So, what's the agenda for tonight? Bank robber or street dealer?" Samantha walked into the garage hours later. She immediately found her voice drowned out by the methodical sounds of attacks landing against a punching bag.

Athien stood in a fighting stance as he punched the bag, his feet planting him as an L at all times. He did a sequence of movements he'd been taught, and soon enough the sweat ran from his brow, beading, before falling down his face in a stream.

"Hi Sam," Athien stopped his fury of attacks, and the bag swayed after he stepped away from it. "Neither, actually, Helm." He pointed at a file open on his pc. Samantha leaned forward to read it.

"Helm, ex-military, skilled fighter, weapons training," She read through the document. "You think he's got to be working for someone else." Samantha took a breath and placed the document back in the filing cabinet as Athien took off the straps around his hands and wrapped a towel around his shoulders. "Who, the Caretaker?"

"Maybe," Athien muttered, unconvinced that that was the only angle. "Once we take him down, we'll be able to move up, into the actual CBD, take some real damage to the Order and crime as a whole. Athien switched his shirts quickly, a loose blue gym shirt to a black button-up, his tracksuit pants matching.

"So, what do you think I can do to help?" Athien laughed out loud, he couldn't believe Samantha was still in on the business, after the house was attacked. He looked at her, standing there, shoulders squared, looking like she could take on the entire world.

"You can help me, gathering research if you'd like, that file isn't large, and we'll need a name, a real one, to be able to truly stop Helm." Athien paused, flexing his eyebrows up and looking at her quizzically, to see she understood, as he continued. "I'm going to take a hit at Mordacai, once he answers, but you could have a look at a couple of the sites we've seen Helm, or others have seen his soldiers, around the city. Just," He paused again and this time looked pained, worry seeping into his face as it screwed up, he thought over how to say it. "Be safe, don't get into any fights that you can't handle, okay?" She nodded in answer and stepped forward, arm out in a salute as she did so.

"Ready for duty, sir. Is Kali getting in on our action?" Samantha stood down again and went over to the open tool case. Her eyes nervously going over the few knives and other small, concealable gadgets and weapons that were housed there, as Athien suited himself up.

"She'll be in when I've got a track on Helm, or arrested Mordacai, depending on what happens there," Athien answered somewhat gruffly, pulling the chest armour over his head.

173

"Well, how do you think it's going to go?" She decided against taking any weapons and stepped away from the case, letting Athien pack a few into his side pockets and slips between the combat suit crevices.

"I think if he is against me, he'll tell me where Helm is, and if he isn't, we'll soon find out," Athien said menacingly. At the same time, he put on his helmet and checked the street for people. "At least it's not raining."

"Okay, I'll check out these places," Samantha held up the document again and pointed at the names at the bottom. "And get back to you, as soon as you're done beating up that terrifying man." She half-muttered. She felt her hair raise as she remembered his goons almost coming through the door at her, Athien driving them back as she'd escaped.

"Okay Mordacai, where are you?" Athien muttered as he walked out of the garage. His phone to his helmeted head as he rang the shady killer and moved towards the car out front. He carefully ensured there was no one on the street watching his movements.

After half an hour of driving and a set of cryptic sentences, Athien appeared on the most southeast street that interlocked the CBD area to the rest of the city. He'd worked out Mordacai's trail without much difficultly, not even seen from the range of vehicles and officers that took their late-night drives in similar directions.

"Mordacai!" He shouted, seeing the big man standing just down a side alley, tucked away from the silent street, as if he always expected to be jumped, even though he was huge. *Probably packed to the brim with all-sorts too, I'd imagine.* Athien checked the street and the small park across the road for other people, but couldn't see any in the poor lighting.

Mordacai's frame shifted as Athien shouted his name to the wind, and he seemed to convulse slightly as he heard it.

"Shut up, you moron! Do you want to get us both arrested? Or killed? This is the CBD we're talking about." Mordacai whispered harshly, his voice almost carrying higher than Athien's shout as the two intersected each other, gruff and squared up.

"Where's your men?" Athien whispered back, his own voice deep and sharp. Athien slammed his fists against his sides as he stood there, watching Mordacai's every move, in case it was a trap.

"Men? What makes you think I have any soldiers here? I can fight for myself, you know that I only have to take out my revolver and shoot at your head a few times, like I did back then? Jog that memory of yours?" Mordacai's words dripped sarcasm and boredom as he remembered the day they'd met and the death of two of his workers.

"I've been shot in the head before," Athien said darkly. "Why wouldn't you have men?! If there was a slight change in your mind that you couldn't put a shot in my head before I downed you, then you wouldn't have come alone." Athien smashed the side of the wall as he finished talking, re-enforcing his strength as he eyeballed Mordacai.

"And why would I think that my esteemed client here, would be out to get me, as he so obviously is here to do?" Mordacai stooped a little, his back arching forward as he mocked Athien, who flared in response to the behaviour.

"Don't play dumb with me, Mordacai, I'm sure you're the reason that Helm hunted me, found me and tried to kill me, otherwise, why would he show up?" Athien grabbed Mordacai's robust frame and hoisted him slightly by the collar.

175

"If I've barely made a dent in what I believe looks to be a huge operation?" Mordacai squirmed away from Athien, spitting directly onto his chest as he pushed off of him, stumbling backwards and almost toppling over as a result.

"You fool, have you never been in business, you take out a competitor, someone has to fill in the gap, or there's chaos among the lower life forms. I saved this city by taking over the Caretaker's business." Athien howled as he came at Mordacai, who, beginning to get worried by the anger exhibited in Athien, decided to take a few steps back.

"So you admit it, that you sent Helm after me!?" Athien swung at Mordacai, his right hand formed into a fist as he hurled it straight towards Mordacai's face.

Mordacai slipped his head low and raised an arm, blocking the attack as he sidestepped, hit by a kick to his side. He dropped to the ground a meter away and coughed empty air.

"What the hell! No, I didn't send that nut job after you, no way, I told you, Helm is a contractor. If I can't find his client on the streets, I have to network with the people behind doors." Mordacai stood as Athien heaved, coming forward with both fists clenched again, a snarl on his face.

"That's an excuse for you to say you still know nothing about him, it's been weeks!" Athien kicked out, his foot hitting the wall behind Mordacai, who flinched from the attack, stumbling away as Athien's full weight came down upon him. He kneed Mordacai into the wall.

"You suck, you know what," Mordacai coughed as he slumped down from having the wind knocked out from his lungs and doubled over. "I was playing fair, but frankly, this is unacceptable. If you won't be friendly," He gestured a hand in a forward stroking fashion further down the alley. "Then

I won't either." Athien backed away as he heard footsteps, two gun-wielding bodies filled the skinny alley, walking in formation. Their sights set on the vigilante who'd wailed into their boss.

"Boss, you want us to shoot?" Athien heard the bigger of the two, who walked in front slightly, speak up and continue to walk towards their boss. His head darted from the small fire escapes above his head, to the bin that lay not ten meters behind him, for protection.

"No, you idiots, don't shoot, don't, don't move, just stay there and keep those guns trained on this sucker." Mordacai chocked for a moment mid-sentence and barked his orders, arm held up in full stop fashion, as he attempted to straighten himself and stand against the Athien.

"For what your name seems to imply, I don't think you got the message on what protection means." Mordacai sniggered to himself, before becoming very serious, all traces of anger and laughter gone from his lips.

"My name is mine, its meaning is mine." Athien retorted, noticeably disturbed by the attack on his name as his head snapped down for a moment. Then, his fists uncurled, as he breathed at Mordacai.

"Fine, but, by the gods my word is mine, I'm NOT your enemy against Helm, so get off that high horse I know you vigilante types are fond of and help me kill the guy." Mordacai sincerely opened his hand and held it out for Athien to grasp. Moisture from his sweat built into the crevices as they locked hands together, Athien's savagery lost as he watched the guns, further than he could reach comfortably.

"Then, give me something, or he's going to strike something or someone again, no matter what, and we should be there

177

to stop it, or save ourselves if he's after us." Mordacai shook his head as Athien spoke, amazed that the first thing he was hearing was an order from the man he had guns being pointed at.

"You know, you've got quite a bit of gull, to position yourself in front of guns, and try to further your own agenda. I'd say it's admirable, but it's just kind of stupid to me." Mordacai ignored Athien's request and instead decided to counter it with his own question. "How did Helm even find you? The first time, right? You'd never seen him before?" He waited for Athien's confirmation response, then nodded and walked a little closer to his men, he waved them away.

"I don't want to push my agenda, I'm simply asking a question that we need answered, unlike the one you just asked. It's obvious, Helm followed me from a couple crime scenes, it won't happen again, I swear." Mordacai again nodded, a finger crossing his bearded chin as he began to circle in a tight loop, just off to the side of Athien's position.

"Why did you stop in front of an Old ladies house? Hmm, I heard she's the, Nan, of some genius or rich boy, or something. Lucky odds, I suppose?" Mordacai leaned against the bin and watched as Athien began to explain himself.

"I was just driving, when I noticed the car behind me, I turned into a driveway, to collect my thoughts and ready for an attack." Athien dodged going into further detail with the story, but gave enough, so that didn't look like he was trying to not answer the question.

Mordacai looked confused, but saw another thought as he began to feel satisfied.

"And, once more, if you forgive me asking, but, why did she just, happen to have a rocket launcher?" Athien scoffed as he looked about the alley, quick thinking proving once again his saviour as he answered the question.

"She didn't have a rocket launcher, the lady had an old, malfunctioning fireworks launcher that she used in the extremist of circumstances," Athien said offhandedly. He shrugged as Mordacai gave him an incredulous stare as if, that was just over too over the top for an explanation. "I talked to her and read the police report." He added for good measure, as Mordacai stood again, overwhelmed slightly by the enormity of coincidences that seemed to occur within the tale, but that all made sense.

"Okay, that's more info on a simple development than I ever wanted to know. Now, perhaps we should touch base on the reason we're all actually the best of friends, eh?" He said, motioning for Athien to follow him as the two gun wielders travelled back up the path ahead of them.

"Helm. Yes, how are you going to get more information, and where should I be hitting in the meantime, to get the most out of his goons and get him angry?" Athien followed, his head slightly lowered.

"What is it with you and hitting things?" Mordacai raised his hand as well, as the two of them joined the others and came out of the alley, into the light of two cars, driven by Mordacai's lackeys.

"I've found it to be a powerful motivator," Athien said stiffly, weary of the four other people who all stood around the cars, guns visible on each of them.

"Fair enough. Now, as to what you should do?" I think that you'd better take a trip up to the Docklands, I've got a decent amount of knowledge to know that things come through that port that definitely shouldn't." Mordacai stepped up to the closest vehicle. The driver started it as he stood on the step up. He looked over the car door at Athien, who held back a while off, not wanting to go any closer to the already quite vulnerable position.

"Docklands? Seriously? That's a little cliché, don't you think?" Athien said, his voice all too serious, despite the joke-sounding question. Mordacai chuckled as he sat in the passenger side seat and motioned to the other drivers to get going also.

"Believe what you believe, maybe there's nothing there, but, like I said, it's all I know right now, give me a couple of days to get it all worked out, and we'll go from there," As Mordacai closed the door, the car rolled forward to turn. He saw Athien's head cock slightly to the left. Mordacai opened his window and spoke again to the vigilante. "Don't worry, I've been working this, industry, for years, I know how the criminals down here think." The car turned on and left the alley and Athien behind, as he watched them go.

"I know how the criminal's mind works all too well, Mordacai." He said to himself, going for the radio on his chest, to relay his information to Kali or Samantha.

I hope her findings are going well.

Samantha had heard Athien step out of the shed, the car started and then she was left alone with the locations he'd written down.

"Okay, Samantha, you can do this, it's just, asking some random people questions and getting the lay of the previous fight scenes." She did up her leather jacket, black centred with yellow arms and tied her long hair into a bun, then stepped into Kali's old, tiny car and drove away from the house.

Her first destination was the scene Athien had been at the other day, where he'd been just before being inevitably followed by Helm and his soldiers.

And almost killed! Lucky he and, Kali had whatever that messed up plan was. Seriously, who has time to build a homemade rocket launcher? She asked herself many things as she parked Kali's car a little away from the scene, avoiding the onlooking stairs from several strangers.

The street was barren, trash littered one side from years of spoilage from nearby businesses and the brick buildings that encompassed the scene were almost dangerously in bad repair.

Samantha came across the opening to the site that Athien had dropped in on the people he'd believed to be working with Helm. She immediately began looking around, not able to see anyone that might pause or take note of her. Samantha looked at the gate, two times her size, and started to climb it.

You only live once, right?

She landed on the other side, slightly slipping on the way down and grazing her knee, but not enough to cause her to slow or inspect it. Samantha wandered into the now abandoned-looking factory plant. She was unsure of what to look for, and so started by looking at the outskirts. Then she worked her way into the centre, where she believed the fight would have gone down.

As Samantha searched, she began to wonder, not for the first time, how Helm had been able to track and know precisely where Athien had been. Her mind stretched for answers as she walked, convinced that there had to be some kind of camera or monitoring device of some sort at the very least.

No way a guy who can fight like that, can just randomly pop up out of the blue, he must have been following, and maybe he was already here?" She reached the centre of the warehouse space, and sore the blood and scuff marks, mud trailing higher and more profound than anywhere else, where Sentinel had fought the criminals.

"So, this is where you were conceived as a threat to the big bad, heh?" She asked no one but the mud, as she knelt and tried to analysis where it was going and had come from, some trail.

Finding nothing to support her theory, she abandoned the mud, proceeding to check the surroundings for any lights, flashing or otherwise. She looked around the crates and storage boxes around the space, finding most of them empty and rusted out, or in the containers, rubber and broken plastics that looked like they'd been there for years.

"Well, this seems to be a waste of time." She said aloud, surprised by the fact that as she'd spoken, she heard a frail, far-away sounding voice speak somewhere close by. Samantha once again walked around the crates, careful this time to keep herself hidden as she watched the gates and warehouse doors and windows.

Maybe he was inside or, just, passing by? Samantha began to question whether or not this place had any importance to her investigation, and stood to leave, her feet dragging loudly across the muddy ground.

"Where are those noises coming from!?" She muttered loudly, remembering to keep her voice down as she still didn't know if anyone was there or not. As she'd been walking, it was as if her steps were echoing off the ground.

Ohhh! Her eyes widened as she kicked a crate and the noise echoed from behind her, quite, but audible as she turned back towards the warehouse.

Samantha jogged softly towards the warehouse, her eyes darting to each entry and the windows as she sought for the object she believed was remaking her sounds.

As she entered the building, she noticed how much it contrasted to the outside appearance and the yard. The interior was clean, with wooden floors, counters and plenty of palettes, ready to be carted out to ships or trucks. Samantha carried herself up the closest flight of steps, just to her right and across the loading bay inside. The upper floors were covered from view entirely from the bottom but, her sounds grew louder and more echoed as she travelled more hastily up the steps.

"Aha!" She exclaimed, seeing the device seated on the chair and facing the window out into the yard. It was a massive stereo system, which seemed to have the capacity to hear and record everything that transpired around the entire property. Samantha could tell by the wires that crisscrossed the floor and lead out of the room. The storey was so covered in wires that it took her a minute to figure out where everything pointed to.

There were wires in the entire warehouse and, in the yard, two receivers she hadn't seen were positioned on the broken light posts that would have lit the area.

"Whoever ran this place certainly had a problem with trusting other people." She said, going back to the stereo and bending down. Her hair slightly covering her face as she flicked the off switch and let her noises well away into the darkness.

Samantha took out her phone then and took photos of the

device.

Wonder if whoever it was who did this has kept any storage of the sounds? She asked herself, stepping gently on the cords as she proceeded into the room that adjoined this one.

She opened the door, not realising that no sound cords from the device had come through here as she did so.

"Well, you're not Sentinel." She was met with a frail old man, sitting behind a broken, leather sofa, holding a shotgun towards her face. His face had shown worry the second she'd walked through the door, and Samantha noticed the trigger finger he had was already halfway through its pull.

Samantha ducked as fast as she could, rolling like her acting classes had taught her and nimbly recoiling behind the broken desk that sat in front of the sofa. It offered little protection from the shotgun just on the other side of the table, but was something.

"Sorry, no, no I'm not Sentinel!" She tried to breathe deeply, hands over her head as she awaited the expected shot, and found none forthcoming. Behind her, she could hear the sounds of cracking bones as the elderly man stood from behind the couch and rounded her side.

She backed away, turning around to hide behind the right side of the desk as he came around the left. She heard a chuckle.

"I guess, ya could still be working with him, couldn't ya?" When he heard nothing from her, the man shook his head and stepped away from the table, the shotgun butt sat at his right elbow, while the end sat on his left hand, ready to be hoisted if need be. "If I wanted to shoot you immediately, I could have just done it through the table, missy." This time she spoke up, her voice back and breathing slowed after the initial thought

184

of a quick and unexpected, painful death.

"Or, maybe you're just a bad shot and want a better target." She replied haughtily, expressing her displeasure at having a gun pointed at her. The old man raised his eyebrows a few times and shrugged to himself, unsure of how to proceed.

"True, that's a funny way of looking at it, but, think about it, would I seriously want to deafen myself for the rest of my miserable life, just to shoot an errand girl?" Samantha stood up quickly then, defiance creeping into her bones as she looked curtly towards the old man, who didn't move or raise his gun.

"If you didn't want to be deaf and you aren't going to shoot me, even if I'm helping a vigilante, then why do you have a gun, would you have shot him?" She clenched her fists and almost snarled at him, surprising herself with her ferocity.

The old man displayed signs of worry, he looked at the door and seemed to contemplate going for it, his second gaze rested on the gun, and then he looked back at Samantha.

"I, I was going to defend myself with it. If he came barging in, wanting answers I couldn't give, that's why I'd set up the device the minute I heard him come in the first time, there was someone following Sentinel, the whole night." The old man slumped slightly against the wall he was near, the gun end dropped to the floor as he held the butt with his hand still, finger off of the trigger.

Samantha's anger staggered, as she immediately saw the sagged eye pockets and weak stance, the man was undernourished and afraid of dying. She could now easily understand that, at least on a small level.

"He can be a little rough, I've heard." She thought over what he'd said for a minute, as the old man regained his composure and was once again able to stand normally, using the gun as a cane of support for his legs.

"Yes, I saw it first-hand. The night those ruffians had locked me up here, and the night that he'd come down to destroy their operation. However, it appears that he might have been tracked by the person who was following him for too long." He nodded downwards, using his head to point out the paper on the sofa behind her, which showed this morning's date, only just readable, in the low-level lighting of the room.

"Ah, but, do YOU know who was following him?" The old man nodded, turning his back to Samantha as he looked out the window, towards the yard she'd been in earlier.

"When Sentinel came in, it was like a fireworks display, he hit, broke and damaged a lot of goons and cargo for this place, there was a lot of blood." He paused, as Samantha came up to the window and looked out too.

"But, I didn't see any blood in the mud down there?" She wondered aloud, eyes still searching the scene, as if she should be able to spot the blood on the ground from up here.

"Yeah, you wouldn't either, because, after he left, the others came." Samantha, very confused as to where this narrative was going, searched the man's face for traces of a lie, or anything that would label him mad. In her eyes, she was both pleased and slightly scared, to see nothing out of the ordinary.

"Soldiers, fully kitted with guns and helmets, the real stuff. They walked into the yard, came from two cruisers, as the others left to follow Sentinel, didn't see the guy in charge. Still, I heard the gunshots as they killed the already damaged souls that had been in the yard at the time. They were good too, cleaned it all up, removed the broken equipment. Made it look like there hadn't been anything wrong done there that night at all," He paused for a moment, his eyes closing and opening multiple times. "Not even Sentinel's mess, could be seen. My boss, the one who locked me in here, he'd left only five minutes before the first attack, boy am I sad about that?" He finished his tale, ending with a funny-sad smile, that made Samantha look down into the yard again and imagine the people who had fought and died there.

"Do, do you know where they took the bodies?" She asked, already expecting to know the answer as she looked out to the small river that rested close to the back of the warehouse property.

"If you think that they chucked em in the river, naa, these guys didn't want to be seen or tracked, ever. They picked em up. Then another car came round later, maybe, an hour or so. Picked up the broken and injured. I tell ya, it was carnage." He backed away from the window then, done with seeing and remembering the attacks.

Samantha followed, aware that he'd left the gun propped up on the wall next to the window.

"I can imagine." She didn't want to, but the events were evident in her mind, the rushed movements, the people piled into a black car, just like the car she'd seen at Kali's house the day before. She hesitated before asking, but she needed to know, Sentinel would want to see the attack and what happened after.

"What's on your mind now, I know it's gruesome, but, look who you work with, that guy doesn't keep his hands clean, does he? No killing, but he sure does pack some punches," He coughed for ten seconds after speaking, it was then that Samantha felt the cold had begun to linger in her fingers and toes.

"Do you have any video of the event, of what happened

after, Sentinel left?" She paused for a moment before saying the name, surprised at how quickly she'd forgotten to think about who was under the mask.

He pursed his lips together into a frown. He nodded at Samantha, standing again from the couch as he leaned over to the desk. He revealed a disc hidden in the left-most draw of the wooden feature. The old man reached out to her, unable to step away from the couch. His body swayed even when supported.

"Thank you, he'll, want to see this." Her stomach lurched as she spoke and Samantha only just managed to stop the bile that had built in her throat. The old man winced as he thought he was going to be vomited on, and shielded his face, for a moment, before dropping it again and sitting firmly.

"There's no problem with not wanting to know or see the ugly that some people inflict on the world. Hopefully, your friend there doesn't let the power that comes with strength go to his head in his fight against the tidal wave he faces." Samantha looked where the old man pointed and saw on the mantelpiece of the room, above a dead fire, there was a wooden sheath. Over what she could only assume must be a sword, which the old man was currently staring at, his face blank.

She turned to leave, having received much more than she'd wanted to and sure that she'd bothered the old man quite enough. Still, as she turned to leave, she took in the full disarray of the room and wondered why a man as frail and old as he was, would be in a place like this, to begin with.

"What are you doing in this place anyway? If you don't mind me asking." She heard a huff come from the man, but he stayed seated and only turned his head a quarter way around, so that she could see he was talking and knew it was to her.

"There's not much point in me saying if I don't mind or not, because you've already asked," He paused to let that sink in, then continued. "But, it wasn't my choice, I was asked by someone to come here, and now that I have, I'll head back to my home city, with this lovely blade again." He motioned with a flick of his head, up at the sheath on the mantel. Then went silent again.

Samantha wondered what was so special about it, for all she could see, there was an old leather-covered handle and what looked to be a hard, rock-like case that made up the sheath.

"I could help you get there, if you'd like, I'd like to help you, for not shooting me and giving me this," She held up the disc, even though he couldn't see it. She took her eyes off the sword and looked at him. "Please?" The old man stood then, slightly straighter than he was before, and seemingly taller. He grabbed the blade from the mantel and stood still in front of Samantha, who was somewhat uneasy, seeing the shotgun within easy reach.

"Alright, I know from experience, that when someone such as yourself offers a hand to help, that they mean, they will. No matter what, and so I'll take you up on that offer." He walked towards her, actually smiling, and held out a wrinkly hand when he was close enough. "My name is Alaistair, and it is a pleasure, too." He coughed again, breaking the younger spirit he now seemed to possess for a moment as he covered his mouth with the other hand. "Pleasure to meet you, Miss?" He questioned, looking slightly down on Samantha in a scholars way. Samantha's uneasiness slipped away as she took his hand and in turn, introduced herself with a flourish and a short bow.

"Samantha," She hesitated, but then continued, not believing that this man ever meant any harm by her. "Samantha Dickens." A spark of recognition entered the man's eyes as he gave a devilish grin and turned her around, going for the door, despite the still complete darkness outside.

"Ah yes, I know that name, very well." They exited the room and then the warehouse, with a quick detour to the office, so that Alaistair could pick up the key to the front gate. They exited with ease, passing not a soul in sight. She didn't ask how he knew her name, it was a common last name to hear of in Alazarath and the world.

Samantha drove Alaistair to the airport herself, relishing in her adult age.

"Congratulations on getting the part, I just hope that your friend can make do without you now," Alaistair commented when she told him where she'd have to be going.

"That just also happens to be the exact, expensive city, filled with dangerous villains and super-powered beings that I need to get to. Perhaps we could travel together?" Samantha turned him down with a gracious shake of her head and some kind words about wanting to stay in Melbourne longer.

"You have a safe trip back to Alazarath now, Alaistair, hope you've got someone there that is expecting you." She waved from the door to the seating room and went to leave, hearing his voice ring down the corridor, full now, with mirth and laughter.

"Oh yes, she's been waiting quite some time for my return." To which Samantha shook her head.

What a strange and, curious old man.

"Guess I'll go back to Sentinel now, he should be done his interrogation."

17

Chapter 17 Conversations

Athien and Samantha sat at his computer set up in the garage of Kali's house. They'd relayed the information that they'd learned, Athien and Mordacai's deal and Samantha's discovery of the file and the weird old man. Now they shifted through the video footage she'd gathered.

"There!" Samantha called, as she saw Helm's vehicle drive up, seconds after Sentinel had run from the scene after extracting his information. The image wasn't the best, due to the lighting around the trucks and brake lights, but they were able to identify one of the number plates.

"I see it, let's get this printed and get it to someone who knows where it comes from." Athien printed the screen, pressing a hundred buttons at once that meant absolutely nothing to Samantha. She instead continued to watch the video on fast mode, to see if she could gain anything else from it.

"Wait, who do you know that can trace number plates?" She asked as the printer behind the pc screen whirled to life, and Athien reached over to grab the print out. His face lingered on hers as he sat back down again, working out his answer.

"Not tracking it, simply whether they've seen it, and if they have, I could get a tracker to it, then, we could find Helm." He nodded, as he reassured himself, Samantha thought, she'd seen him do it before.

"Hey," She raised a hand and caught his shoulder, holding it tight enough to know she wasn't going to let them leave, just yet. "Why don't you send an electric copy?" She asked first, taking his mind off the thing he'd had it on the whole night.

"Because, I haven't set up a decent enough security protocol system to not allow myself to be hacked, yet." He smiled, knowing what she'd just done and that now, she'd make him do it, instead of going out to give the picture to whoever it was needed to see if.

"Then you're going to do that. Right now, instead of going to Mordacai or whoever in this criminal gang you're working with." He laughed, sitting back down and placing the print out on the table between them. He opened up the network settings to create a Virtual Private Network and another program that Samantha didn't recognise.

"Athien, do you think that Sentinel can beat Helm? Is that what's on your mind?" She asked suddenly, not truly sure of how he'd respond to such a personal, self-doubting question, and her thoughts were confirmed when he winced and gave a pained smile.

"I know that I can beat him, it's just, the guy has some skill, I didn't expect to have an obstacle like this so early into the run." He huffed down and sank lower into the seat, mind going back through the fight he'd had previously with Helm and the moves that the foe had produced.

"It's not like he's a martial artist, Helm has been trained

for military, every move he made against me was to deliver the most pain and create the largest wound that he could with what I gave him. Others I faced, as The Shadow, when I worked with the Order of Mark, they were usually just, people, or slightly trained martial artists. Not a lot posed a challenge. I guess I underestimated how many people I'd fought with my training and how many more people there are in the world." Relieved to have that out, Athien sat taller again, but his head still drooped slightly as his lips curled.

"That's fair enough, you went from mercenary to criminal highjacker, there's going to have to be some growing pains," Samantha said. At the same time, Athien's eyes fluttered around the screen, searching for something that he had to click on.

"Yeah, well, it's ready to send messages to the criminal underworld," Athien said light-heartedly, opening a private email tab and entering the email he'd been sent by Mordacai. "Or, you know, to one, criminal in particular." Uploading the picture took seconds, in which time he flicked back his short hair three times and looked at the tool case at least twice.

Never realised how used to talking face to face with people I'd gotten.

"Ok, what are you going to say?"

Athien crossed through into the kitchen after sending the message, feeling very uneasy by the natural simpleness that came with an email, it was something he hadn't done in a long time. Samantha followed soon after that. The two of them awaited Mordacai's message.

Kali was sitting at the bench, knitting as she watched the sports channel, a football team lead by a considerable margin, and it wasn't her team as she yelled, in her own, quiet voice;

"I've been watching you play for years, and you still can't kick a ball straight!" She turned as she heard them enter, and immediately went back into knitting mode, pretending to not have been watching the screen.

"Kali, I didn't know you watched football!" Samantha sat down with her and proceeded to cheer when the losing team managed to kick a goal, making Kali much happier as she smiled and looked over to Athien.

"You really shouldn't lean, you know, it's bad for your back." Athien straightened his stance the second she said it, and sat down on Kali's other side as they watched the advert play over the football.

"So, when are you going to be returning to Alazarath, it's on Wednesday, isn't it, which makes it, two days from now, factoring in the ten-hour difference." Athien checked his watch as he asked Samantha, counting the hours on the hand to emphasise that she didn't have a lot of time left.

Samantha continued not to watch the T.V and didn't react to his question, besides letting her smile droop slightly.

"I guess, I haven't given it a lot of thought really, but I thought, it might be helpful to stay down here a little longer. For a week at least." She looked at the other two, her eyes wincing slightly as she expected a barrage of complaints from either party.

"But, it's your future, acting. Sam, it's what you want to do, isn't it?" Kali looked confused, her eyes creasing down her brow as she looked at Samantha with a mixture of confusion, and also softness and, something else.

Is that pride? Samantha decided not to dwell on it and to instead conclude the conversation as fast as she could.

"Yeah, it is something I've wanted to do for ages, but, helping people, is also something that I want to do, perhaps even more than to act." She watched as Athien and Kali both nodded and then looked at each other, as if there was some kind of agreement going on between them.

"Sam," Athien began. "Can you be sure that you'll still have the part, if you pass it off for a week? While your efforts and help have notably been valuable, you do have another life, a soon to be successful one at that." He stopped speaking and waited for her to answer, while Kali sat back and continued to watch the game, keeping either eyes both on the two of them at the same time as well.

After a while and multiple kicks scored by both sides, Samantha got up and left the table, her phone in hand as she walked away. Neither Athien nor Kali followed, and they sat in silence as there was the sound of dialling coming from the room beyond the kitchen T.V, Samantha's room.

"She's probably ringing up the agency that hired her," Athien stated after another minute, his phone buzzed as he spoke. He looked down to see who had messaged him.

"I hope so, she should not be out there, with no fighting experience, her charm did well in this last escapade, but, what happens next time, Athien?" Kali watched him looking at the phone and see her as she spoke.

"Well, that's the idea, she doesn't get into the mean and hairy fights, but, if she stays on, I guess I'll train her. I don't want her to be doing the same thing that I'm doing though." Athien read the text he'd gotten, it was from Nicola.

"Athien, I've just met up with an officer out in the centre of Melbourne, near the Eureka Tower. By the sounds of things, there's a satellite that's going down, please, call when you can. Nicola." Athien read. He wondered what either of them could do in that scenario, but he was sure what she could do then and there.

"Get out," He sent back to her, then, seeing that she wasn't answering immediately, he added, "I'll be there shortly." Kali, still watching him text, took his shoulder in absolute disbelief. As he looked intently into her eyes, he could see genuine worry for him swimming out.

"You are not, going to try and blow up pieces of a satellite! It's huge, and going way faster than you can." They both heard Samantha as she finished up the phone call in the hallway to the other room, seconds away from walking in on Kali's death grip on Athien. Another message popped up on his phone.

"Yeah, that's why I've got someone who can move faster than anyone else can, on my side." It was then, as he pulled her arm off his shoulder that Samantha came through the doorway. She grinned happily.

He looked down, eyes rolling from the sudden chaos that was brewing around him.

"Mordacai, wishes us happy hunting," He held the phone up so that Samantha could see, showing the exact car, registration and a location underneath the day photo. "But first, I have to help stop a satellite from destroying Melbourne's biggest landmark." He didn't explain that Nicola had asked for his help, just exited the room. It hadn't even been twelve hours after taking the suit off last night, after his talk with Mordacai.

"How are you going to do that!?" She called out after him, looking back at Kali seconds later and finding her already shoulder-shrugging towards Samantha.

"That boy has a death wish, I wasn't sure until now, but he definitely wants to die in some horrific, spectacular way." She huffed and grabbed the car keys from her side table as they both followed Athien's direction into the garage, his car already leaving the drive. The tool case was open, and his bag was gone.

"Shoot, Athien!" The two searched the news to find live updates as to what was happening.

18

Chapter 18 Zip

The city was busy. As Athien drove, he'd usually find it somewhat difficult to navigate quickly around the slow-moving traffic. Tonight, with the blocked routes and chaos of a Sunday night, it was almost impossible to get anywhere within a decent time.

All the lights were chaotically bright, sirens breathed in the air that wasn't taken by horns.

The building he parked at was strategically in the centre of a busy shopping sector of the city, near the Central plaza and station, on Swanston Street. He walked by the hordes of people going about their early night business, not paying him any special attention as he entered the building. It was a large corner shop for a phone company that had a giant electrical billboard at the front. Athien had been here once before, at the start his campaign as Sentinel. It used to be one of the Order of Mark safe houses.

Something he'd learned from being a mercenary, there was always someone in a safe house, even if it looked empty, it wasn't. People had littered the five-story building the first time he'd been in. As well as guards that attempted to kill him. Athien had stopped them, the last act he'd committed as his former identity. Then he'd reworked the security systems and traps so that only he knew where they were and how they worked.

Athien entered, climbing the stairwell of the building quickly, passing the wooden frames full of pictures of long-dead people. Within the next room, there were storage racks. Lines of canned food, medical equipment, computer and other technology and finally, the things he'd come to grab;

"Weapons." He said quietly as he quickly browsed the front of the cabinet, which consisted of mostly different small firearms and one rifle. Athien grabbed the side of the cabinet, scratching the green, chrome paint off slightly as he flicked a hidden latch and swung the front backwards, revealing a secret compartment.

He let the door bang against the wall and immediately saw what he'd come for. A mini rocket launcher.

It was among other, high tier weapons. Athien wrapped the strap of the launcher around his shoulder and made his way to the roof of the building, his carry bag with the Sentinel uniform in tow. He changed before going through the door.

The city lights etched off every surface, blinding, as he donned his helmet and exited the building. Grapple gun in hand, he quickly surveyed the land. Of course, with the police on high alert and the city ready for a meltdown, he theorised it wouldn't be as odd as usual to see a man in combat gear gliding down from the rooftops.

Athien grappled himself from the building roof to the alley diagonal from him, which was between two large buildings. As he descended, the cord on his gun held and the air rushed into his slightly open mouth like a hurricane, threatening to pull off his cheeks. He landed with a thud and rolled, pressing a button to disconnect and rewind the cord of his grapple as he walked. Athien moved slowly at first, to see if any rushing camera people were following, then faster as he reached the end of the alley.

The ruckus was almost overwhelming, even with the police cars everywhere and the warning sirens, plenty of people still stood about the streets as if it was a regular night on the road.

"This is impossible," Athien muttered as he stepped onto the street, following the queue of people that were walking in the same direction as he needed to go. All things considered, he managed to get quite far, all the way to the next street corner, before someone noticed who was passing them.

It was a young man and women, they'd been walking slower than the rest and Athien had passed them, his bag briefly brushing by them and causing him to be seen. He picked up speed, nothing he could do to stop the madness that would soon take to the streets, but, he could at least distance himself from them.

"Hey! It's that vigilante, what are you doing on the street!?" The couple began to scream it at the top of their lungs, phones practically jumping out of their hands as they caught live footage. Footage of the masked vigilante just, casually fast walking up the street.

He felt a rough push from the side. Athien decided it was a good time to run as someone next to him, a tall woman with jet black hair, attempted to grab at his bag. Her face contorted in surprise and fury as she sought to be the one seen taking down the vigilante. Athien pushed people as the onslaught of beings that were parked between him, and the next street corner seemed to grow in mass and volume. They took up every inch of his path.

He felt an arm wrap around his neck as he jumped through a group of people ahead that had only just realised what the commotion was about. Only just managing to get away, after quickly jabbing the man in the ribs. Slowing the others that approached from behind.

Alright, this is not going to work. Athien made it to the next street and decided to run into it. Instead of waiting for the traffic lights and getting crushed to death by the mob that was attempting to swarm him. He lurched onto the road, bag swinging wildly as he weaved past a fast-moving car that was heading towards him. Another to the side of that honked furiously at him as it passed.

He took out his small phone as he made it to the middle. Athien used the divider between the two to shield himself from one side and defuse the other from wanting to run him over on purpose. His phone was nearly ripped from his hands by a passing motorists wind funnel.

"Look, this is Nicola, and I can't come to the phone right now, busy being smart and running around the place." His call went to voice mail, and he hung up, dashing to the other side of the road as there was a lull in traffic.

Thank you. Athien screamed to himself, as he made it to the other side in one piece and noticed the lessened crowd that littered the sidewalk. That said, they were all ahead of him this time, having been notified by their social media and the ruckus he'd caused down the street.

"Get out of my way!" Sentinel's voice came out as Athien ran towards the pack, his arms waving as he worked his way forward. He stepped onto the bike tracks along the road, to avoid the people who were coming towards him.

The traffic picked up again, and Athien found himself with his choices running thin. He could try for the road again or, run through civilians, damaging his already disgruntled public opinion. Athien called the number again, his feet angling more towards the road even though he heard the vehicles honking angrily at him. This time he heard a quiet yelp, as the audio on his phone was turned down, but he made out Nicola's voice as he turned it up. The crowd almost upon him.

He turned onto the road again, stepping behind a car, picking up speed, faster than he'd run before, but still far slower than any vehicle on the road. The people ahead tried getting him on the bike tracks, not daring to brave any closer, but this pushed Athien out into the centre lane, where he knew he'd be in the most danger.

"Athien! How are you! It sounds deafening where you are, and, is that people screaming that I can hear?" Athien ignored the question as he heard a rock, thrown by one of the people he'd now left behind go smashing into the car that was right beside him, causing the driver to freak out and stomp on the breaks.

"Nicola, I need help, now, I'm nearing the corner of Swanston and Elizabeth, oh, actually, one over from that, can you get me?" He knew she'd be confused by what she saw, but, there was literally no time to explain as Athien nearly lost his footing to a stone and fell beneath the car behind him. Athien caught himself though, and amid the buffering sounds that came from the other side of his phone's connection and the blaring of the horn behind him, Athien became disoriented in his surroundings. Athien fell back, back in the centre of the busy road.

This was a terrible idea! He felt worried as he saw three police cars appear, two from behind and one in front, about to cross into the wrong side of the road, so they could pin down his movement.

"Please, Nicola, hurry." Athien stood, tall as the cars approached at high speeds, blaring sirens and screaming out their windows for vehicles and pass-Byers to move aside.

"Sorry it took so long!" Athien saw a gun point out of the window of one of the cars behind him as Nicola's voice came screaming out of the phone. Her voice was high pitched as she sprinted to his location. Athien ducked, rolling himself over the divider and into the new waves of undisturbed traffic on the other side of the road. The officer didn't shoot, and Athien was immediately sideswiped, his body twirling rapidly as he was hit and flung against the divider, dazed by the sudden glancing impact.

"Stop moving, put your hands in the air!" Athien felt his heart racing for the first time in a long time as he felt the barrel of a gun tap the back of his helmet lightly. His sight was blurred, but he could make out the boots that rested on the ground in front of his face down head, at least two sets of them were right on top of him.

Athien felt the world slow for a moment, as he recalled the last time Nicola had run by close to him.

Suddenly, he was on his feet, held up by her shoulder as she looked at the officers, their guns just lifting from where his head was a second ago, as she slowed down.

"Sorry officers, but I need this one." She sped up again as they reacted, their guns moved to train on her as she spoke, and was gone from the scene before they could talk, vanishing in a bright blur of colour, like the lights of the passing cars.

"You're wearing a mask now, nice," Athien noted out loud, still slightly dazed as he tried to keep up with the world that moved about them so fast that not even his eyes, with the chip from his father in his head, could keep up. Nicola laughed, her voice only slightly resembling a Gatling gun being fired. She slowed her speed as they passed several streets and entered a quieter square devoid of people.

"Yeah, I'm aware, thought it was about time I stopped zipping about like I was someone normal. I might as well wear a mask." The mask was a pink colour at its base, but was splotched with green and yellow metal paints that made each colour stand out by itself.

"It works for you," Athien commented as he came back to normal speed, looking around to check where they were and where all the people were. "Oh, we're at Eureka, so, the police have actually abandoned the entire area." He commented, seeing the giant building looming above them like a beacon to the satellite, which Athien could only just see, as it hurtled down towards them from the stratosphere.

"Hey, this is exactly the gear that the vigilante I was with the other night was wearing!" Nicola accused. Athien didn't make any agreeable movements.

"Nicola, look, you get everyone out of here, leave the rest to me." Athien started to walk towards the building opposite the Tower, unshouldering the bag as he did so. Nicola sped past him and landed in his way,

"What are you going to do? And, how come you didn't tell me you beat up people, huh?" Athien took her shoulders and dropped the bag, which landed with a heavy thud, though it didn't have far to fall considering its size, Nicola looked into the bag and, her heart froze.

204

"Yes, I have a rocket launcher. I'm Sentinel, and yes, I'm about to shoot that rocket into a thousand pieces to ensure that Eureka doesn't break into even more." He dragged his sentence out as he spoke and then dropped his arms, waiting for Nicola to say something, as the satellite drew nearer.

"Wa, what!?" She held up her hands, throwing them exasperatedly around as Athien monitored the square. Shops still had open doors, and the Tower was lit up like a beacon as the moon began to appear amongst a sea of clouds.

"I need to be up on a building before that satellite gets too close, sorry, but I'll explain it all to you later." He went around her, headed for an open shop right ahead.

"Wait, why not take the Tower?" She asked, still following him, now confused and desperate to see the satellite not hit anything. Athien holstered the bag and looked over his shoulder as he continued to walk.

"The elevator is down. It would take too long to get up the stairs. In emergencies, they're shut down." Nicola jumped to Athien as he turned back, unsure whether he'd thank her or not for what she was about to do.

"You're SO stubborn, I can get you up there, you just need to ask." Was all she said as she did exactly that, not giving him a chance to argue as she half dragged, half carried him towards and into the Tower.

Athien's eyes adjusted themselves to attempt to catch up with Nicola's velocity, an experience he was still getting used to as he lost his footing again and again. Her speed hindering his ability to land steps.

"Here we are." Athien dropped to his knees, legs bruised lightly from the few bumps as she'd gone too fast around corners, his hands blocking his ears as her voice came out like a meat grinder, threatening again to break his eardrums.

She released him on the topmost floor of the building, with the glass box of the observing platform to their left, jutting out of the buildings otherwise rectangle structure. To their right, Athien could see a service door, probably locked, leading directly to the top of the skyscraper.

"Thanks for not making me deaf." Athien stood, slightly shakily as he proceeded to make his way for the service door. Nicola stayed behind him, air coming into her lungs in giant gulps as she fought for more breath.

That's the last time I run up these steps. Nicola thought, remembering the problems they'd caused her as a child. She always slipped or fell on them, no, even with the ability to run faster than anyone alive, she still couldn't take the stairs.

"Well done, I'm not sure how long that took, but it was quicker than my eyes could see." He heard a wheezed out;

"Thanks." From Nicola, then tried the door to the roof. It opened, and Athien was surprised, looking about the floor for a moment to see their security parameters.

"For a huge landmark, visited by millions per year, this place doesn't have the greatest security features." He walked through the doorway and up a set of steps. The hallway and stairs weren't well lit, and he cast a torch about as he began the climb, ready with the rocket launcher at his side.

Nicola had never been to the sky deck, so, after she was adequately breathing, her heartbeat at near resting point again, she stepped to the left. Nicola walked out, onto the glass square that put her right above the square they'd been in earlier.

"Wow." She exclaimed, acting like a swivel as she looked about at different angles. She saw the streets alight and full of people, except right beneath her.

"Wait, what." Nicola had been staring at the ground below her, absent mended for a second. Then, in another, there was somebody there, blue light around them only just enough to illuminate them. She pressed her face against the window, trying to get a better look as they walked towards the building, looking up at the building, like they could see her.

They disappeared below her, heading straight for the Tower. Nicola stepped away from the glass and walked towards the door. There was no way they could get up to Sentinel that fast, what with the elevator being down.

Right? People like me aren't that common.

Athien had positioned himself at the centre of the building's rooftop, the rocket launcher on the ground in front of him. He waited as the satellite plummeted down towards him.

"You planning to blow up the building after you're done saving it?" Athien turned, glad that he had the uniform on as he rolled over the rocket launcher. Moving away from the voice that had come from nowhere.

"Who the hell are you, and how'd you get up here?" The figure before him was clad in a dark costume, a full-length cloak and mask covered and obscured most of his features, but Athien could hear the baritone voice. The two stood towards each other, Sentinel aiming the weapon towards the smaller body and the newcomer, simply flexing his fingers as he watched.

"Bit extreme, isn't it, to hold a rocket launcher towards someone?" They held up their hands in mock surrender, alerting Athien.

Must have some kind of power, perhaps they're like Nicola.

"It's never extreme, to point a weapon at someone you don't

207

know, especially when they can move without being seen." Athien stood, taking a split second to look up at the satellite, before focusing back on the task ahead of him.

Did Helm send them? Does he have supers in his gang?

"Perhaps, you just weren't looking hard enough, too focused on, other things," they gestured up, towards the satellite, now heavily distinguishable from the stars behind it. "My name's Zip, that's all you need to know. Now, tell me, are you a friend? Or Foe?"

19

Chapter 19 Reaction

Athien started as Nicola slammed threw the door behind him, catapulting her forward. She rolled to recover.

Athien kept watching Zip as he pulled his hood over his face more and looked at the newcomer.

Athien noticed that his legs were buckled as he looked at Nicola.

Weird looking at another person in a mask, I can't stare down their eyes, not precisely, harder to feed their fear.

"I'm going to blast that giant piece of metal out of the sky, I don't care what you call me. It'll devastate the city if it hits." Athien stood, aware that Nicola was up and possibly seconds away from charging into Zip, who had now turned towards her slightly.

"Uh ha, and, what's her stake in all this?"

Nicola stood straight.

"Hey, I saw you on the ground, not half a minute ago!" She called to Zip, even though he was right in front of her, and she began to walk forward, her right hand pointed at Zip, as if he were a ghost.

"Stop there." Said Zip, pointing back at her.

Athien didn't know what to do in response to the newcomer.

"No way, look, Sentinel here is going to stop that satellite from hitting the Tower. Now, I don't know how you got up here so fast, but you'd better leave here, just as fast." As Nicola continued to move forward, Athien felt her nervous and worried tension boil. Zip took a step back, both hands facing forward towards Nicola as she moved.

"Stay back! I'm here to do the same." Zip's voice held power behind it, his words a threat, as he took another step back, full attention now on Nicola as Athien turned to his side.

Athien looked up, and saw that the satellite was entering his aiming range, the faint sound of roaring speed as it rushed down to earth. He turned, seeing both Zip and Nicola getting heated up over each other's presence, and charged at Zip.

"To hell with this!" He roared, letting the rocket launcher go as he leapt towards Zip, startling him and Nicola, as he re-entered their line of sight.

Athien landed a fist against Zip's face, instantly cracking the mask he wore and propelling him off his feet and towards the ground. As Zip fell, bright light escaped from around his body, faster than Athien had ever seen, and then, he was gone.

Like a puff of air, the light that had shone so bright a moment earlier vanished into thin air, leaving them alone once again on the top of the Tower. Athien sighed and turned to look at Nicola, who looked just as surprised as he did over the disappearance.

"People can do that? Athien watch…." He heard Nicola start to shout, but then the noise was lost to him, as he felt something charge down on his spine, and like lightning, he turned, seeing a Taser poking his back as Zip fell on top of him from above.

"He can teleport!" He heard Nicola shoot, as he fell to the ground, the suit discharging most of the energy but his head buzzed like wildfire.

Nicola had watched as the mystery boy disappeared, then seen him appear again, just as if he was the air. He landed on top of Athien, using the Taser in his hand to hurt her friend.

"Get off of him!" She yelled, angry that she hadn't reacted sooner. Nicola, charged full tilt at them both as she sought to dislodge Zip.

"Nope!" She saw Zip, his hands already off Athien before she'd even started running. Light had engulfed his body, but she was closing, much faster than he was disappearing.

"Got you." She stated, feeling his clothing, the cloak and a jacket underneath, as she bear-hugged him and began to push away from Sentinel.

Zip panicked, never having encountered someone who could run faster than he could travel, he exerted even more energy. The light grew from not just him, but Nicola too.

"Wow." They both exclaimed, Nicola, slowed as she attempted to stop them both from going off the side of the building. At the same time, Athien could only just make them out, his body still nowhere near being able to react as quickly as his eyes could.

"Stop!" His voice carried with time, but Nicola heard it, just as she realised what was about to happen as they both stepped off of the building's rooftop and into thin air, falling.

Athien tracked them, but instead, turned away. He watched the satellite continue it's plummet towards the city, instincts telling him to shoot it down, but also wanting to help Nicola.

"Shoot." He felt himself again, which meant that Nicola was

out of range, or not using her abilities. He lined up the rocket launcher, prepared the shot.

He aimed, wide off centre as he marked for the satellite's trajectory and speed, slightly uncertain whether or not it would be able to make the journey against gravity.

He fired, forgetting the sound the weapon made as the shell left the carrier. It rocketed off into the air, and Athien's ears immediately rang from the cacophony of noise. His shoulders concaved as the force pushed him onto his back.

"Watch out!" He could barely hear the sound, let alone where it came from. Acting again on instinct. Athien rolled away, curling himself into the smallest shape that he could muster. Then, something immediately landed where he'd fallen. A large thump occurred.

"What are you doing, you'll make the damage worse?!" Athien stood, his body thoroughly battered from the last few day's events as he saw Zip appear behind where Nicola was. She was sprawled on the ground where she'd fallen, but otherwise looked unharmed —The grapple gun cable in half beside her, one end still down the building.

"I didn't see you doing anything to stop it." He heatedly pointed out, the launcher on the ground, smoking slightly, as the two confronted each other, the rocket shell still heading up, the satellite almost upon its arch.

"I was, I was going to teleport it, back into space! Send it up! Not all over the city, this place is uninhabited at the moment. That was the point in evacuating it!" Zip was noticeably furious, as he stepped up to Athien, uncaring of his taller stature and burlier shoulders.

"Do it then! What are you waiting for?!" Athien pushed him, hard and Zip fell backwards to the ground, Nicola re-righting herself as they all heard a terrible explosion.

The shell exploded, making contact with the front of the satellite, right on its dome, and sent a shockwave through the air as it did. It hit everyone but Nicola, who saw it coming as her heart picked up pace, she hid behind the doorway as the puff of air shot towards them.

Athien and Zip both pressed their bodies down as hard as they could against the ground, but were unable to save themselves from the near undisturbed shockwave. It ripped them from the roof the second it caught under them both.

They yelled, thrown from the edge of the other side. Athien managed to unclip his grapple as they fell and was surprised to see that Zip hadn't immediately teleported himself, as the smaller figure fell, dazed from the impact.

"Hey, Zip!" Athien clawed at him as they fell, reaching terminal velocity as Athien worked to get them both to safety. He worked rewinding his grapple gun as they fell, and as soon as it was, he fired.

"Uhh." Was Zip's response a second later, his eyes opening wide as Athien caught him around the middle, aiming for one of the window bars of the building.

It caught, yanking Athien's arms, hard. He managed to hold his grasp, and they half plummeted, half glided towards the windows two floors below where the grapple had caught to the building.

Athien turned them around, using his shoulder to smash into the glass, jarring instantly as they managed to break through and they fell among shattered fragments of the heavily dense glass.

"Thanks." Athien looked up, seeing the glass on the other side of the floor, the pieces of satellite falling around the city.

Zip was ahead of him, light breaking the darkness and sight of falling fire as he teleported again.

"Looks like he knows what he's doing," Athien commented. He coughed as he felt for any breakages in his shoulder, rolling onto his right side so that he could breathe properly.

Nicola ran from the Tower the second she saw that Athien had pulled out his grapple. She quickly attempted to figure out the map of carnage that the satellite pieces would take. She ran from the Tower rooftop, route planned out.

Nicola reached the end of the stairs, exhilarated by fear as she breached the doors. She headed east from the observing block, the furthest piece she could see falling had been heading in that direction.

Cars on the road were being abandoned as fiery bits of metal rocked down towards her at high speeds. She was able to see the back end of the satellite, as it fell towards the Crown Casino.

"Gotta go faster." She muttered to herself, figuring that there had to still be tens of thousands of people in the casino. She ran into the building, to the top floor and was about to rush the first person out of the room, when a familiar figure appeared in front of her.

"Gidday, speedy." Zip waved at her, as he faced the corner window, his hands raised, light already ebbing from his entire being and filling the room as the piece came closer to it.

Nicola ran out of the room again to see what had happened. Getting back outside, she saw that the piece was midway from being teleported itself, Zip using his ability on it instead of himself.

"That's awesome," She ran from the casino to the next scene, which, Zip had gotten to the rest way faster than she did.

214

"And that's, not so awesome." She said as she ran towards the final scene. The piece was far too close for her comfort as she reached Federation Square, people already sprinting towards the exits slowly, to her anyway.

She grabbed the few close to the centre first. The most she could help at a time was two, momentarily speeding up their walking pace a hundred times faster, before going right back to the next few. The piece fell quickly, which escalated her time, but she was able to almost empty the entire Square, before she realised she wouldn't make it.

"No!" She moved quicker, the heat from the satellite piece proving to be hard to handle as it came within jumping range. She couldn't get underneath it without feeling like she was going to burn up.

After a final hurtle through the arena of smoke and heat, she came out the other side, slightly charred and smoking, but otherwise fine. The satellite collided with the sidewalk seconds after she escaped.

Nicola was flung through the air, like a rag doll, as the metal smashed down. It immediately embedded itself deep in the ground, sending a cloud of ash and dust hundreds of meters in each direction. The small shockwave from the little piece was enough to make her feel a break in her arm. However, she'd landed on a concrete poll at the start of the square and laid there, dazed, as people on the sidewalk began to figure out what had just transpired around them.

"Well, that could have gone a lot worse."

Athien coughed, standing after he'd seen Zip teleport away and walked to the window in front of him, seeing that the fireballs were out of the sky. There was smoke raising blocks away, near Flinders Street Station.

"Good, they got all the people to safety." Athien unhinged the helmet he wore, checking the room for security cameras first. It came off, the clip slightly jarred from the amount of knocking around he'd done over the night and as he pushed his hair back, he breathed deeply.

"Time to hit Helm." He said, picking up his grapple gun and making his way, slowly, down the stairs, replacing the helmet as he touched down on the ground floor. He got a text as he left the building, Nicola, her name appearing on the screen.

"Are you ok? I'm sorry I didn't come for you, but we saved all the people! Oww." Her text said, leaving Athien a moment to answer as he looked for people walking by.

He saw none, and replied to the message quickly, heading back to the Tower so that Nicola could hopefully run him back to the safe room he'd gotten the launcher from.

Thanks for the help, maybe next time, we call in the Teleporter first. Athien wrote as he walked, sending the message as he turned around the corner of the building and came to the first line of police tape.

Could you get me to a place? He sent as Nicola replied to his first message, his back stinging slightly as he bent under the tape and threw himself over the second one, leaning on the wall when he finished.

"Yeah, he's with me now, the police are not shooting at us, surprisingly," her message began, then; "Sure, Eureka?" He smiled, appearing in the still abandoned Tower square.

Police sirens came from all sides.

"Yeah. It's good that they believe that you both helped." Athien wrote, as he felt a slight disturbance within time as she neared him again.

They will certainly not respect me, for a long time, at least. He thought as Nicola arrived, mask slightly askew as she beamed from ear to ear, ecstatic.

"Alright, where do you want to go, oh fugitive of the law, and, where is that launcher?" She asked, mid-way through her sentence, side-tracked. Athien pointed above them as she huffed in response, legs already bent as she made for the top up the stairs to retrieve it.

She arrived seconds later, with the weapon back in its bag and at Athien's feet, who smiled with gratitude.

"Thanks." He said, shouldering the heavy weapon as he prepared for travel. Nicola breathed deeply for a moment, then they both heard the sounds of sirens get far too close. A vehicle turned into their street.

"Alright, where are we off to?" She held his shoulder, ready to run, as they both saw the front of the car come into view, officers already looking in their direction.

"The corner of Swanston and Bourke, the one with the giant advertisement board." Nicola nodded but stopped a second too long, collecting her plan of travel, as one of the officers pulled himself right out of the window of the still-moving vehicle and shouted.

"Stop! Vigilante, you're under arr....." His sentence was blotted out as Nicola stepped forward, her entire body ringing with power as she left the scene. He fell from the window as the car came to a stopping halt.

"Detective, you all good down there?" The other officer sniggered behind his younger partner's back as he got up from the ground.

"We'll get him, eventually," Said Detective Billings, embarrassed and angered by his failings. "And, this never gets back to the office, understand me?"

"Will this," Athien started to say as they moved towards the building. He stopped, before the next word left his mouth. The door before them slammed shut behind them seconds later. "Will that, ever get boring to you?" He asked, quickly looking about the floor and check for the traps he'd set.

"No, I don't think so, it's such a thrill, to be running that fast, moving like you're the wind. However, I almost got burned up with that rocket, if Zip hadn't of teleported it into space a sec after it hit, I might not even be standing."

Athien motioned to her, gesturing for her to slow down, before walking up the stairs.

"Really though, step lightly, there are traps in this building." *I wonder how much she'll want to hear about this place.* Athien wondered, as they both walked up together, Nicola busy staring around the space to ask questions or see his somewhat worried glancing.

"Alright, so why does this exist and how come you know about it?" She asked immediately as he entered the storage room. Nicola stayed by the door. Athien propped the weapon inside the still open cabinet and closed it, before answering her question.

"It's a long story." He said simply, leaning against the wall as he thought about all the things that had happened to get here.

"Well that must be an understatement, Athien, do I WANT to know, why you're in a storage bunker, in Melbourne, with bigger guns than I've ever seen, even on the internet?" Athien nodded, smiling to himself as he took off the helmet and looked at her.

"Probably not." He huffed, laughing lightly as he unbuckled the two belts around his waist and took off his combat suit. His shirt and pants were ruffled and torn from all the explosions and fighting.

Nicola stepped into the room, looking about the corners and dark shadows as if someone might be hiding there.

"I'm not part of a gang, if that's what you're thinking." Athien took his jacket out of the bag he'd had his combat suit in and replaced the items inside it, the zip only just fitting as he had packed it so roughly.

"Athien, I'm not sure what to think. What are you going to do with all this, stuff, I mean, why?" She stuttered for words as Athien hefted the bag up onto his shoulders. "No, actually, I do want to know, what in the world made you collect this stuff, how, did you manage to sneak it in here, I know your dad is rich, but you?" She stopped, voice still even though he could hear a slight ounce of betrayal in it, as she looked back at the cabinet of guns.

"This, all of this," Athien gestured around to the whole room, including the cabinet and the bag he held. "Isn't, didn't belong to me. I, took it," He refrained from telling her about the guards, he hadn't wanted them dead. "From some very, very angry and evil people, who bought me, while I was overseas, climbing the Himalayas." Athien stopped talking, giving her enough information to absorb as she stood there, looking at him with newfound clarity and, confusion.

"You were, bought, like, sold to them? How does that happen, in the Himalayas?" She sat on a box in front of him, now invested in hearing his tales.

But, Athien looked at his phone and attempted to soothe her curiosity.

"Nothing exciting really, I fell down a hole, found something I shouldn't have and was captured. After being forced to fight my way through an arena of combatants," He paused as she looked confusedly at him. "I'd been training around the world before this. With the help of this other fighter, only the two of us survived, and were then bought by the highest bidder." He stopped, taking a breath as Nicola interjected.

"Ok, that's enough storytelling for today." He made for the door, as Nicola caught his arm and held him in place for a second.

"I'm, really sorry that you had to go through that." She let him go and followed out the door and down the stairs, not wanting to be caught in any surprise traps on the way down.

"The past is behind us, not much to do now but, keep moving forward." He wanted to tell her about everything now, the seed of thought, of having someone know what had happened over the years he'd been travelling, but he refrained from it.

I've already probably spooked her, no need to flatten her with stories that she, or anybody, wouldn't want to hear. Athien stepped into the street, Nicola behind him as they looked down the alley and searched for people.

"Looks clear." He entered the alley, jacket swishing.

"Alright, are you good to get home from here?" Nicola asked as she started walking ahead of him. Athien looked about the street, basically empty but slowly filling now, as the scare of the satellite had ended.

"Yes, my car is just around the corner." He said absently. Nicola turned away, and Athien stopped her just before he felt the energy begin to surge within her.

"Thank you, and I'm sorry I told you my story." She smiled, even though he could see the look through her smile. It was a mixture of fear and confusion.

"Don't be, what else is a friend for, but to share burdens with?"

20

Chapter 20 Adjourned

Athien began his jog the next day, starting from the house, turning into the street and down to the tramway he took to University. His body was still sore from the events of the night before, bruised badly over his ribs and legs, with minor bruises and a cut in his shoulder.

"Hi! How is your morning?" He made casual conversation with the neighbours as he went by, focused more on his breathing over the actual conversations, as his heartbeat with a steady rhythm.

He made it around the block with ease, chest slightly heaving and breath coming out in puffs of grey mist as he re-entered the property.

"Hi Sam, what are you doing up this early?" He said, spotting Samantha, standing on the veranda, her arms crossed and a frown on her face.

"Well, let me see," She stepped into the early morning light, and Athien immediately realised the seriousness she held within her voice and stature. Her shoulders square and eyes staring him down. "You ran off, we couldn't find you, and the city was hit by a giant satellite, which was blown out of the sky AND to top it all off there's videos of this women, who could run faster than I could see." Athien winced, imagining them both out there, looking for him in the horror that had ensued, from his actions.

"Well, to be fair, I had no idea, that there was going to be someone there that could just," He sought for a word that didn't sound like it came straight out of a science fiction book, and couldn't find one. "A guy who could teleport things across space, like, that that was a thing." He shook his head, annoyed that not even the Order had told him about Zip, when they'd seemed to have a date and number for every powered hero on the planet.

"Wait, so, you're the one who blew it up, sent that giant hunk of metal hurtling out of the sky and into all of us, normal civilians on the ground below?" She huffed, and Athien smiled slightly, before quickly hiding it.

She's not angry. Athien had seen Samantha angry, when he'd broken her swing as a kid, and her glider when they'd been gliding in England years ago. She boiled up and became haughty in both those times. *She's just expressing her worry.*

"Yeah, that was me, then I got blasted off the Tower. Nearly fell to my death. The day was saved by a Teleporter who then saved the city better than I would have. With that fast women's help," Athien clapped her on the shoulder and held her there, locking eyes. "Don't worry, I'm mostly fine, just a few bruises."

Samantha's eyes creased downwards as she looked at him, concern turned to relief in an instant as she brought her arms around him and hugged deeply.

Athien's face screwed up for a second as he wheezed, pulling her away slightly, but not enough to make her release, she felt

222

his discomfort.

"Oh, just a bit of bruising, huh, and, how many ribs have gone with that?" She stepped away and shook her head, seriousness gone as she pitied his pain.

He keeps this up for a year, and there won't be a speck of him that isn't covered in bruises. Samantha moved to lead him into the house, the front door banging slightly into the wall as a slight breeze swept into it.

"Sorry, but I've got to get the stuff in there," He pointed at the garage as he spoke, "Into the car, Kali is going to take it to the new, lair, with me." He avoided speaking too loudly, making it sound more cryptic than a new garage on a property he'd decided to rent.

Samantha, looking mockingly hurt, pouted at her cousin.

"What, am I not cleared to hear where this new lair will be?" She asked, hands on her hips as Athien stepped back towards the garage.

"Well, I don't know whether or not I can trust you, do I?" He took another step back and bowed fully to her.

"Wow! After what I know already, I would hope so!" Her voice raised, gaining hem look by the neighbours across the street, as the kids there stopped playing with their ball to look over at the shouting teen.

"Of course, of course, please. I can't have the whole neighbourhood knowing about it. That would defeat the purpose of moving," Athien pulled up the garage door and stepped within it, his eyes still trailing Samantha. "Maybe you'll have to find it, increase your detective skills." He stepped into the garage and let the door fall.

"Hey that's not very..." He voice was silenced over the closing door as it slammed into the ground and locked, Athien surveyed the area within and categorised it into the trips that he would take.

Later that day, Kali came to the Garage, done with her work as a nurse. She looked at Athien's immaculate packing, every item inside the room, besides the tool case, was boxed or folded to the smallest it could be.

"Well, who taught you to pack? They did a good job of it." Kali pushed one of the boxes, testing the weight, as Athien loaded the final contents into a small box.

"It was something I had to learn, The Order hated tardiness, even more so than they hated miss fires and failures." He kicked off the wall, feet planting hard on the ground as he took the box in his hands and carried it to the car, opening the garage door as he went.

"Well, that was dark." Kali picked up a box herself and hefted it into the back of the small car as Athien went back for another. Samantha arrived as they finished loading, her head buried in the phone in her hands.

"Hey, Athien, you read or seen the news today?" Athien looked up from the front of the car, his hand on the ignition.

"No, I was actively avoiding it." He smiled and left the driver's door open, walking around to Kali's side as Samantha stepped down from the veranda and showed them her phone.

"New Heroes spotted in yesterday's disaster, no casualties reported," The title read, and Athien read on as it explained the cause of the scene and more details on the heroes. "A rocket shell was fired into the sky as the satellite fell to earth, sources show the attack came from somewhere in the centre of the city, but police are yet to find the source or the shooter. But, this turned into a success, after experiences all over the CBD report a fast women and a teleporting, cloaked figure, rescuing countless lives and destroying the satellite pieces amid bright shots of light." Athien finished reading as the article went on to show shaky videos and photos of a black-cloaked figure, bright light ebbing from his body.

"Wow." He said, seeing the end of the passage as he stepped away, one photo of Nicola. She'd saved the final group at Federation Square, her body slowed as she'd been knocked off her feet and onto the ground, looking up into the lens of the phone.

She's going to need a better disguise if this is going to be a thing. He nodded as the others finished the passage.

"Well, good to know, I've been sidelined, once again." Samantha and Kali both exchanged a look, Samantha putting away the phone and Kali moving towards the driver's seat of the car.

"Well, did you expect anything more, all you did was make the matter worse?" She said, seating herself within the vehicle as Samantha joined, smirking and Athien hung his head in defeat.

"I don't want any recognition. The police already hate me enough as it is, no need to make it worse." They all set off into the street, the car driving slower than it would usually, the back setting close to the ground with the weight it carried.

"So, how far is it to this new base?" Samantha asked, the car turning into the main street, behind a slow-moving tram that stopped at the pursuing lights.

They arrived at a newly made garage, set in front of a new, two-bedroom house only fifteen minutes from Kali's and closer towards the centre of the city than before, in the suburb of Richmond. Athien lead Samantha through the front door, heading around the house in a short tour, before they unloaded the car, Kali staying at the wheel.

"It's not big, but that suits me just fine," Athien stated, putting a box down at the far end of the garage and accidentally knocking the table over at the same time.

It landed with a soft thud, however, as Samantha managed to catch it with her foot, arms still loaded with a box.

"Yeah, I can imagine you in here, in the dark being a moody vigilante. Surely there are better ways of protecting people as well as taking out this Order you're so hell-bent on smashing." Athien frowned, standing to go back for another box.

"It's not here, the Order," Samantha stumbled for a moment as she stopped to listen. "They're in Alazarath, this," He gestured with open arms at the room and outside. "This is, was meant to be a warm-up, training for the dangers of that city, not a crusade to end all crime but, things change." It was Samantha's turn to frown as she took in the depth of Athien's time he'd spent thinking about all of this.

"Oh. Well, in that case, I suppose it's a good thing that Helm's giving you so much trouble. Otherwise, you'd be worse off when you inevitably move back to Alazarath."

"Yeah, that's right, in a way. People like Helm, people who prey and destroy other's lives shouldn't exist to begin with. It's good for me to fight them."

They finished unloading and drove the way back to Kali's house.

"Hey Athien, remember that whole, not being seen thing you were talking about?" Samantha said as they travelled, not knowing that Athien was listening to the radio as it broadcasted the news, just as much as she was.

"Police have revealed footage of their encounter with the fast girl and her accomplice, the known criminal and vigilante,

Sentinel. Who has managed to dodge police several times in acts of vigilantism. They also revealed, footage of Sentinel and the girl, as they met in the Eureka Sky Tower, minutes before the satellite was blown into pieces." Athien groaned, wishing he could have gone through and scrapped the security of the officer's car before they'd left.

"Well, it doesn't matter," He said, bravado proving his weakness as he straightened his back, aches echoing throughout his body as a result. He saw both Samantha and Kali look back at him, Kali through the rear-view mirror and Samantha by turning back. "What, I have no intentions of being beaten up again tonight, three days in a row of that and I might just die."

"Sssh, sssh." Samantha quietened him as she listened in on the radio again, the reporter still talking about the night's events, her voice slightly raspy and quite over the thumping car's driving.

"We've heard that Aust Electricals, the builders of the satellite have sent a hate-filled message to another news outlet. They have reportedly discredited the broadband service that had helped put it into orbit and for the heroes that helped save the city last night. Their agenda set on suing all three for the loss and destruction of their millions of dollars of construction." Athien whistled as Samantha did the same, with Kali lifting an eyebrow in his direction as they neared the house again.

"Sounds like your head should be down lower than it already is." She said, leaving it there, not wanting to make an even bigger deal of what it would mean if Sentinel's identity was ever discovered.

"Yes, I'll keep a low profile. Now, let's go do some research on Helm's lab, before I go scope out its workers tonight."

Athien tapped Samantha's shoulder encouragingly as they both leapt from the car.

"And then we'll be able to get you back to Alazarath, before my school starts back up again." He finished as they went inside, using each other's phones and maps of the city to develop a rough idea of what to expect within the layout when Athien approached it that night.

"Alright, time to go." He stated, leaving Samantha and Kali at the dinner table hours later, his plate of food finished clean.

"Hey, you're taking me too, who's going to watch your side without the computer here, I'll have to go to the other place." Samantha piped up, following him down the hall, even though she had a relatively good idea of what he had to say on the matter, with what happened last time he'd sought Helm.

He'll say no, wanting to protect me. Athien stopped at the door when she spoke, his back still turned as he looked at the moon, crescent-shaped almost and right above his head, in front of the house.

"Look, I don't think that's a good idea," *knew it.* Samantha square-shouldered herself, ready to argue the matter, before Athien even started to explain. "Because I think Helm could be monitoring the networks surrounding the base, like that old man you met was. Tracking you to the new base would be terribly inconvenient," Samantha relaxed a little, her face showing notable surprise. "Besides, I've got to look after you, not let you do everything that you wish to do." She slapped him, an annoyed look on her face, knowing he'd take it all back and wanting to see him squirm a little.

"That was almost a good speech, you're so mean!" Athien laughed, stepping past the walls of the house and onto the veranda.

228

"You know what, that was, and I'm so sorry, I take it all back," He slowed, turning the corner as she followed him, expectance in her eyes. "But, you're still not coming. Good night, Sam."

21

Chapter 21 Boom

Athien pulled out of the driveway of his new hideout, the neighbourhood a lot quieter than Kali's, with only three houses actually on the street he was on. The land around was still mainly for sale. His scanner jammed the limited cameras and communications as he drove the long way to Helm's base, which was inside an old factory outlet near the docks of the Murray River.

On the way, he passed over the highway. His radio picked up signals from the receivers of the cars below, one of which was the same report he'd earlier, on the lawyers now hunting the others and himself. Athien cracked his neck in anticipation, turning the radio off for the drive, so that he could remain focused and ready for his scouting mission.

"Well, that looks quite a bit bigger than it did in the pictures," Athien stated, pulling off the road and down a side alley. The walls of the base he was seeking to spy on lay high above. It was old, rusted metal that creaked with each sway of the wind.

He stopped the car, lights off, then checked the area. Nothing and no one catching his eye except for the broken glass that sat across the entirety of the alleyway as he changed into the Sentinel uniform.

"Kali might kill me tonight, if Helm doesn't." He stepped out, the glass fragments cracking under the weight of his body and splintering even further as he walked to the end, opposite to the direction of the base.

Time to count your troops. He briskly found the side of a building. In two bounds Athien was atop the small structure, able to see the other roofs across the street now directly in front of him. Athien laid himself against the roof, the tiles beneath him proving uncomfortable but, still intact as he didn't slide off of the roof. He pulled out a small set of binoculars from the belt on his side and looked at the base, the moon shining bright just at that moment as the clouds passed by beneath it.

"There's certainly a small army here Helm, what's your plan?" Athien asked himself as he looked, seeing the wall covered by four soldiers, all in identical features except by height. He could see into the building that was beyond the wall, its second level also guarded by at least two guards that circled the halls.

I wonder if Helm is in there right now, with this many of them to guard the place, it's hard to believe there's not something precious to him here. He thought, not seeing the black armoured, masked criminal anywhere among the others.

Athien stayed there for a long time, two hours going by without him falling asleep or even yawning. He watched the patrol times, the switches between guards and every weapon that each one carried.

Over twenty people, guarding something, that isn't in one spot and carrying enough firepower to take on the city itself, for a while. Athien summarised, mentally cataloguing the data he'd collected as he slipped a little down the tiles, testing their strength. Then he began the climb back down the wall of the building. The moon had meanwhile slid back behind clouds, reminding Athien again, that he would need to develop some infra-red vision goggles to help with the lack of light.

His feet crunched onto the glass as he landed, jumping from the top of the door frame to get down faster and placing his covered hands on the ground to steady himself. A slight slip had almost ensured he'd over correct himself and fall face first.

Guiding the car out of the alley, Athien almost missed the one individual who stood on the street not a hundred meters down the road. Their body was built like a brick, rectangle and heavily blunt, the head covered with an orange, fedora hat which stood out amongst the dark street like a sore thumb. Athien lowered the lights of the car and eliminated as much of it that could reach him, lowering the light blocker in front of his face as he approached the moving figure.

The brick of a figure came closer to the road, as Athien sped up the vehicle, his gut telling him that this meeting was not a chance encounter. When the car was within a few meters range, Athien turned away and looked hard at the road, as if he was finding it hard to stay awake. He was hopeful that the character didn't see the dark helmet in replace of the hair that should have been on his head.

Something is off about him. He looked back into the side mirror as he passed, the figure right behind the car. Athien sighed, happy he hadn't just got into another fight.

"What the...!" He yelled, foot slamming on the peddle as he saw the figure double back, running at the car like a bull and catching it in smooth strides, feet spread wide as they closed the now five-meter gap in a second. Athien saw the figures' fists rise, as he proceeded to bring it down upon the back of the car.

The car's trunk slammed into the ground and Athien, his body akin to a doll in a box, went straight up and against the roof, banging his head hard against it. The car's front rose into the air until it was almost fully erect. Athien's body bashed against the wheel and the airbags as they deployed against the force.

Heavily dazed, but still able to move, Athien opened the door to the car and flopped out onto the street, hearing heavy footsteps coming up from behind the second he touched the pavement.

"There you are, she said that you'd be coming around here soon." The voice that spoke behind him was gruff an deep, deeper than Athien had ever seen as he got to his elbows and knees, ready as his slightly spinning head could ever be.

"Who the hell are you supposed, to be?" Athien slapped his head, vision foggy as his attacker's foot reared up behind him, ready to break his back. Where he knew he'd have very little chance of surviving.

"You can call me, Boom." Athien stumbled forward as the leg came crashing down upon him, managing to half roll, half flail fast enough to avoid the attack. He landed on his side, head aching like a thunderclap had sounded right beside him. He rolled, his body now facing up and towards the looming figure, whose face was etched with annoyance at not crushing him.

Standing over him, Boom was a giant of a man about a foot taller than Athien and the body of a tank. He looked like a hitman, staring Athien down without even blinking.

"Boom, wow, that's the second most original name I've heard in the last two days." Athien got onto his feet, arms arched back as he prepared to propel himself up, Boom right in front of him and rearing his foot for another kick.

"That's not very funny." He kicked at Athien as he rose from the ground, just able to catch the leg as it aimed directly for his head, threatening to cleave straight from his neck. He held on tightly, positioning himself quickly as Boom lost control of his movement, not suspecting the grapple.

"Who cares?" Athien said gruffly, struggling to keep the leg up as Boom attempted to break his grasp.

Boom began to pull his leg in on itself, the rest of his body coming forward to start punching Athien if he didn't let go.

Athien's head throbbed severely, and as he stepped back from the fists that curled towards him, he felt a quick was of nausea cross his throat and mouth, bile building from the shock of the car attack. He let go of the leg, letting it fall as he stumbled back, Boom's fist flying forward but too far away to be able to connect.

"Got you." Athien's eyes widened as Boom's fist stopped early, too early.

What are you doing here? He couldn't react, as something hit him full force in the chest. Athien flew backwards ten feet, landing with his back against the ground. He was only able to spare his head another banging from instinct, his hands moved with his body as he fell and managed to cradle it.

"Aha!" The wind escaped his lungs in one short volley, leaving him winded as he fought to stand, vomit rising from the impact and the swelling he could already feel atop his head.

Boom stood back, his arms pulled into a boxing stance with his feet, waiting for Athien to rise again. Athien did, slowly and while coughing.

"What are you waiting for? End me here." Athien was on his knees, his arms shaking as he continued to rise. Boom continued watching, his face grim and severe, lips a straight line.

"I was told you'd have some fight, I'll wait to see that before I snuff you out." He flicked a finger, and Athien's eyes focused in on the movement, seeing a little, spontaneous shockwave appear as the fingers collided.

Powers. Athien rose faster, his breathing getting faster as he sought for more oxygen.

"You'll never get the chance again." He snarled back at the bigger man, Boom responding with a nod and grin, full length, as he flexed his muscles and cracked his neck.

Athien took a step, then another and then leapt towards Boom. An angry yell splitting his lips as he came forward, blinking rapidly as he calmed his breathing.

"Come on!" Boom roared, colliding with Athien.

Boom's fist came towards Athien, who grabbed it, turning around slightly as he dodged the attack and threw the arm around, putting Boom off balance. As Boom fell, he smiled again, and Athien managed to step and duck away from the explosion that hit his side, glancing him as he did so.

"Stupid power." Athien grabbed Boom by the back of his jacket, the buttons holding tight as he managed to heave him towards the ground.

Boom caught himself, swinging around on one foot as the other hit Athien's left one and kicked him into the ground. Athien hit the ground hard again, this time running his chin on the stone. Blood sprouted from the cut he received, and he rolled to avoid Boom's massive stomp attack, followed by two explosive punches that cracked the ground.

Athien stood again, blood spilling onto the ground as he launched a series of attacks against Boom, colliding over and over with the bigger mans' head and chest, driving him backwards.

Boom held up his arms to hinder Athien's advances, covering his centre and occasionally jabbing as the Athien darted around him, using the bigger man's size as a weapon.

"Stay still!" Boom roared, stopping amid the turning attacks that Athien was throwing and punching out into thin air.

Athien turned to the side, his wounded shoulder facing away from the blast. Boom's fist exploded, more potent than any of the previous attacks. It sent rocks and debris flying as well as almost knocking Athien down again.

He backed off, thinking, as Boom barraged down the street towards him.

His attacks are too strong for me to fight him head-on. Boom swung at him, and Athien sidestepped the attack, his right foot sliding back and then his left as Boom came in for another strike.

But he has to send the explosions in a specific direction. He realised, watching as Boom's explosive punches pasted him without incident as he continued to outmanoeuvre the attacks. Instead, the explosions hit the ground or walls of the buildings they passed as Athien continued to go backwards.

"You shouldn't leave your attacks so open." Athien smiled, causing his chin to bleed more profusely and his headache to cloud his vision for a moment.

I've got him. Athien jumped left, seeing Boom going for a right hook explosive punch. He carried the arm around as it came, Boom too slow to react to the counter-attack as Athien drove the hand around his body. The explosion aimed right at Boom.

Boom howled as his body was hit, sending him off his feet and across the ground, where he slid into a wall. His head collided with the glass of the shop front they'd moved next to, shattering it and spraying him with tiny particles of sharp glass.

Athien wavered, staggering as he waited for several seconds, sure that Boom wasn't going to immediately get back up and try again. When Boom didn't, Athien went down on one knee and held back more vomit, his head beginning to spin harder from the loud sound that was created by the explosion of glass.

"I told you that you wouldn't get another chance," Athien said after he knew he wasn't going to fall unconscious. He stepped up to the downed foe and inspected them.

"It was fun, though." Athien heard a croaking voice mutter from within Boom's mouth, though it moved very little and his eyes only fluttered.

"Who are you working for, and what is your real name?" Athien asked, forcing his voice back to its usual gruffness as he began to question him. Boom's eyes opened as he heard the question. He attempted to push himself up, only making it partway before he realised the glass now sticking into his hands.

"And why, would I tell you that?" He asked, giving Athien a pause as he thought about an answer.

"Because, if you don't, I'll make sure you can never use that explosive power of yours on anyone ever again." Boom's eyes widened, and he immediately looked at his hands, both bleeding lightly and fuzzy through his eyes.

"That's, fair. But I'm sorry, don't know the name of the

237

women who hired me, she was a client, and I let her go without a paycheck closer." Athien looked at him, confused.

So, he's a bounty hunter?

"Your name then?" Boom shrugged, even with his sore hands, he managed to find the pocket on the front of his jacket and held it up for Athien to take. When he realised that Athien wasn't going to come forward and take it, he threw it onto the ground far enough away that it was a bother to pick it up. Athien obliged.

"Baethan Alexanda and associates," Athien read from the card. "We handle your needs, when the big laws can't," He threw the card back at Boom when he'd finished, disgusted by what he saw.

"You kill people for your clients, a hitman. Well, Baethan, we'll see what the police have to say about you when they pick you up." Athien's face twisted up as he felt the blood trickle from his chin, his eyes watering from the sudden realisation of how much pain he was in.

"Baethan goes to prison, and Sentinel doesn't learn about his employer." Athien scoffed, as he kicked Baethan hard.

"You said you didn't know who hired you." Baethan nodded his head slowly, waiting his time to explain himself.

"But I can find out, if you die." Athien brought his foot up and kicked Baethan in the face, sending him into unconsciousness.

"That's not going to happen." He tied up Baethan with difficulty, and called the police. Then managed to get the car started and left the scene, the jammer running to ensure that this time, he wasn't followed by anyone. The crumpled boot of the car stood out like a beacon, crumbled by the first punch, but luckily Athien wasn't far from home.

22

Chapter 22 Anticipation

"Kali? Is that you?" Athien spoke over the phone as he drove back towards the new base, his head throbbing heavily and a shirt wrapped over his chin to stem the bleeding. He heard a noise on the other side of the phone line, but it took a moment for Kali to answer.

"Athien, you sound hurt, what happened with your scout out?" Her voice was partially warm, and also held a little snark to it, sounding like she'd expected him to not take it easy again.

"It went well, but I ran into an unsavoury customer." Athien's voice slurred, vision swimming for an instant as Kali sat up from her seat in front of the car in the garage. Samantha nodded off on the spinning chair beside her aunt.

"I'll be there soon." She grabbed her nursing gear and some clean sheets, prodding Samantha as she slept to let her know she was in a hurry and that she wouldn't want to be there.

"What, would I do without you?" Kali chuckled as she clambered into the car. Athien meanwhile peeled off the boots he wore and stepped down on the gas, pushing the damaged vehicle over the speed limit on an empty side road.

"You'd most likely die. Now hop off the phone, before you take out an old grandma. I'll meet you there in ten." She ended the call and move out of the garage, the car skipping as she pulled away, her small convertible eating into the gutter as she straightened herself.

Athien put down the phone and focused on arriving to the garage in mostly one piece, his mind foggy as he almost turned down the wrong road.

Wow, this is worse than being poisoned. Athien sniggered, finding the thought amazingly funny, remembering an old memory...

He'd just been bought by the Order, was sleeping in a pleasant room after trying to escape for four hours, dragged back and beaten each time. He'd drunk a glass of water and found himself immobilised on the floor for the better part of an hour as his body wriggled and fell unconscious, while his capturers laughed at him....

Kali opened the door to the garage, careful to turn on the light as she entered. She nearly over ended herself over a box that was sitting right in front of the door. Her equipment in hand, she raced to the table and folded it down, in the centre of the room.

She heard the car as Athien approached the house, the usual purring replaced by a gut-wrenching splutter as she saw the door open behind her. Kali placed the bandages and implements she thought she needed all laid out on the table.

"Poor car." She muttered, seeing the beauty she'd had since she was a teen almost fail to make it through the garage door. It spluttered again and died, lights fading and causing Kali to blink rapidly for several moments from the blinding.

"Thanks for, coming." She heard Athien's weak voice before

240

she saw him, her eyes widened as she saw the back of the car, the boot caved in at the centre with the metal stretched inwards.

Kali grabbed Athien as he opened his door, balancing himself against her back as they both walked to the table. Athien was still covered from chest to feet with the combat gear he wore as Sentinel.

"Athien, what happened to you!?" She exclaimed when her eyes finally rested on his face, as he attempted to lay flat on the ground, his back began to spasm for a second as his head rested on it.

Athien's eyes rolled back before he jerked upward as Kali put his jacket under his head. The muscles in his neck finally loosened themselves. Kali got to work, immediately going for the bleeding cut that ran down his chin, the scarf falling onto his neck and blushing his skin with blood.

"Explosive punching freak." Athien was halted from speaking more as Kali pushed his mouth gently shut, her cloth, damp with water cleaning the wound as Athien winced from the pain. She stopped cleaning it after a few seconds, watching for how profusely it still bled, before going for a patch, the bleeding mostly stopped.

"There, don't worry, it'll be a scab in just a few days." Kali left that, moving her hands down to his chest as she sought for a clip or something to get the giant suit off of him.

"Sorry, I'll get up." Athien sat up, his head spinning. He held it with one hand as Kali helped take off the suit, one hand and then the other.

He lay back down again as she inspected his torso, bruises from the nights before newly darkened and one, where the stab wound still healed, was a deep purple with a pink centre. Kali winced at the injury, patching it with a smooth, soft covering and then looked at Athien's head, which was swirling.

His eyes darting around, Athien had never felt so much pain before.

"This might sting." He heard Kali's voice, but couldn't see her as he realised his eyes were close, fatigue taking hold as he felt a needle stick into his neck, in the vein on the side.

Athien's pain finally ebbed away slightly, slowly, as he felt a tear cross his cheek and his mind slip towards the void. Kali stood back as he fell into a sleepy trance, the drug she'd injected him with taking longer than she'd thought possible to react in his blood system.

"You're a stubborn one for sure." She felt the top of his head, gloves on as a slight trickle of blood-streaked along the middle of Athien's hairline and dripped to the floor. She did what she could for the swelling, cleaning the scalp and washing the hair to remove any chance for infection while it healed. Patching it with a cream that would harden enough to seal it in.

Athien woke twice during her cleaning and operation, within half an hour of the two-hour limit the drug was meant to last, his eyes stirred as she'd begun to roll him to the side.

"Athien, this will make you sleep, and I need you to go willingly, take time off when you wake up tomorrow, there's going to need to be some time for healing this body properly." Athien nodded as he was rolled onto his back.

What are these? Athien's mind wandered as he let his body sleep. The pain was sent all over his body, inspiring a scene that was equally as painful as the one he had experienced tonight to play out in his mind.

He saw himself, a younger, happier version, as he stepped down the giant steps that lead up towards Prometheus's Tower.

His father's hand was over his own as they'd walked away. The moon shone brightly as they walked, the blacked-out limousine his father had always driven in parked right outside the stairs, a chauffeur ready to drive them home for the night. *Why, does this seem so, real?*

Dream Athien was eight years old, he summarised, wearing the same suit shirt and tie that he'd worn a lot that year and walked with a spring to his step. Dreaming Athien noticed the man standing a little down the road, watching them intently.

Watch out!

He attempted to call out, sensing danger before the pair had even seen that the man was there, hands poking deep into his pockets as he watched.

"Can I help you, sir?" Athien smiled, hearing his father's voice ring out in the dream, asking the man that had been watching them and the chauffeur looked into the review mirror, to where his client was looking.

The figure walked out of the shadows, Athien's body out of the dream jerking as he was surprised. Helm walked out from the shadows, the random man gone as he stalked towards the car at the same speed that Prometheus and Athien did.

"Excuse me, but." Athien watched as Helm pulled out a gun, his mask glimmering from the light of the moon as he shot towards the two above him.

"Move!" Athien's body jerked violently up as he yelled out of the dream, feeling another spike of pain as the bullet pierced the younger him inside the dream.

Kali jumped back as she finished packing up and throwing out the goods she could and couldn't use again, his body lurching nearly entirely off the table as he yelled.

"Athien, calm down." She said, instantly placing a damp,

warm cloth on his head as she felt a fever crush into his head.

Athien's body returned to silence, his mind quiet and devoid of dreams as his heart beat too fast for him to count.

"It's only a dream."

23

Chapter 23 Preparation

After sleeping for a several days in major sweats, Athien felt slightly better from his bout with Boom. He awoke mid-morning 6 days after the incident, having spent the last day reading and eating.

"Listen, Kali, I know it's a little more expensive than what it was previously, but I hope you can be comfortable with it." Athien held Kali's shoulders as he stood in front of the car he'd had wrecked by Boom. After his headaches and pains had subsided, he'd hired a fitter and fixer to replace the boot door and upholster the insides of the car as well.

"It will be fine but, what are you going to use for your," She lowered her voice, so that the two workers couldn't hear and whispered; "for your exploits." Athien smiled, relieved that his chin felt only slightly irritated by the cut he'd received.

"Well, that will be coming in tonight as well, so I guess you'll have to wait and see. Let me just say it's mobile and still drivable." He stepped away from the car, messaging his shoulder.

"Well, at least your money is being put to good use, I think your father will be happy to see you're alive." Kali smiled as she looked back at him, knowing fully that he still hadn't contacted Prometheus after the expo that they'd been to weeks ago.

"That's, not," Athien wrung his head for a moment before he closed up again. "I've been busy, and of course he's paying for it." He answered gruffly.

The car mechanics finished up their work an hour after, and Kali took her car for a test drive to ensure it was still in workable order. Meanwhile, Athien continued to do what he'd been doing for the last day, new learning material that had been put up over the previous week. Samantha worked building her audio files for the off-screen tapes she needed to record.

"Well, that's all done." He said, submitting the assignment and closing down the coding apps he'd been working with. The computer he used pinged with an alert as he went to shut it down.

He redirected to news.au and looked at the new alert.

"Police raided an old warehouse on the docks of the old Melbourne Murray River." Athien bolted from his seat, sending it spinning backwards as he read the report, which went on to explain the event in detail.

They broke in, immediately shot at by the soldiers inside and causing chaos on the river, leading to two trucks leaving the yard and several deaths, with three reported police deaths. Athien cooed as he saw the photos of the damaged scene, damage on the wall and rooms evident.

"What were they thinking?" Athien hit the table in his room, angry that their deaths could have been saved if he hadn't of waited. He stepped away from the screen, mind quickly set

246

on training as he sought to get away from the knowledge.

"Hey, what's your problem?" He met Samantha in the lounge as he passed and almost too absorbed in his walk to notice her presence.

"The police failed, so I'm off to train, see if this head can take it." He pointed to his head, the cream Kali had used to seal his wound still slightly visible through the thick hair he possessed. Samantha followed him as Athien moved through the area and into the hallway without stopping.

"Wait, you should be resting for weeks, after the damage that you've managed to survive this month," She entered the garage behind him. She stopped at the door, Athien's hands already beginning to wrap the straps he'd saved there. "And shouldn't Helm be going underground, the address you took a look at days ago was ransacked by the police." She stepped down and watched as Athien finished wrapping one hand, moving to the next with speed. The old bed that had been leaning against the wall for the week was the only thing that Samantha could see he'd use as a punching bag.

"Yeah, that's where the police failed, which means that tonight Helm will most likely come back and take what he needs to from the docks, the police won't stand a chance, even if only a handful of men survived the attack on them. They're not expecting it." Athien finished explaining as the last strap wrapped over his wrist tightly.

"Look, I understand why you're upset, kind of. But you can't take on Helm by yourself. Especially not with his soldiers with him." Samantha said bluntly, moving forward as Athien squared off against an imaginary person, his right leg falling slightly behind his left and forming an L shape towards Samantha.

"I have to go after him, and don't worry, if I get into trouble," Athien said, already securing a way to make her feel calmer and more at ease. "I'll give the Nicola or that Teleporter a call." He began punching the air, his arms folded inwards towards his body and cocking out with every punch. He began holding the punches after he hit, then his arms curled back, and he'd used the other hand.

Samantha doubted he'd ever call them for help, but was reassured by the fact he was at least admitting that he now had allies that could help him in battle. *Unlike me.*

Her self-doubt caused her to frown as she thought it, Athien catching on immediately to the negative thought. He continued to punch forward, mixing it up with an occasional uppercut or a front kick, his toes angled upwards as his foot came forward.

"Don't worry, when I fight Helm, I'll beat him this time, I'm even going to pack some, insurances that should secure that victory." He smiled as he continued to punch out at nothing, face forming back into a straight line again as he concentrated, mixing more variation into his attacks.

"Well, if you can fight him half as good as you fight that shadow, then I wouldn't be surprised if you annihilated him." Samantha stepped in front of him and put her hand up, just when his arm came out to punch at nothing, striking her hand instead. Athien smirked as he attacked again, and she connected with his fist. "Wouldn't this be better if you were training with a real-life person, not whatever your imagination can conjure." Athien's smirk widened as he followed her train of thought, punching faster.

"Well, I have a fairly good imagination, and it helps when I can imagine the exact size of my opponent." He referred to

Helm, then took a half step back and kicked quickly towards Samantha's head. Her arms coming up in a defensive position as her body arched to the side, the kick flying through the arms and knocking the shadow down as they passed over her head.

"Uh-huh! And was that you kicking his head right off his shoulders?" She asked, laughing while she stepped away again and straightened her form. Athien stepped back as well, enjoying this more than he'd admit but glad that she was joining in, his thoughts delving between her, the news and the image of Helm coming towards him.

Shoot. Athien froze for a moment as Samantha came forward, his vision spun as he remembered the vague dream he'd had when Kali had put him under with the drug.

He held his hands up, pausing Samantha's approach as he banished the dream from his mind again. Something deeply unsettled him each time he remembered it. Which had happened multiple times since the first event…

"Well, that was odd, you kind of froze there for a sec, are you okay? Your headache return?" Samantha's smile had faded as she'd waited the seconds for him to be ready again, he shook his head.

"No, it's not back, it was," He paused again, then swung at Samantha's middle. She took steps back to avoid the attack and huffed ad he continued. "Just a dream I was remembering."

They continued to spar lightly with each other, as Athien gauged how ready he was feeling to fight in the fight he presumed to be only hours away. Eventually he moved to combos as Samantha practised small blocking techniques.

The sun ebbed towards the middle of the window plane at the back of the garage as they paused sparing, both having worked up a sweat. They rested on the floor, before a voice called.

"Hey Athien!" He heard Kali's voice coming from the front of the house, precisely behind the wall which the side door rested on, her voice sounded concerned.

Athien leapt from the ground like a rabbit, curling his legs underneath his body as he sprang across the ground, heading for the front door.

"Yes, what is it!?" He yelled, opening the front garage door as Samantha scurried to follow.

As he left the room, he felt the unusual warmth of the nearing winter's sun, a slight breeze catching his hair and making him squirm slightly, the cold reacting with his cut. Kali was standing next to the front door, but the concern wasn't for her. It was directed at the two men that stood in the driveway.

"It's here early then." Athien smiled and waved to the two motormen, their mechanics wear showing clearly. Between them both was a silver motorbike, wide and long, with a stocky build and thick metal covers over the actual slim design.

Two men smiled and came forward, the one on the right, thick handed, shook Athien's while the one on the left held a clipboard with signing papers on it. American branding showed clear at the title section of the page.

"Hello, Mr Dickens, we presume?" Athien shook hands with both men as he looked past them and at the shiny silver bike that he'd bought.

"Yes, that's me, on this continent anyway." He smiled at the two, conscious of the Band-Aid he had patched over his chin.

"Ah, yes, it was good to hear from you again. It's been a while since we've had to deliver out this far," The one holding the paperwork began to prattle. Athien gave him a stern look, creasing his eyebrows and frowning for a split second. "But yes, here's the paperwork." He corrected himself and held the click board out for Athien, who took it and signed quickly, familiar with their clauses from a job he'd done with the Order.

They might have been terrible people, but their contacts and suppliers, some of them are good ones. He gave the paperwork back and stepped between them, his left hand out and gliding over the front as he inspected it for his wants.

"You put in everything?" He asked, looking at the underside as he lay on the concrete to inspect it. Both workers answered simultaneously.

"Of course, down to the nuts and bolts that tie the plastics together, under the metal guards, of course." Paper worker stepped around the bike and into Athien's eyes as the other walked past and turned their car on again, enveloping the street with the roar of the engine as it started.

"Yes, it's the most individual, custom made bike we've ever made, doesn't look like any brand not even our own." He winked as Athien caught his eye, and the two shared a nod.

"Well, thank you, two fine gentlemen, again, it has been a while, and we'll have to do another build again someday." Athien kicked the back wheel of the bike as he led them both back to their car, already ready to take it for a drive.

"Well, to be honest, Athien, I hope you DON'T need another build for quite some time, she's practically a mobile tank, what you've got there." Athien laughed as they got into their car, relishing in the particle ability he'd now have in the nights that followed.

"True, until next time, Mechanics," He waved as they reversed down the driveway and turned off to the left of the house, down towards the tram road exit and out of sight. He looked at

"Do you like it?" He asked, back at the bike and twisting the throttle key, eyes shining as he remembered when he'd drawn up the plans for the vehicle.

Only a year ago, how time flies when you're busy. Athien thought, hearing the engine purr to life with an electric humming sound that wasn't much louder than a kettle boiling.

"You know you're underage to be riding that, right?" Samantha looked at the bike more closely, seeing what the mechanics meant. The usual plastic coverings on the bikes sides and front were reinforced with metal covers, strengthening it, so they didn't bend at all.

"Not at all, I got my Learners."

He returned a minute later, the magnetic plate in his hand as he slapped it onto the vehicle's back. Athien sat on the bike, ready to take it to the new base as the sun broke through the cloud bank and shone for the last time of the day.

"Oh, since when though!" Samantha's smile grew wider as she saw the absolute glee in Athien's often too serious face. *He is excited from this bike!*

She clapped as he did two laps up and down the street, the bike was quick to turn and speed up, and Athien did a rapid drift to finish off the ride. Surprising both Kali and Samantha.

"Those don't look like rookie moves to me," Kali said bluntly, but didn't push the subject as Athien's happy face came back into view.

"I'm ready now, just got to wait for the police report, make some adjustments to the bike, and I'll have Helm nabbed." He walked up the drive, clapping Samantha on the shoulder as she looked surprisingly after him.

"Since when are you optimistic?" She asked, his body already disappearing past the door frame and into the hallway of the house. Kali followed as they all entered the house, closing the door as the last strands of the sun's rays passed below the house's roof and vanished from view.

"We'll be coming with you tonight Athien, no way you're facing that monster alone." Kali stood in his doorway as Athien put on a thick, black sweatshirt and combed his hair backwards. He felt a few strands of hair reach longer than the others as he brushed through the cream.

Gonna need to cut this again.

He looked at Kali and agreed with her.

"Yeah, thank you both for this, it's going to be good to have you both there." Athien suddenly brought himself right next to her head, whispering urgently into her right ear. "But, if something happens, I want you to make some kind of mechanical or digital malfunction happens. it's an off chance, but if it happens, I don't want either of you seeing it." He stepped away as Samantha's footsteps echoed closer to the kitchen wall next to Athien's.

Kali's face went ridged, but she nodded curtly, believing his words to be an extremely caution-driven measure.

"Alright, just, make sure you beat him this time," She smirked uncharacteristically, before saying; "I don't want to have to fire a firework projectile at my nephew." She let Athien pass, and Samantha turned the corner towards them at the same time. She had her satchel slung over her shoulder.

"Ready?" She asked, radiating after Athien's happiness had spun around the house.

"Yes, it's time to hunt this man until he drops, tonight, Helm's going to prison." Athien grasped his fingers together as he

253

made a dramatic pose, causing the others to laugh, before he stepped away and walked back down the hall.

"Well, we'll see you in fifteen minutes, Athien," Kali called as they went to the garage door. Instead, Kali retrieved the keys and brought them to the car. They heard the motorbike start from outside and saw him drive down the street, a small device similar to the one he'd put in into Kali's car to down connections visible on the left handlebar.

"We're going to have to be fast, no guarantee he's going to wait around for you again, especially not with that fire in your eyes." Samantha sat in the passenger side of the car as Kali jumped into the driver's seat, eager herself to take the car for a test drive. It had been some time since she'd driven it at all, without its new updates.

They met at the garage, Athien already decked out with a reinforced make of his usual Sentinel costume. The difference was he'd gotten a chin guard strap and another belt, across his left shoulder, where a set of two twelve-inch knives pointed towards his centre.

He bowed to them as they entered, waiting until they'd shut the door, before he breathed again and continued to set up his PC monitoring screen. To the right, he had news reports from over a hundred sources and on the left, audio channels and police reports, though he'd only found three channels.

"Wow, that's a quick set up," Samantha said, only briefly understanding what she was looking at on the two-meter widescreen. Athien explained it to her.

"So, you're both ready for this? Keep an eye on the news and scanners. I'll check about his previous location, see if he really is going to hit it, or just terrify the police that are still investigating the scene." Athien grabbed his helmet, dusting it off slightly as he awaited their responses.

"Yeah, we've got you from a technical standpoint." Samantha stalled for a moment as Kali put a hand on her shoulder and continued for her.

"If you catch onto him, call your new friends." It wasn't a hope, Athien heard the concern they both felt for him in their pleas and nodded.

"If I catch him, it won't take them long to find out, and they're a little quicker than I am with travel." He replied, revving the engine as the garage door opened behind him...

24

Chapter 24 A gritty defeat

Athien sped down the busy roads towards Helm's previous base, the clouds above still casting some orange glare that was lessening, as the sun descended further under the horizon. The lights of the cars he passed shone brightly against the silver of his bike. He stood out like a beacon, black and grey against the yellow lights.

Athien had blast painted the bike a black chrome colour, patchy, from the rush he'd had to get on it, but enough so that it wouldn't immediately stand out to the builders of the bike.

The cops will be more afraid of Helm then of me, at the moment. He swerved between two large conveys and turned right, heading two blocks over from the actual crime scene so that he could monitor the sight before trying the enter.

"That's a lot of police." Athien had hoped that he'd find the sight mostly emptied by this point, but the entire base was lit up when he climbed the same alley he'd been in two days prior.

Police officers covered all floors and the ground around the base, forensics and investigators still hard at work finding evidence.

They won't find anything of use, that's the kind of man Helm is, this might not have even been somewhere he needed. He thought, looking for the lead captain of the investigation, which he found by looking for the person who was surrounded by the most people.

"Kali, is there anything on the radios?" Athien talked into his radio, seeing the full-faced grimace that the captain exerted upon the officers h spoke with. "Because this guy looks like he won't be leaving here for a year or two." There was a ruff skittering sound as someone ran over to the radio, and Athien heard Samantha's voice over the radio first.

"Athien, sorry, didn't realise we hadn't put the radio on the station." She took a deep breath, and Athien heard her put the radio down on the table then. "We've seen nothing on any sites or media, but the police are still looking about the city for the two cars we sent them pictures of, but there hasn't been a hit yet." She paused, reloading the screen to confirm her thoughts, and still didn't see any mention of the masked soldier.

"Don't worry Athien, he'll be there, somewhere, no way can a criminal like him keep away from the city." He heard Kali over the radio, sounding distant from the table as her voice echoed.

"Keep me posted, I might do a little more scouting from this side." He turned off his radio and listened as theirs noised out, before rising and moving closer to the crime scene. He could hear chatter from below his building as he reached the end of it, cramping low to avoid detection from their eyes and cameras as he poked his head out.

"We can't see hide nor hair of why this place was of any

use, to anyone, but if they were willing to kill so many cops, they could have at least left something of value!" Two officers, a short, balding man and a taller, dark-haired women stood below him, drinking coffee while they were on break.

"Yeah, well if they try again, we'll get the back up, and we get the armed forces ones," The man was saying, spilling his coffee as he passionately, angrily spoke. "You know what I'm talking about, the heavy hitters, exactly what should happen right now." Athien's eyes furrowed as he thought about the implications of the arrival of the armed forces.

It's already annoying having to dodge the police, let alone have them actively fighting to kill me. Best be done with Helm as fast as we can. He thought, continuing to listen to the conversation.

"And, to think, two days ago, we had a satellite, an actual satellite, crash into the city, I tell ya, we might be entering the end times." Athien saw the shorter man grab at a small cross at his throat and whisper something to himself, as the other officer looked away and up the street.

"Grim, Grim! Car fast approaching on the north-west side!" Athien snapped to attention, as the female officer leapt to her feet and rushed to the other side of the street. Her partner spilled the rest of his coffee as he rashly pulled for the handgun at his side, sensing the danger as a black car drove, speeding, down the road at them.

"Clear the road!" He yelled, keeping himself on the right side as other officers noticed the immediate danger and reacted; meanwhile, Athien did likewise.

He leapt from the building, back down the alley and rolled to recover, going straight for his armoured motorbike as he anticipated a drive-by shooting.

"Kali, something is happening, Helm or his men are here."

He yelled too loudly into the radio as his bike purred to life and he sped through the alley towards the scene,

"Wait, how! There's nothing on the radio…. Athien, watch out!" He heard Samantha shout as something played off the radio in the garage.

"Shooter in a black vehicle, send back up." Athien breached the street, just as guns were fired at the base, the officer on the other side of the road ignored him as they focused fire on the bottom.

Athien drove down the road on the left side, only noticed by the driver, who hadn't yet reacted to the speeding bike that was headed straight for their car.

"Shoot, stay away from me ya vigilante, this is a police crime scene!" Athien heard the officer yell but paid no heed to his words, both the officer's and his focus absorbed by the shooting car, which was just beginning to swerve towards the walls of the base. The driver dodged Athien's motorbike just as the car roared into the street.

Guns fired, and the second floor of the base was riddled with bullets. Luckily, they were mostly undercover as the female had given them enough time to react with her quick sightedness. The car stopped firing as it passed Athien, who stared up at the driver's window and through, spotting Helm. The masked man was lingering in the back of the vehicle.

He turned around sharply, wide shots fired from behind him and also hitting the car's side. The damage created many holes as the vehicle passed by, speeding away from the scene. Athien followed in hot pursuit as the vehicle turned into the street, he stepped onto his bike and it roared to life.

"Can't let him get away!" He shouted into the street, dodging faster as more cars approached him. The truck edged into the left lane, causing other drivers to spin out or just break.

He heard the radio signal splutter and die between himself and Kali, and looked on at the vehicle with newfound concern.

Athien closed the gap between himself and the big car. He jerked the handles to the side, grazing the fence of a clinic they drove by as a gun poked out the side window of the van.

He pushed the bike faster, as he caught the glint of the window sliding down on the left side of the car as well and heard the first shot fire. Its arch was too short, but skipped off the road and rocketed into the bike on an angle, scratching the bike but otherwise just making a sharp sound.

Athien re-centred the bike, streamlining himself with the car in front, only half a metre from it, when the door opened. He was momentarily blinded, some source of bright light seeping out over him as they opened the doors, his bike careened towards the left as he sought to break it.

"Shoot him!" He heard someone inside the car yell, the doors closed to halfway as Athien poked back out the left side and unsheathed a dagger from his chest. Athien aimed for the centre of the doors as the left side shooter poked out again.

He threw the knife, bullets scattered off the sides and front of the bike as Athien twisted the handle to avoid the first volley. The blade twirled twice through the air and struck the floodlight that was through the doors, shattering the globe and sending sparks flying around the back of the car.

"What the hell!" The gunmen stopped firing as their car swerved dangerously to the left, hitting several mailboxes and sending the few travellers on the pavement scattering. They were heading for the busy city streets, now only a block up.

Athien knew he had to destabilise the vehicle, or stop the soldiers before they made it into the city centre. He took a risk, using their dangerous position to come up right beside the car.

His head was under a window as he matched speeds with them, but he could see the gunmen, through the rearview mirror.

"Helm!" He yelled over the roar of the vehicles, half-standing on the bike as he reached up, his elbow smashing through glass.

The commotion in the car was hectic, Helm was on the right side, and between them were two soldiers, then two at the front and one at the back, holding his hands with tears in his eyes.

Athien grabbed his second knife, wielding it in his right hand as he sought to plunge it into the soldier closest to him.

"Turn!" Helm barked at the driver, his arm snaking past the headrest of the driver's seat and gripping their shoulder with force. The wheel was turned and the vehicle shot to the right, heading into Bourke Street, as tonnes of cars appeared to their right and left. Athien sliced once at the soldier, landing a hit over their chest, which only scratched the combat gear they wore. Then Athien had to step down and managed to swerve into Bourke Street too, his bike almost colliding with a lorry that was poorly parked on the side of the road.

The truck wasn't so lucky, turning again to attempt to get through into an adjacent street, and collided headlong into a car that tried to brake beside it. The two vehicles combined their forces and slammed into a traffic light post, as Athien slowed on the bike as fast as he could. He turned into the street, passing over the curb and sending people into a scurry that were already dodging the crashing vehicles.

Athien passed Helm's car, which came off the side of the heavily bent pole and went up, landing heavily on its side before sliding, a metallic scraping sound filling the street. Flaring sparks skated off the road.

The other car hit the wall of the corner building, a small store, smashing through the glass midway up but otherwise stalled by the brick foundations.

Athien attempted to cover his ears as the clash occurred, but found that with the helmet on there was only a certain amount he could change with regards to sound. The massive smashing of metal and glass was enough to cause a sharp ache in his eardrums, and the two cars came to abrupt halts. The other didn't get further than the lamp post that Helm's car had guided it straight towards, folding around like a lollipop as it stopped instantly, crushed.

Athien wasted no time, even with the glass, a small fire from the vehicle and the shouts and screams from those around him, he ejected the key from the bike and stepped off. His eyes set on the vehicle wrapped around the traffic light.

Smoke curled from the engine and Athien was very aware of the eyes that weren't running, as they eyeballed him from behind. He wasn't the only one who had moved for the car, and two other people were already at the driver's door side. An old man, white hair flowing down his back and a young women, sweat dripping from her brow as she'd been running and had crossed the street to help, attempting to pry the door open though it had caved inwards from the impact.

"Break the window and pry it from the inside!" Athien took charge of the event, breaking his usual code of silence to civilians as he made contact and motioned with his arms for the people to break away.

The car began to smoke even worse, switching from grey to black as it bellowed from beneath the engine and crossed into the street, people already filling it up in attempts to see the accident.

"Sentinel..." He heard the old man mutter, his breath heavy as he stepped away from the vehicle. Athien propped up his elbow and slammed it into the window to break it, ignoring the man's surprised and somewhat fearful voice.

I've got to save this guy, any others? He thought, briefly looking through the window. He found no passengers.

When the glass shattered inward, he could clearly see the driver sat and slumped forward. Athien scraped away the glass and stuck his hand behind the door, feeling for the dint, finding it, and after a short, quick punch into the handle, it opened. He stepped away from the door as the young women came forward, grabbing the driver with the old man's assistance, with which they managed to lower him to the ground successfully.

Athien looked at where Helm's car had crashed, finding everything above the wheels of the vehicle covered in the smoke from the driver's car he'd just saved.

"Kill him and be done with it." The answer he received was all too clear, as Athien turned and ducked, sensing the danger as Helm's soldiers progressed into the street. Four soldiers exited the smoke.

Athien could hear their feet falling loudly as they began to spread out in search of him, the street erupting back into chaos as the guns were revealed.

"Stop right there, lower your weapons." Athien had no idea who the officers behind him were talking to, and he didn't care for the minute as his concentration was on a too close soldier. Luckily they froze as the police officers shouted.

Time to get to work, best not to let the officers get shot. He stooped down further, hands brushing the ground as he rose, diving quickly out and under the soldier. They saw him, too late to react as Athien's quick and strong arms wrapped around their weapon. He sent it flying in an instant and pushed them back in the process.

"Trust me, dealing with me is much better than attempting to deal with them," His sentence came out purposefully antagonising as he sought to rile the soldier up. The thought of a fight that wasn't against a satellite or super-being was propelling him into a warrior state.

"Stop! Put your hands in the air!" Athien heard another officer call out, hurried steps that counteracted all the others he could see and hear by running towards him, not away.

Athien ducked, slightly late as his focus was split by the officers, and re-centred on the fight at hand, other soldiers pinning the police down with two warning shots from the sides.

The soldiers' arm snaked past Athien's side without any effect, besides putting them off balance. Their gut was left wide open as Athien plunged his counter attack punch straight into their rib cage, driving the air from their lungs as quickly as it had entered. The soldier fell towards the ground, one knee keeping them up, as Athien's voice interrupted his attack to the back of their head.

"Told you." He struck, landing a crushing knockout against their skull. The body fell limp a second later, as a foot came flying into view from his side.

"Take this you fool, Helm's taking nothing from you any-more." Another soldier, one of the flanking shooters, shouted as Athien blocked the attack, his mind whirling as he figured out a countermeasure.

"He never has," Athien said aggressively.

Why didn't you try to shoot me, I saw you coming from a mile away? He looked back at where the shooter had been, finding another in their place and this one's gun at their feet.

Athien caught the leg of his attacker as they sought to regain their balance, heavy footing proving their downfall as Athien drove the leg up. They fell onto their back, prone to his next attacks, but not helpless.

"Damn it!" The soldier's voice rang out as they rolled from the fall, avoiding Athien's axe kick, fast approaching as they kneeled and half-stood, hand going for their back as he approached.

Please just be a knife. Athien dodged to the left, fearing the incoming attack, he'd seen the sheath as the soldier had rolled. The soldier's arm came out, slicing in an open arch to slow Athien's approach, who wasn't even in range yet and closed the distance. Athien caught the arm with the knife as it came around the soldier's body, his fingers driving into the vein that he knew resided in their wrist. He found it and pulled the hand down and across his body, throwing the attacker off balance, dislodging the knife from their grasp.

"That was fun, try again next time." Athien smiled, fully in the moment as he drove down on the fallen victim, who was cradling the pinched nerve of their wrist even as Athien knocked it away and punched him out.

Around him, he could hear the gunfire going off periodically as he stood over his downed attacker.

The other two flankers came into view, and a quick look behind told him that the police were more concerned about saving the civilians and protecting the streets than dislodging a wanted vigilante.

"Alright, you two, get him now." Athien heard the familiar, deep voice even before he saw Helm, standing inside the still clearing smoke, arms wrapped together. He dived backwards, seeing the guns of the two shooters as they began their trail towards him, about to open fire as he rolled away. Athien hid behind the cover of the car that had smashed into the traffic light.

Bullets skittered and wedged into the road and concrete path as the soldiers fired towards him, police and others around reacting with terror at the gunfire. The sound rebound off the windowed skyscrapers and echoed around the city.

Athien ducked out of habit, the bullets bouncing and punching into the car as the soldiers continued to fire, despite his cover. The police, hidden behind a car just behind him fired single rounds at the attackers, missing their marks. Athien watched as one officer dodged a shot, then pulled their partner down as another went over their heads.

Sliding around the car, Athien gauged the distance between himself and the first shooter, both having stopped to reload their guns undercover.

It's only a few meters. Athien ran forward, leaping from cover. The other shooter saw him break from cover and shot towards him. Bullets crossing the path faster than Athien could dodge. As he made it to their protection, he felt the familiar pull of bullets penetrating his combat gear. He felt pain, at least one shot had struck home against his side, blood trickled down his right as he appeared on the other side of the car he'd rolled to and surprised the shooter positioned behind it.

"Stop firing." He said simply, taking the gun before it could be fired and he punched the soldier in the face. Their helmet dinted inward slightly as their head folded down, dazed.

266

Athien threw the body into the ground and grabbed the gun, positioning it on the top of the car and aiming towards the other shooter.

Let's end this, Helm. He'd lost sight of the leader, but was too focused at the minute to check the perimeter for Helm as he fired. Two bullets firing into the ground at the shooter's feet.

The last soldier saw Athien's gun a second before he'd shot, stepping off one foot as he stumbled to get away from the open gap. Two bullets scaring him as they hit the ground. The soldier fell back, gun aiming at the corner of the car, into the sky, where Athien should have popped out to continue the attack.

I'll get this one. The soldiers' disillusions were quickly quietened as Athien ducked low, appearing below their aim. He rolled past the car and kicked out. The gun flew from the soldier's hands, over their head, and they felt a leg give out. A horrible crunching sound occurred shortly afterwards as Athien leapt away from them again.

"You shouldn't have come here," Athien muttered.

There's a lot of police here now, but, where's Helm? Athien saw the street the truck had come off was utterly cut off, police guarding it and the road he was currently on, from the other side too

No way had he got out, in a building... He lost his train of thought, eyes racing to catch a shadow that had moved on the ground in front of himself. Athien stepped to the side of the car he'd been behind, further into the street, as a body crashed down next to him.

"Nice, thanks for those free tips." He heard Helm's deep voice speak from behind him as he turned his body back to face forward, hand going for the knife he still had in its sheath.

267

"What tips?" Athien growled back, shifting his weight into his back leg, the knife positioned at his neck height, pointed towards Helm's.

Helm charged, done with words as the police at the edge of the street collected the two soldiers close to it, still down from Athien's beat down on them.

Helm's body came in at high speeds, fists balled up and firing forward like a cannon.

Athien blocked the left punch with his right arm, switching the knife to his left hand as he sidestepped the second punch and wedged the blade towards Helm's centre. Helm managed to worm his body around the blade, catching Athien's arm with his right hand. He knocked the sword away, knee rising and colliding with Athien's open stomach. The combat gear cushioned the attack, but Helm's strength still pushed Athien back.

Air escaped Athiens' lungs with a burst as he back-peddled away, eyes set on the knife now sitting behind his attacker.

Helm came forward, giving Athien no time to draw another breath before another flurry of attacks came towards him.

Athien brought both arms together like a shield, using them to absorb the two punches Helm threw at his face. Athien toppled the stronger fighter.

Helm's back hit the ground, but his legs caught around Athien's as he'd come down to punch Helm's prone state. Athien was unable to get away and fell next-to the criminal.

The two struggled, leg wrestling for several seconds, their feet kicking out at each other's groin and stomach areas as they attempted to gain ground and escape.

Neither was willing to break, but Athien managed to collect Helm's straying arm with a heavy boot kick, causing Helm to roll away and escape the leg war. Helm's back arched forward as he cartwheeled away, he landed on his knife.

Helm waited a second, enough time for Athien's already moving body to stand, before he picked up the large bowie knife on the ground. His feet became planted horizontally to each other with his left shoulder facing Athien.

It was Athien's turn to charge, his body shifting from foot to foot as he slightly zigzagged towards Helm, his hands moving like a windmill in front of him as he attempted to put off Helm.

This isn't going well, the police might shoot us both if I don't finish him soon. Athien thought, a step away from Helm, when the knife Helm held slid from his fingers, his wrist snapping back. The blade wedged itself through his combat gear and into his shoulder.

Shoot. Athien lurched forward and punched out, leaving the knife in his shoulder as his other arm collided with Helm's mask. He felt a crack in the bottom right half of it as Helm stepped away, stunned by Athien's ignorance. Helm jumped forward, grabbing at the knife that was in Athien, he pushed away, punching and kicking as Helm gripped the hilt. Helm hit him over and over again, berserk as his eye appeared under the broken mask.

Athien stood, nearly motionless as he was forced to pull the knife from his shoulder. Thundering pain erupting up his arm. He sneered at Helm through his helmet and readied to charge the man as his relentless punching seized.

"This is my city, soldiers win battles, not schoolboys." Helm spat over Athien's helmet as he yelled, pushing the vigilante back and onto the ground. Athien fell on his side, keeping the knife in hand as he attempted to roll away.

Athien's shoulder crumbled as he tried to roll and he landed on his head, pausing for just a moment to clear his thoughts, anger turning his saliva bitter.

"Get over yourself, puppet," Athien said, spite fuelling his anger as he moved to stand again. His bleeding shoulder anchoring him as he pushed off from the ground.

"What!" Athien's eyes widened as he half stepped, half stumbled away from the kick that almost slammed against his rear end, and Helm's body went wide as his anger seemed to rise.

Athien felt the familiar swimming feeling he'd found after fighting Boom days ago, his eyes blinked rapidly as Helm approached again. His eye appeared red to Athien.

There we are. As Helm's knee came up, arms reaching for Athien's shoulders to drive the knee into his ribs. Athien caught the knee mid-movement, pushed it down and, using his thicker helmet, bashed Helm with a head butt.

Helm staggered backwards, hands going up to his face as he felt for where the mask had broken. Athien was finally able to see the concern in his opponent's eyes, but also, the unrelenting rage that bellowed from them.

"So, there's a face under that mask, is there?" Athien looked at the street to his side, the police and two soldier's back to trying to shoot each other, but the other side was still very much focussed on the fight in the middle of the scene.

"I'm no one's puppet!" Helm yelled, his hands both unfastening the two blades he had strapped to his side, as Athien re-focused and charged again.

Helm sliced with both arms as Athien approached, his zigzag approach quickly defeated as Helm's blades caught his gear and sliced slightly through his right arm. Athien punched Helm in the gut, ducking under the third knife attack, but

Helm pushed down with his chest and knocked Athien away again.

One of Athien's knives slips off the side of Helm's gear, and the other only wedged into the patching of the re-enforced backing.

Athien stood tall again, backed into the truck's roof as it lay behind him and deflected Helm's next attack hit the roof.

Athien then formed a knife with his hand and wedged it up and into Helm's elbow, right where another cluster of veins were. Helm dropped the other knife mid slice attack.

Athien, taking advantage of Helm's open middle, launched a massive bombardment of attacks, hindered by his injured shoulder. His heel faced Helm's face as it collided with skin and jaw.

Helm fell back this time, and when his back hit the ground, Athien felt something different, not just the tiredness from the battle sinking into his bones. As he looked around, he felt a sense of proudness in his work.

"You should stand down now, Helm, there's no way that you're getting out of this." Athien stood over the dazed villain, Helm's eyes swimming as he attempted to clear them by blinking, arms already preparing to spring him back up and continue fighting.

"Not. Going. To happen." Helm's voice broke between the words of his sentence as he stood, shaky, but otherwise ready to keep going. Athien took a step forward and, bringing both his hands together, smashed them down on Helm's back, who crumbled under the attack and slummed back to the ground, eyes closed in defeat.

Above him, Athien heard a helicopter as its blades spun between the skyscrapers nearby, news channel anchors already attempting to disobey police orders.

His shoulder began to throb heavily seconds later. The adrenaline was already slipping away from him as officers approached from all sides, guns trailing on him and fingers on the triggers.

"Who is in that chopper?!" Athien heard one of the reporters scream at the police over the noise of the blades, the camera's pointing up at it and Athien, as police closed.

"Sentinel, put your hands in the air! You're under arrest." He heard the officers approaching, but was still watching Helm, who was not moving, besides the slow, laboured breathing visible from the rise and fall of his chest.

"You should have fought harder for your spot, Helm." Athien muttered, louder than he'd intended but still not caught by the viewers around him. Athien kept his hands by his side, looking down at the ground as the officers got closer and closer to his spot, guns still pointed directly at him. His shoulder panged severely, but it was something that he could focus on, rather than the guns of the officers.

I don't see much of a way out of this. He'd done what he came to do, but dodging twenty shots that could be fired any second seemed out of even his range of skills.

"Don't bet on my arrest, Sentinel, I'll be onto you again, soon." Athien heard Helm's voice, barely above a whisper, as the downed villain's eyes stirred.

"We said, put your hands in the air!" Athien slowly moved one hand up the other hindered, his feet separating slightly as he prepared to get behind the truck for cover.

"What the hell are they doing?" The officers behind him stopped, their guns pointed down, as a shadow was cast on the ground, a body hanging outside of the helicopter. Athien didn't see it, taking the surprise that had distracted the police.

He ranfor cover.

His body slammed against the side of a vehicle, as he expected the sound of gunshots. After a moment, he slipped to the front of the vehicle, hidden, from the other eyes on the scene. Athien took a look at his shoulder, finally, seeing that the wound created by the blade had gone right through his armour and wedged firmly into the muscle, which was torn, thanks to Helm's attack.

Gunfire erupted behind him, and he heard screams echo from all sides as whatever had been standing in the helicopter dropped onto the road. Athien turned, grimacing as his shoulder panged again, the wound now covered by spare cloth he'd ripped from his gear, as he stepped out to confront the situation.

The police officers on the road were being engaged by a being Athien had attacked before. Metal claws on their hands and feet and a metal beak jutted from a heavy-looking helmet. Vamp stood before him, his body worming around the officers as they attempted to stop him, his claws ripping through cloth and tissue as he attacked, unmercifully.

25

Chapter 25 Sentinel and the...

Athien slowed. For a brief moment, he was climbing the Everest Mountain, falling down the hole again... He saw the forge, the cage, a suit of armour in a coffin, metal, under stone older than anicent egypt. He saw the arena, when his ally, Mask, gave him a dagger, and as he doned his green and red mask, as they'd all made their own, he felt something. Power. Athien had fought like a hurricane, stabbing and kicking and hitting, but never killing. That which he'd sworn he wouldn't do, but had to, under the order.

Bile filled his throat as he opened his eyes again, and saw the same, desperate image, in the fight Vamp was having with the police. Athien stood, and roared.

"Vamp!" Athien came forward as officers scattered from the onslaught. Vamp wobbled slightly on his feet. Athien imagined him smiling as he approached.

Vamp's head snapped around as Athien approached at a quick jog, fearful of Vamp's tendency as he saw the carnage of the mad man's attacks. Vamp followed Athien's movement and waited until he reached near to kicking distance before he struck out.

Athien's front leg came up as his other curved forward to knock the new villain onto his back.

Vamp catapulted forwards as the leg made contact, using the defused attack to move even faster, his claws dragging across the ground as he shot towards the running officers.

"Oh, this is so priceless!" Curling back one hand as he wracked it across the back of an officer, kicking another as the first fell and disabling both of them. Then Vamp turned back, facing Athien with a glint in his eyes like stars.

"Stop." Athien picked up the knife he'd wielded against Helm, his blood still on the weapon as he faced off against the crazy villain. Vamp smiled wide, his jaws opening as he did so, showing a ridiculous, slightly blood-covered face underneath.

Vamp ran forward, arms drawn down again as he prepared to mince Athien with his claws and a slight bubble of saliva appearing under the helmet he wore.

Athien dodged the first swipe, but was surprised, as Vamp didn't swing with the second one, but pushed him instead. Athien fell, shock registering only after he felt Vamp's clawed hands over his arms. He was pinned.

"You're looking a little worse for wear this time around, Sentinel." Vamp brought up one hand, Athien busy attempting to squirm out of the hold. Vamp curled down all but one of his left-hand claws, looking directly towards the stab wound Helm had dealt earlier.

"Get off me, and I'll let you…" Athien gritted his teeth and stopped as the claw split the cloth he'd put over the wound and entered his shoulder. "I'll let you live." His body shook involuntarily from the pain it was receiving as Athien managed to free one arm. He held Vamp's, before the claw could dig any closer to his bone.

"I don't think you have any power to be making those threats." Vamp's other hand came up, clenched in a fist as he punched down against Athien's already bruised chest.

Athien consciously screamed, egging himself on as he tried to move. Using the knife in his hand, he snaked it up and cut just above the upper side of Vamp's arm, causing Vamp to waver as his second punch rolled off of the vigilante.

Athien's vision fluttered momentarily as he saw a moment of weakness in his enemies guard.

"Sucks to be you." Athien spat, seizing the opportunity to use his free hand and push against Vamp's chest. The criminal looked concerned for a moment.

Vamp's smile was still there, though he looked more deranged now, chuckling softly to himself as he saw the small trickle of blood that ran down his claw. It shone bright red with Athien's blood.

"I bet it would." Vamp retaliated, his claws by his side as he stood, in a horse-riding stance, his feet planted wide in a horizontal gap as he faced Athien. Athien brought the blade up again, gesturing it at Vamp as he took a step forward.

"I told you to leave this city. You're insane." Athien charged forward, not giving Vamp the attack of opportunity with those claws he was so fond of using. Vamp's arms came up as Athien's foot came up sharply, closing the distance too fast as he knocked into the claws and pushed Vamp backwards.

Vamp stumbled, conscious of how far he'd been pushed as he turned slightly, seeing the police officers behind him, aiming their guns straight towards his location.

"Fire!" The commanding officer shouted, his handgun shaking slightly as he pulled the trigger, aiming for Vamp's head as the beak closed again.

Vamp crumbled to the ground, dodging the first wave as Athien followed suit, the bullets flying over both of them and smashed the glass of the short skyscraper opposite.

"This isn't your city to command, Sentinel, not yet." Vamp shouted, his body up again as the second volley crossed over them and he began to sprint towards the officers.

"Stop shooting!" Athien yelled, switching the knife to his left hand. He aimed at the middle of Vamp's simply clothed back as bullets went past both of them and clanged off of Vamp's helmet. Athien threw the knife, it's hilt spinning over and over the blade as it made its way through the air, and imbedded deep into Vamp's back.

Vamp's body fell suddenly and softly, as his claws lifted past his chest, which hit the ground first. His lungs erupted, air escaping out all at once in a crescendo. Athien ran to the side, his aggravated wound now bleeding rapidly, but he caught it all, soaked in the still clinging cloth he pulled back over it as he hid from the officers.

"Going to take more than that to stop me!" Vamp's voice rang out, his hand clasped a remote that Athien couldn't see, and pressed a button on it.

The helicopter above them exploded, the blades, still spinning at high speeds, smashed through the glass of the skyscraper to Athien's side.

"Stop him!" Athien yelled at the officers, breaking cover as he saw the small van that had been parked on the side of the road, ever since the fight began. It sprung to life and wheeled forward.

Vamp stood, staring daggers in Athien's direction. Then he was off, and running to the van. Athien went to follow, but the helicopter's cockpit landed on the ground seconds after and exploded, blocking his path to the criminal.

"And you're dead…" Vamp's sadistic voice climbed over the smashing sound of metal on concrete and the roar of the van's revving engine. His claws were out again as he reached for the captain and group of officers that had attacked him.

I need to get something long ranged soon. Thought Athien, his eyes travelling over his belt as he sought for a weapon he could shoot or throw. The officers fired back, but Athien saw at least four of them fall to the claws, as Vamp ran around the broken helicopter and dodged the frenzy of reporters at the border of the zone.

Athien vaulted the barrier, grabbing the gun out of an injured officer's hands. He aimeed it at the side window of the passenger seat. *If I stop the driver, he won't get away just yet.*

Athien aimed and fired, the shot going through the side window and then through the front of the vehicle, smashing both pieces of glass and causing the driver to swerve. It didn't do enough, as he fired a second shot and missed. Vamp held tightly onto the back of the vehicle. His claws dug into its side as he was so perilously close to falling back on to the ground.

"Hey, that's my gun!" Athien dropped the officer's gun, pondering whether he'd be able to catch the car if he made a break for the bike. He also knew well that he'd most likely have to fight the officers present and take the long way around.

I wouldn't make it, but, maybe someone else could. Athien thought about Nicola, wondering if she'd been watching the live coverage.

Officers finally reached Helm. He'd been able to stand by himself, bleeding from the face, where the mask was broken, and he was hobbling on one leg.

278

Athien felt metal tap against the back of his helmet as he watched Helm's arrest. The last people around the scene fell back as several police officers came forward and surrounded Helm.

Other officers were already being lead to hospital vans. Athien saw no one trying to catch Vamp as he got away.

"Sentinel, you're under arrest." Athien put his hands to his head, thoughts racing as he came up with a plan to escape his capture.

"Sargent Rock," He started, seeing the badge on the officer standing to his side, handcuffs out and already heading for his hands. "I suggest you back off, with all due respect, what I proved tonight was that you need me. I didn't see any of your officers taking down an ex-commando or Vamp." His voice came out arrogant, but also, thoughtful, and Sargent Rock stopped for a moment, the officer behind Athien chipped in then.

"You were speeding and, you used an officer's gun." Athien shook his head. The media around him were still filming, spotlights put up by police illuminating the scene and making Athien's gear look even more rugged than it was before.

"Then you'll find my money in your mail within the day, and, let's face it," He risked a look back, as both officers took a step away from him. "You wouldn't have made the shot either, too busy trying to end one issue when there were more at play," the officers huffed, and a few even had looks of bewilderment. "There isn't a law against defending the defenceless, yet." Athien's voice seemed to carry further than he'd intended, reaching the people beyond the officers, and everyone heard the shouting that began next.

Several people were shouting around the police barrier.

"Is that what you think you're doing, criminal?" Sargent Rock clipped one handcuff over Athien's wrists, his arm having to rip the hand away from Athien's shoulder.

The wooziness was starting to worsen in Athien's head over the loose of blood. He chuckled nevertheless, easing himself into the cuff but keeping his other hand gripped hard against his helmet as another officer moved for it.

"Look around you Sargent, what, do you think!?" The officers didn't know what to do, without their commander there, he was too busy trying to arrest Helm, who was struggling.

Suddenly, Athien saw a reporter break from the pack, their cameraman stepping over the barrier as the officers stood facing him. The reporter stayed back enough to not be arrested straight away herself, and spoke through a microphone.

"Sentinel, please, do you have anything you want to say to the city?" Athien looked at them, surprise echoing through his brain at the direct question, he hadn't thought about the media coverage at this new level of goals. He took a few deep breaths, pulling an arm off his right one as he broke from the officers and stepped forward, composed, despite the pain in his shoulder.

"My name is Sentinel, as I'm sure many are now aware." He began, police grabbing both his arms and holding them behind him, but not stopping his speech, as the crowd quietened to listen.

"I'm real, what you see and will see are my actions to help this city. To stop its enormous increase in crime. Help against the criminals who hold no heart to it," He paused again, letting his words sink in as he spoke deeply and concisely. "There are others with me, and together, we hunt those who commit crimes, so, they should either get quite, or enjoy what time they have left, before I come knocking." He felt something, the air slowed slightly as he finished speaking, but by the time he figured out what it was, Nicola was already standing by his side.

"We're here to help." Her voice was different, higher pitched. Athien briefly spotted her new attire, a jacket and pants, green and pink, suiting the sparkling mask she wore.

"Yep, that's the idea." Another voice said from behind him. The building crowd suddenly shifted away as a blue light emitted from behind Athien and the police, near Helm, who had finally been zapped by a Taser and dragged towards a van.

"Who are these people?" The reporter, taken aback by the newcomers but fast to continue her interview, doubtlessly there were plenty of people in the studio that were awaiting her return.

"Step back." One officer stepped in front of the cameraman and reporter, who both just sidestepped him and awaited the answer to the question.

Athien looked at Nicola, who shrugged slightly, still unsure of what her name would be, and then he looked at Zip, who stood back a little from them but was very much expecting Athien's response as well.

Athien turned back to the reporter, officers just clipping the other cuff to Helm's wrists off to the side. The restless crowd and reporter all listened.

"We're," He paused, unsure of what he was about to say would paint himself and the others in a particularly useful light for the rest of their lives. "We're the Underdogs, and we're here to help this, the great city of Melbourne."

281

Amidst the flurry of cameras and yelling from all members present, Athien could see the proudness that Nicola exerted. She was absolutely beaming as she made her way around the police. There was no array of bullets fired, no harsh yelling, the officers just didn't know how to respond to the situation, as their commander ignored the spotlight altogether. His broad hat seen from the back of the van that held Helm, but otherwise, not present.

They heard officers scurrying to catch them minutes later, but by then Nicola had run him off, and Zip had disappeared.

Athien clambered onto his bike after he lifted it from the debris it had been wedged into, the police too busy at the scene to impound the flash looking vehicle.

"I'm going to have to get a better stamina gauge, if I'm going to be running you from scene to scene. Aren't I?" Nicola joked, surprised to see both Zip and Athien nodding when she looked up again.

"Yeah, and you both, are going to need actual uniforms, if this is going to be an actual team. I can't have you both being discovered in attempts for the police to find me." Athien said grimly, though his face beamed with the biggest smile Nicola had ever seen him wear.

"I don't know what you're talking about, yours is the one that's in shatters." Zip protested, his voice a drawl but the excited look in his dark eyes gave away his true feelings. Nicola put her hands on her hips and looked down on the shorter hero.

"Uh-huh, sure thing, Zip-Pa." She pronounced his name with a drawn-out P and shrunk away as his hand quickly lit with the blue energy he used to teleport.

"And, you're going to need a code name," Athien said,

pointing at Nicola as she shied away from Zip.

"I know, I bet that Underdogs takes off with the media, they always seem to like teams," She sniggered, steal beaming. "That was well thought of, Sentinel." She was careful not to even stutter, keeping his secret identity as it was, secret.

"Well, you'll have to come up with something for you, separate from our," Athien brought up both his hands, his shoulder surging with pain but less so than it was before. He made curling finger gestures as he continued.

"Team name. Something that tells people, that it's you they see in front of them, not Bolt, or one of the others." Nicola grinned, jumping up and down after a few seconds of thinking, her heart racing as she almost went into her faster mode.

"I know, I know!" She exclaimed.

Athien flicked the ignition pedal on his bike and then left it on stalled, interested and thinking of what she could have thought of, even though he felt he had a good idea.

Her heart always speeds up whenever she runs, or so she says, feelings of elation. So...

Athien's thoughts were interrupted as Nicola jumped into the air a final time and landed, her feet flat on the ground, facing both Zip and Athien.

"Heartbeat!" She squealed slightly, delighted with her choice of name, which received a brief nod from Athien.

Thought so. Thought Athien, readying the throttle as the streets ahead of the alley they'd gone down were filled through by police and emergency services.

"Bit long, isn't it?" Zip asked, his voice sounding playfully as he teleported away five meters, sensing Nicola's annoyance before it had even arrived. Nicola whirled around, her eyes wide with shock towards Zip.

"Isn't yours a little short? Come off it." She proceeded to speed herself up and catch Zip, who had begun to glow again. "Ha! I'm faster than you." She exclaimed, grabbing him around the middle and accidentally throwing him into the ground as Athien rolled forward on the bike.

"It's perfect, both of yours are, and as for my, attire," He said, looking down and plucking at the ripped and shredded combat gear as he spoke. "I'm already working on moving away from this standard gear, but my next suit will take a while." He watched as they stood together again, looking like old friends, despite Zip's withdrawn behaviour bouncing off Nicola's loving and heartfelt one.

"Yeah, that might be for the best," Nicola said, her voice ringing shrilly as she slowed down again. Both Zip and Athien covered their ears for a moment to stop the ringing that echoed around.

"Never going to get used to that," Zip said, actually laughing, as Athien patted his helmet, the ringing noise still going on through his hypersensitive senses.

"So…" Nicola stood between them both, one arm draped around Zip's shoulders, the other almost pulling Athien straight off his bike as she leaned them all together. Athien's shoulder spiked with pain as she touched it.

"Please don't touch there." He interrupted Nicola, lightly pulling her hand slightly up, over the back of his shoulder as she continued.

"Sorry, so sorry, but," She made them wait a second longer as she flashed another monstrous smile.

"What happens next?"

Acknowledgements

I thought this book would never be released and it's thanks to the many minds that have allowed me to bounce my ideas that I've been able to create a linear storyline to be followed.

First thanks goes to my family, who've been kind and supportive enough to not yell at me whenever I say "what about this…" and who've inspired me to no end in pursuing this, the world of storytelling. From the editorial help to the fantastic dinners we share, there is no better company that a writer could ask for.

To the three Musketeers, the 3 writers of whom I've had the brilliant pleasure of meeting over the years and the core fellows that have made my plans make sense. Though the three of you have never met, Cordell, Conner and Josh, you've made this ride a lot smoother and crazier for me. A special thanks goes to Josh, who's been reading my writing since before it was legible and will heed my call no matter the time of day.

To my friends, Jackson, Michael and Eli, who all helped with heaps of the science and scene breakdowns.

(As well as allowing me to design characters off of them)

Also to my University roommates, Henry, for discovering I wrote his as he's 300 times in the first draft of the story and offered the first critique of the story. Manny, for working with me at 2 am on Helm and Sentinels' fight scene and Daniel. He got us all playing D&D together, which really settled those otherwise work filled University nights.

I'd also like to thank my English teachers from high school, Miss Massaro and Miss White, who gravitated around me and even allowed our classes to do some creative writing outside of the curriculum. To a third-year teacher who allowed me to teach a writing class in year 6, I don't remember why this happened or your name but I'm so glad that it did.

I'd also like to shout out to all the beta readers and people from the Nanowrimo community for helping me commit to writing this series and pushing me all the way here, a fantastic support group for any aspiring writer.

Lastly, I'd like to thank you, the reader, for taking the time to read this book and follow me on this journey as a writer. The road's a lot brighter with you behind me, and I really hope you enjoyed reading this story as much if not more so than I enjoyed writing it.

Carpe Diem

About the Author

Brodie Selzer grew up in rural Victoria, Australia. He spent his early years unaccumponied by technology, and spent a lot of time creating adventures in stories and games outside. From this, he began to write stories at the ripe old age of 8. Now 21, Sentinel is his debut novel, a story inspired by living in Melbourne during his studying of Cyber Security. Brodie enjoys a range of music, animations and video games, and spends his time being inspired by them, while working on his books.

Look out for;
  Sentinel 2 Underdogs
  Coming 2021

You can connect with me on:
🜨 https://www.bselzer.com